BOY CAESAR

By the same author

Jeremy Reed

BOY CAESAR

Peter Owen
London and Chester Springs

PETER OWEN PUBLISHERS
73 Kenway Road, London SW5 0RE

Peter Owen books are distributed in the USA by
Dufour Editions Inc., Chester Springs, PA 19425-0007

ISBN 0 7206 1193 8

A catalogue record for this book is available from the British Library

Printed and bound in Great Britain by
Bookmarque Ltd, Croydon, Surrey

For Lene and Moo

'Only by going too far will you get anywhere at all.'
— Francis Bacon in conversation

Introduction

Elagabalus, or Heliogabalus as he is better known because he worshipped the sun, was Roman emperor between the years AD 218 and 222. Literally 'Boy Caesar', he came to power at the age of fourteen and was brutally assassinated by the Army shortly after his eighteenth birthday.

Born in Emesa, Syria, he was an essentially benign ruler, remembered for his notorious extravagance, fanatical devotion to his own solar god – to whom he erected temples in Rome, the theatricality of his appearance and his same-sex marriages. An idealist, who had his mother introduce a woman's senate into the rigidly guarded male hierarchy dominating the Roman Empire, the pro-feminine Heliogabalus alienated both the ruling classes and the drive-unit behind their power – the Army.

Popular with the people on account of his generosity and relaxed system of government, Heliogabalus fought no wars and conducted no personal vendettas against his enemies. Little is known about his life before he became emperor, but the historic impact of his short reign was such that his name has become synonymous with decadent hedonism.

Heliogabalus liquidated a fortune even greater than Nero at the height of his spending. His dramatically colourful reign, recreated here and given the contrast of a 21st-century journeyer in the process of researching his life, is aimed at giving Boy Caesar another bite at the apple.

I have, throughout the novel, taken the liberty of fusing classical and modern times in Jim's reading of Heliogabalus, a method of dissolving past into present and present into past not dissimilar to the technique employed by Derek Jarman in films such as *Caravaggio* and *Sebastiane*.

Jeremy Reed

Thanks to a joy in death or in the new, despite bereavement, and in contrast to ordinary life, all moralities had broken down. What prevailed was the joy of the transsexual, of the requiem, of the kamikaze. Of the hero.

– Jean Genet, *Prisoner of Love*

I

The year is AD 218. From where he stood, pointing his left cheek-bone up for the mirror, Heliogabalus was aware that he was being watched. The sensation frisked his nerves, causing him to freeze. The idea that there was two of him, and that the other meant trouble, had been cooking in his unconscious for a long time.

He could hear the rain outside knuckling the little yellow pom-pons of flowering mimosa. The unseasonable rains had been returning day after day, the rapping staccato of brilliant showers seeming even to break into his sleep and make noise in his dreams. He was fourteen years old. So much had happened already that he remembered highlights in his life with total recall.

For weeks now, encouraged by his mother Symiamira and her entourage of lovers, Heliogabalus had dared to entertain the hope of becoming not only emperor but caesar. Was he not, after all, reputed to be the illegitimate son of the butchered Caracalla and as such the last of the Antonines?

No matter how tenuous his claims to the imperial title, he knew instinctually that he was about to take up with his destiny. It was somewhere out there on the exhaustive highway that led to Rome. His mother had fed him with ambition the way a slow poison accumulates in the system. It was she who had condoned his wish to make up like a girl and live out his same-sex attractions. She had fine-tuned his aesthetic, allowed him to wear her dresses and been right behind him in his fanatical devotion to the god Elagabal. But more than anything she had impressed on him his difference. He was set apart, she claimed, by the data in his blood. An emperor's sperm had patterned menus in his genes.

His imagination had needed little prompting. Already he saw himself dragging it in front of the Senate. It was his plan to affront their machismo by insisting that women should be introduced into the governing body. He had it in mind to subvert the whole gender-bias on which Roman society was founded. In the hours in which he was thrown in on himself and had nothing to do, he would create scenarios in his head, like shooting random footage. In these documentaries he was invariably in the process of entering Rome, and to his astonishment there was nobody there. He had come to a dead city.

Alone and waiting for his tutor to return him to the world of Ovid's *Metamorphoses*, he busied himself regrouping a vase of candy-pink peonies. The cerise, fist-sized flowers were the colour of sunsets he had known while out riding, the sweat stinging his eyes as he pushed a strawberry roan to overkill in the foothills. His mother had taught him always to be alert to his destiny. For years he had devoted himself exclusively to the cult of the sun-god Elagabal, worshipped at Emesa in the form of a black phallic stone, universally believed to have dropped there out of the sky. He was, as he reminded himself, blood of the Emesan dynasty as well as an emperor in the making. But he was, above all, impatient. The over-bite he brought to life was a response to the feeling that he would die young. He could get no purchase on the idea of growing old and of his biological arc peaking.

When his tutor came into the room it was to complain of the violent rainstorms. Despite the use of a saucer-shaped orange umbrella, he was wet through. Heliogabalus had a lot of time for the unorthodox Serge, a man who pointed up the aesthetic aspect of every study. Serge reminded him at times of the little incidental detail used to decorate an almond cake: the cherry dipped in alcohol.

'We'll look at what Ovid has to say of Tiresias' encounter with the snakes today,' Serge said. 'But there's important news awaiting you, and the lesson may be cut short. Something to do with war and the necessity to act fast.'

'How I wish they could get it over quickly,' Heliogabalus said. 'I've no interest in politics.'

'We live or die by affairs of state. You must learn at all times to be diplomatic.'

'But I won't be manipulated,' Heliogabalus fired off, feeling his individuality come up in a rush of confused emotions.

'These are dangerous things for a young man to say,' Serge cautioned, the tone of his voice implying a shared complicity of ideas.

Heliogabalus could hear the big rains washing the glass conservatory. His mind jumped to Ovid's story of Tiresias and how the latter had undergone a sex-change after disturbing two snakes mating in the forest. The way he interpreted it was to read the encounter as a metaphor for the subject's initiation into the underworld mysteries. Tiresias in being changed into his opposite was also engaged in the process of becoming himself. Serge had encouraged him in his particular take on the theme of transformation, a subject so dear to Heliogabalus that he could place himself in the story and imagine the powerful hormonal switch triggered in his endocrine glands. He had wanted to call musicians in and make a performance of the scene, but Serge had advised against it, saying that the intentions could be misinterpreted.

Quickly establishing a groove for his line of enquiry, he asked Serge why it was that Tiresias had hit out at the snakes with a stick. He couldn't see for himself why this act of violence should have occurred. 'Why did he do that?' he asked. 'Sex is hardly abhorrent in any form.'

Heliogabalus realized the moment he had spoken that he should have sat on his views. His tutor's signal this time was to avert his eyes and look away, the adopted gesture counting for more than words.

'I'm inclined to think,' Serge said, 'that we can interpret Tiresias' stick as symbolizing a caduceus or magician's wand. You will recall that after eight years of experiencing life as a woman the scene repeats itself. Tiresias goes back to the same place, encounters the identical snakes engaged in sex, hits them with his stick and instantly reverts to being a man.'

'The way I see it,' Heliogabalus said, 'is more to do with the Dionysian mysteries. If Dionysus is a man who wants to be a woman while remaining a man, then Tiresias also fits this description.'

'Dangerous subject for a youth,' Serge commented. 'Ovid himself, remember, died in exile in the Black Sea.'

Heliogabalus smiled. He liked pushing boundaries with Serge and adopting cutting-edge theories that upended his tutor's beliefs. He knew, too, that his pro-gay expressions were received by Serge with a tacit but secret air of approval.

Serge looked away again. The inconsistent highlights in his hair were to Heliogabalus a sign that his tutor paid insufficient care to the consistency of dye. He could see too many dark roots showing through the blond. Serge looked tired, enforcing the fact that his middle years had come as a source of disillusion. Somewhere beneath the surface, he suspected, was a man in the process of unplugging from the mains.

'We must observe limits,' Serge said, looking out at a dense cluster of magnolia trees, their white flowers fisted to debris by the rain's assault.

Heliogabalus knew that he was pushing an unorthodox line with his tutor, but he could not help himself. If he became emperor, against all the odds, then he would honour Serge and reward him with a suitable sinecure. But he had his own views on the subject and was determined to speak.

'I've written something I would like you to hear,' he said, picking up the notebook in which he had made sketchy impressions of the difference he perceived between right and left brain functioning, a theory that had grown up from his reading of the Greek mystery cults.

'The way I see it,' he said, determined to speak, 'is that the political male, denied access to right-brain hemisphere functioning, with its accent on imagination, feels immediately challenged when confronted by the feminine within his own species. While governments exist to maintain left-side control –'

'These views are not helpful to your future,' Serge interrupted.

'But they are integral to my beliefs.' Heliogabalus took a deep breath and continued, 'It's my contention that Rome with its partially shut down right-brain hemisphere epitomizes government by outmoded machismo. A constitution in need of being challenged by a pro-feminine emperor.'

'I must ask you to suppress such thoughts. They are dangerous to you and a death sentence to me.'

'You can't kill imagination,' Heliogabalus retorted, 'but you can kill the person carrying it. As for me, I couldn't care. If I go to Rome it will be on my terms.'

Serge looked out again through the glass wall at the stripped magnolias. Heliogabalus knew that his sentiments had met with approval, even if Serge would never outwardly condone such ideas. The sky looked soapy with rainclouds. Inwardly he dreaded the prospect of having to take to the field against Macrinus and prove himself to a largely mercenary army.

'There's a line of Seneca's', Serge said, 'which goes "The object of their toil was their epitaph." You may know it, for it expresses the futility of all human aspirations. Don't set out to provoke trouble is my advice. It will come to you in due course, anyhow.'

Heliogabalus had to restrain the impulse to laugh. He had no intention of adopting his tutor's discretion in public life. He wanted to burn brightly and go out in a blinding flash, affirming his vision. 'What really interests me in Ovid, to return to the *Metamorphoses*, is when his characters are overtaken by ritual frenzy.'

'We call it daemonic,' Serge said. 'A form of overreach that exceeds intoxication but has properties in common with that state.'

'I like the idea of the participants dressing in leopardskin and conducting nocturnal orgies,' Heliogabalus said.

'You should remember also,' Serge continued, 'that *orgia* are not orgies but acts of devotion and that *bacheuein* is not to revel but to have a particular kind of religious experience. Ovid is thinking more in terms of what we call inspiration, in the sense of the poet feeling possessed or overtaken by his theme.'

Heliogabalus admired Serge for his unfailing ability to direct ideas into serious discourse. His tone rarely switched from an intellectually maintained gravitas, although he suspected his tutor of being a regular visitor to the male brothel in one of sidestreets in the city centre.

'Madness as an altered state interests me greatly,' Heliogabalus said, attempting to hijack the theme. 'We should differentiate between this and the pathology that labels people mad.'

'You know too much for your years,' Serge replied, again throwing his eyes into a wide-screen take on the rain-stripped garden. 'You speak like a poet. Clearly Ovid has got into your bloodstream.'

'Ecstasy is the state with which I most readily identify,' he answered. 'Doesn't the Dionysian initiate orchestrate his own measure of dementia in proportion to the increased hold established by the god? I believe I can govern a people through imagination, young as I am.'

Serge was about to tone down the recklessness of his pupil's claim, when a servant expressing apologies hurried into the room. There had been a change in events and Heliogabalus was urgently required to join his mother in the left wing of the villa. He knew from the peremptory nature of the command that he was being summoned to fight. For months his mother, fuelled by the ambition for power, had been plotting a strategically devised offensive against Macrinus. He knew that she and her duplicitous circle would stop at nothing to have Heliogabalus appointed emperor. The recent news she had given him pointed much in their favour. In the attempt to increase his popularity with a disaffected army, Macrinus had appointed his son Diadumenis associate emperor, a move so unpopular with the Army that they threatened to desert.

As Heliogabalus crossed the marble floors in the direction of a room in which he could hear excited voices, he was aware once again of the individual destiny he carried. If his grandmother, Julia Mesa, younger sister of the empress Julia Domna, was the drive-unit behind the conspiracy, then he was a willing participant in her scheme. He wished only that he could be proclaimed emperor without having to lead a disabused army into the field. He dreaded the rank smells of horse-sweat, the carnage, hot blood gouting in litres, urine and excrement. Armies carried with them the smell of death, like the murdered body he had discovered on the road one day, with his mount rearing up like it had been electrified. He remembered the stench and how flies had lined the wound, thick as black jelly. If he was to be used as a tool in the political struggle, then he assured himself it would be once and once only.

When he entered the room both his grandmother and his mother came over to escort him into the circle. He could see the occasional raised eyebrow express silent disapproval of his light makeup. He was conscious he would be forgiven these things only if he acquitted himself in battle. That he was queer went without saying; that he had a right to be was something it was necessary for him to prove.

Contrary to what he had expected, it was his mother's lover Gannys who led the way in giving him a résumé of affairs. He was told that the Army had declared him Caracalla's son and that he had a majority support. Macrinus, believing himself invulnerable, refused to leave Antioch and had left his prefect Julianus in charge of the troops. It was important, Gannys emphasized, to capitalize on Macrinus' misassessment of the situation. If they struck now they would have the advantage. At the sight of Caracalla's son leading the Army, it was more than probable that the seasoned praetorians would desert Macrinus' cause and be won over.

All of this made perfect sense to Heliogabalus, who none the less felt totally dissociated from proceedings. He knew that he had to act and could do so only by adopting Serge's advice and sitting on his true feelings. He despised Gannys with the same distaste he felt for war. He resented any man whose body came between him and his mother. He looked at the man's squat, unrefined features and suspected his mother of bad taste. He wondered how Gannys failed to smell him as the intruder on his mother's skin. Incest was another of his secrets he had to bury. He himself would have peeled the offending scent off her like a roll of film and confronted her with it.

After Gannys the military had their say. The rains were expected to move off that night, and plans to mobilize within two days were intended to coincide with a total eclipse of the sun. He was told that he would be closely protected in the field by a number of select praetorian minders but that it was incumbent on him to inspire confidence in the troops by his leadership. The opposition, he was told, were little more than splinter-groups of mercenaries, criminals and soldiers retained on triple pay. The latter wore red cloaks as gifts from the emperor, as part of his spurious claim to be an Antonine, but had little or no reason to be loyal. He was informed that in the event of victory letters would be dispatched to Rome declaring him emperor, before the procession set off on the long haul to the capital.

He listened to what was being said in a dream state. He had so often imagined himself as caesar that he feared the reality would be disillusioning. Part of him would have preferred to keep the fantasy safe rather than act on it. He could hear the rain outside giving over, perhaps as a sign, he told himself, that now really was the time for him to engage with Macrinus. He was bored by the military, caring more for the damage done to the sprays of lemon-scented mimosa and to the smashed torrent of pink camellia heads than he did for their strategies.

That night he went to his mother's bed, determined to talk to her of death. It was not so much that he was afraid, it was more that he wanted to test his ideas on the subject against her own. He found her waiting for him in a purple see-through gown and had to dismiss her advances in the interests of conversation. It was not for nothing, he reminded himself, that his real name was Varius, indicating that he was not only the son of various men but that his mother was notoriously promiscuous.

Symiamira, not giving up on her intentions, lay beside him on a couch, her sinuous body forming the shape of an S placed on its side. He resented the fact that his mother considered her body to be her only instrument of expression. He knew from experience that if he coaxed a little of the story from her interior she would reveal an understanding of life that he had never counted on existing. Her reading of character, learned through her senses rather than her head, displayed a naïve but profound ability to penetrate defences. He knew that when encouraged to give shape and value to her thoughts she possessed a surprising facility to point up the psychological traits in an individual's behaviour. Her essential grittiness was not without subtlety, nor her hedonism without the ability to reflect on her life of reckless excess.

Now that the rains had lifted the heat was oppressive. He sat beside his mother, hardly knowing how to start. He wanted to tell her that ambition and death were one and the same and that the pursuit of office was correspondingly an invitation to die. It was not just Serge quoting Seneca on the subject that had triggered the impulse in him, it was the realization that he might die in the field. The priests of Emesa had assured him that to die in the pursuit of individual destiny was the only death acceptable to the gods; only he didn't want to lose his life fronting an army he despised.

For weeks now the phrase 'What can be better for me than to be heir to myself?' had been coming into his mind, and he still had not succeeded in puzzling out the enigma. He decided to try it on his mother, who was in the process of getting drunk.

He assumed she was not listening, as she closed her eyes and seemed to be wanting to shut him out. Then suddenly, in a voice that seemed to belong to somebody else, she said very clearly, 'Dry stones are not fetched from a stream. You will get to Rome unharmed, but the stones will return to the river.' She sat up as abruptly, looked confused, and said, 'Did I speak? Sometimes I have no knowledge of what I say or where it comes from. Don't take my words too seriously.'

Heliogabalus looked away, his mind elsewhere. 'What you have just told me is not unlike what I have read in Seneca, who says, "No good thing makes its possessor happy, unless his mind is reconciled to the possibility of loss."'

'Your life hasn't begun yet,' Symiamira said, by way of reassurance. She angled her foot in his lap, but he would not be drawn. He sat wondering why his individual role in life should be different from Serge's or his mother's or Julian's, the blond boy who was his lover. Sex, he had discovered, was the gateway to an ecstatic union with death, but it offered him no significant clue to his identity. He assumed that nobody could explain to him the mystery of why he, a Syrian youth who had never seen Rome, should be in line to be its future emperor. If the secret was coded in his genome, then he doubted he would ever know. Like all those before him, he would turn the question over in the dark pockets before dawn or in snatches of self-reflection watching a sunset point up acute orange and vermilion.

His mother looked at him from a place that lacked all signposting.

He was afraid that she was about to predict his imminent death, but instead she returned to drinking and laughed in a manner suggesting she had scared the thought away. 'Men think only of their balls,' she said tersely. 'They attempt to squeeze the life out of themselves, together with their secrets.'

'What are you trying to tell me, Mother?' he asked, the catch in his voice causing her to look at him with concern.

'That you have a rival in Gannys. He has his own plans to become emperor. If we are successful in our claim he will have to be killed.'

'But he's your lover,' Heliogabalus said, shocked by the ruthlessness of his mother's scheming. That life appeared so cheap to her upended his beliefs in its sanctity. He felt suddenly like the casings had been torn from his nerves. In order to make his point he was tempted to walk out on her and on the idea of being emperor.

Symiamira tried again to trigger his sexual interest, but he pushed her away and stonewalled her attempts to coax him into conversation. He knew that if Gannys could be so easily disposed of then his own life would follow. What he wanted more than anything before he died was to know the sort of intense love that his friends had never experienced. That it would be with a man didn't matter; in his mind the bond could only be heightened by the quality of likeness.

He could hear the noises of an army assembling out there in the night: men who were probably unaware of why or for whom they were fighting. Their needs, he knew, were the perennial ones of money, camaraderie and brutally perpetrated sex on the vulnerable. They would be paid with money derived from theft, and they in turn would commit grossly unsanctioned crimes. He had refused outright to study Tacitus' *Annals* or any other martial accounts of the Roman Army's remorseless war-machine. Armies had been consistently liquidated, but an essentially genocidal residue survived and persisted. Scorched by the African sun, gored by stampeding elephants, eaten alive by cannibals, he knew the stories and how nothing ever succeeded in turning the Army around. They were rapacious to the point of fighting their own shadow.

He could sense his mother's feelings of rejection. She got up from the bed and slipped a silk gown over the transparent one. Instead of returning to the couch, she went over to a lamp-lit corner of the room and arranged herself on a tondo of red cushions. She had shut herself up from words again, and her downturned mood showed in the way she narrowed her eyes at the glass.

He felt too vulnerable to risk being alienated from her at such a time. For all he knew, tonight could be their last together, and Serge's teachings had impressed on him that animosity was the wrong state in which to die. He wanted to make it up and went over to her and bruised her mouth with his lips. He knew that his body language would communicate on a deeper level than words. He worked his tongue like a feeler into her palate and withdrew before he got caught up in the erotics of her response. He could feel her mood change instantly, registering how he had succeeded in throwing the right switch.

'I'll follow your advice,' he said, aware of the compromise he was making. 'From what I've read in the histories, being emperor is an unenviable thing.'

'You must never say that to anyone,' Symiamira warned him, her expression so serious that it jolted him out of self-reflection. 'Men everywhere will envy you your position. Your cousin Alexander, although only a child, has an equal right to rule. Take what is yours, and together we will face the consequences.'

Although he knew he was too young to find a similar basis of trust in himself, Heliogabalus invariably turned to Seneca's thoughts as a consoling source of back-up. The line 'I shall never be frightened when the last hour comes; I am already prepared and do not plan a whole day ahead' had worked its way into his mind while his mother was talking. Philosophy gave him a pivot and provided a necessary window between himself and reality.

He left his mother to sleep. The alcohol had kicked in, and she lay face-down on the cushions. He placed his hand briefly in hers, knowing that at some stage of the night Gannys or one of his equally duplicitous associates would force himself on her.

There were lights on all over the villa as he left his mother's apartment and went in the direction of his own in search of Julian. Their brief affair, tempered by mistrust and the fear of being found out, would, he knew, end with his departure for Rome. Julian, with his privileged background, his fleckless green eyes and worrying nature, was studying law, and would doubtless in time become a respected barrister. Three years older than Heliogabalus, and with his father having taken up a consular appointment in Syria, Julian was determined to make his future in Rome.

When Heliogabalus went into his room he could smell Julian's presence. He knew he would be hiding under the sheets, his skin slightly musty with pheromones and a scent that reminded him of the complex notes of vetiver as they came up in the masseur's green-tiled parlour.

Julian pushed his head out from his hiding place as he heard Heliogabalus enter. He emerged like a diver, his hair tousled from friction with the sheets. His quizzical stare took in Heliogabalus with a mixture of fear and longing. He propped himself up on his elbows, his naked torso catching in the light, a leopard tattooed across his right shoulder.

Heliogabalus quickly undressed. Julian had always made him feel like a commoner, taking every opportunity to demean Heliogabalus' family. He had in his assured, logical manner – and without intending to cause offence – stripped apart Heliogabalus' claim to be an Antonine. The line had ended with Geta, he insisted, the younger son of Septimius Severus.

When Heliogabalus attempted to fit his body to Julian's he could sense the resistance. Julian was somewhere else tonight and was not going to give himself without first expressing his feelings. He knew from experience that coming up against Julian's body when he was in this state was like attempting to break into a mirror. He could make no purchase on its cold surface.

'So you're really going?' Julian said in an accusing tone. 'You must know it will all end badly. Reading Suetonius should tell you that. You can't go to Rome as an impostor.'

'Who is to say I'm that?' Heliogabalus said defensively. 'Besides, Macrinus has to be defeated first. You make it sound too easy.'

'You don't really believe that your father was Antoninus Caracalla?' Julian persisted. 'You know as I do that he was Sextus Varius Marcellus. You yourself once told me so.'

Heliogabalus swam an arm out across Julian's chest. He could feel his friend's heart turning over like a motor in its thoracic groove. The thought that it would stop one day caused him pain, in the way that acknowledging love demanded a corresponding acceptance of death. Julian would die, but whatever had passed between them would, he knew, continue to exist in some form of post-human context.

'I have to prove myself to the soldiers first,' Heliogabalus said. 'It's the part I'd rather do without. But if I do survive to be acclaimed emperor, then surely you can find a way to join me in Rome. It doesn't have to be an end.'

'Never,' Julian replied, the force of his conviction allowing for no argument.

Heliogabalus felt the hurt go deep. He flinched inwardly. He took the refusal to be a judgement on the incongruous figure he would cut as emperor. Julian would not wish to associate with bad blood, even if the person was caesar. He lay there listening to him breathe in the dark, their sexual energies put on hold by bad feeling. He could sense Julian weighing resentment against desire, while his own cock remained obstinately hard, its impulses untamed by their differences of opinion. He knew that he should let go and turn over and have Julian make things right through the annihilative powers of sex.

Uncertain how Julian would respond, but willing to take the risk, Heliogabalus went under the sheets and took Julian's urgently demonstrative cock in his mouth. He began fellating it, working on the frets like a guitarist playing the instrument with his tongue. Julian lay back and abandoned himself to Heliogabalus' sensually improvised rhythm. He knew how to create little triggerings in his friend, as the first premonitory hints of orgasm. But this time he intended to leave Julian with no more than the anticipation of coming and in this way encourage his lover to expand his repertoire of erotic play.

Heliogabalus disengaged and worked his head back to the air, leaving Julian with the excruciating ache of arrested orgasm.

'I'll miss you,' he found himself saying, as their bodies interlocked in the dark. But, even in searching out Julian's lips, he felt an underlying sadness that he knew would heal in time and be converted to a sense of painless loss. He had come to think of Julian, like he did of the mimosa, as a transient, intoxicatingly beautiful event in his life that belonged to a certain moment. The idea of him growing old or diseased seemed intolerable.

Aroused, Julian tried to flip him on his stomach, but he resisted, preferring to remain with his lips and to hold to their fierce, interrogative vocabulary. There was the enigmatic taste of Julian's roots on his tongue, that mixed primal scents with the less definable signature of his psychic being. As they struggled to find deeper access to each other, he was aware of how easily love could be transformed into murder. The barely concealed animosity that lived as the subtext to Julian's feelings for him was starting to be answered by his own sense of wounded pride. He resented being thought of as inferior on account of his illegitimacy. He knew it within him that he had a perfect right to be emperor, and the sleight given him by his friend caused him to be brutal in biting the tissue along Julian's nether lip. Both manœuvred for the ascendant position, but neither were going to concede to being fucked. The woman in him had taken offence and closed down the routes by which he usually gave himself with such abandon. Tonight he was going to resist Julian and suppress the fantasy he entertained of himself as a serviceable rent boy: a butch-haired faggot working the bath-houses in the interests of achieving in calculable numbers.

A frustrated Julian fought free of his embrace and sat up coldly. 'Let's forget it,' he said. 'There's too much friction between us.'

Julian's instant cooling shook him. He wanted to live on in his friend's memory like a bruised emotion that took colour when it rained or when a particular mood invited reflection. First love, he

26

had been told, never died; but already he felt a tincture of hate for his resentful partner. It was a hatred so inseparable from love that he felt confused by the dual emotion.

'You'll end up nobody,' Julian bitched, digging at Heliogabalus' insecurity. 'You see, sex will be the end of us both. We'll be forced to marry, and the compromise will show. They'll laugh at you if you get to Rome.'

Heliogabalus moved away from Julian and turned to face the opposite wall. This time he felt irremediably hurt and was determined to reject any attempts at reconciliation. Julian's assertion that he would end up nobody had gone in deep like a twist of wire. If nothing else he had a purpose now: to prove Julian wrong in his spiteful prediction. He would be somebody and nothing less than emperor.

'I think you should go home,' he said, as a way of trying to defuse the situation. 'I need to sleep and have an early start. Let's not end on a bitter note.'

Julian got up abruptly, like somebody running back out of a sea that had proved too cold. He jumped off the bed, his erection still standing in line with his navel. His petulance showed in the truculent way he stood, the left hand angled to his hip, his chin raised as a token of rejection. His stormy attitude, whether genuine or affected, was the invitation to a potentially recriminative scene.

Heliogabalus made no attempt to have his friend reconsider. He watched him put on his clothes with the sort of indignant haste provided by a blow-out temper. Julian's shattered hair was standing up spiky like a dahlia. Every cell of him was on alert, waiting for an apology that never came and which Heliogabalus was determined to withhold.

'Shit on you,' Julian seethed, as he fussed with his shoes. 'You'll be sorry for kicking me out.'

Heliogabalus remained silent. He wanted at all costs to avoid reproaching his friend. He knew he would suffer later for having said nothing and that the minute Julian left he would wish him back, but his mind was made up.

Julian made an attempt to correct his hair, picked up the two books he had brought with him and without turning around hurried out of the room.

Heliogabalus stayed a long time without moving. He settled back on the pillows, stunned by his friend's abrupt departure. It seemed to him that Julian had taken a chunk of the air with him in leaving, for the room was oppressively hot and he had difficulty in breathing. The atmosphere was still charged with the twitchiness of their recent hostilities. He wondered how he would be able to sleep in the aftermath of what had happened. He blamed Julian for having worked on his insecurity at a time when he was most vulnerable. Tonight, faced with the unnerving prospects of going to war, he had needed his unconditional support. That he had been denied it had come as a shocking reminder of the powers of betrayal. He felt as though a nerve had been cut in his body. He had trusted Julian, who in turn had repaid him by walking out with the calculated malice of someone intent on wrecking his emotions.

He wanted on impulse to run to his mother's room and take refuge in her bed. Julian had succeeded in scaring up the sleepy chimeras garaged in his unconscious. They stared out like fat pythons sensing feeding time in a vivarium. Their fangs came searching along his spinal chord, jabbing him with current. In his state of panic he imagined himself being ridiculed by the Army, fumbling in his mount, jeered at for his unashamedly bleached hair. There was so much he had need of keeping under cover. He was acutely aware of his difference and of the need to manage it until such time as he could safely own to his true identity. The men outside in the dark, who had gathered together to logo his name as the last of the Antonines, were of a very different nature. He wanted nothing to do with their coarse masculinity and the values by which they lived. He would go out to join them, carrying a wound he could share with no one.

He called his assistant and asked for wine. His only option, he knew, was to drink himself to sleep. When it came, he drank half of the dust-covered bottle without questioning the contents. The wine tasted of fermented sunlight, with the planets involved in assisting its biosynthesis there in the ageing process. He felt the warmth

catch in his bloodstream and connect with his brain. His consciousness was slowly being dispersed, as the jungled underworld with its
psychic guerillas closed over. His last jump-shot connection before
sinking into sleep was the awareness of a black cube of night sky, lit
up by the fires the military had built somewhere in the surrounding
hills.

2

When Jim cut out of Borders, he headed for the Amato in Old Compton Street, Soho. The purchase he had made of *The Lives of the Later Caesars* linked in directly with the dissertation he was writing on the life of the emperor Heliogabalus. There was so little of a reliable nature written on his brief, scandalous reign between the years AD 218 and 221, and all of it so coloured by the misassessments of Heliogabalus' biographers, that he was glad of his purchase. The only two accounts in English of his life, a largely apologetic disclaimer by John Stuart Hay and a brittle exegesis by Orma Fitch Butler, had done little to redress the damage done by earlier historians.

It was a blowily cold April day. The thin turquoise sky over Soho was frescoed with meditative rain-clouds. Jim looked up at their slow crawl over the West End, their stop-and-start pace resembling articulated trucks tailgating the hard shoulder of a motorway. By the time he reached the Charing Cross Road entrance to Old Compton Street the shower had opened up in a rapid, torrential dazzle. The street was buzzy with its overtly gay community, and Jim made a hurried dash for his café.

He had planned to have thirty minutes reading time to himself before his lover Danny arrived. Danny, who was studying American Literature at King's, was the drop-dead gorgeous love of Jim's life. He pinned the thought of him with arrows and daggers to his heart and lived in an emotional storm of possession.

The café was lively with its student spill of Japanese girls, fastidiously dismantling millefeuilles with the studied elegance of a beautician shaping an eyebrow. Jim recognized the red-haired one, Uchiko and threw a smile at her before taking up with his book. He wondered about the process of reading and what sort of access it provided as a tool to jump across the centuries and handle blocks of deconstructed time. That Heliogabalus had become a fiction, a character in part invented by his biographers, was clear to Jim from reading the contradictions inherent in the works of Lampridius, Cassius Dio and Marius Maximus. Nowhere described physically (did he have blue eyes, green eyes, brown or grey?) and correspondingly deprived of any form of psychological reason to account for his actions, Heliogabalus had been reduced to little more than a set of facts by his contemptuous biographers.

Jim chewed on the notion of history as continuous fiction, an area of study with which he was increasingly preoccupied. If he was to retrieve Heliogabalus from a past to which he had no proper access, then it was necessary in recreating him to make him real. In writing about his subject he would have to earth him in the London milieu in which he worked and lived. That way he hoped to get a better purchase on the youthful emperor he was reincarnating for the purposes of his dissertation.

Taking advantage of the time left to him in which to read, Jim got under way with passages lifted from Lampridius' lacerating account of Antoninus Heliogabalus' short and extravagantly flamboyant rule. Beginning with an apology for being so imprudent as to commit Heliogabalus' scandalous life to writing, the author lost no time in alluding to the young emperor's sexual tastes. After wintering at Nicomedia he was supposed to have conducted himself 'in a depraved manner, being debauched by men and being on heat' to such a degree that the soldiers regretted ever having taken his side against Macrinus.

Jim looked up to check the café for Danny's arrival, then continued reading. The author was not going to let go his acrimony and questioned how anyone 'could endure a princeps who was the recipient of lust in every orifice of his body, when no one would tolerate even a beast of this sort'.

Jim knew very well from less extreme sources that the emperor's slow procession to Rome could be attributed to a variety of causes other than erotomania. The route was a bad one, and the imperial party demanded the sort of luxurious travel facilities and leisurely stops that were not in the interests of speed. He was also aware that coins inscribed Salus Antonini Aug. and Salus Augusti, struck at

the time, suggested that Heliogabalus fell ill some time between 8
June 218 and 1 June 219 and that sickness may in part have been
responsible for lengthening his stay in the East. Jim reflected, too,
on other omissions on the author's part and of how Herodian
claimed that Heliogabalus sent a portrait of himself dressed as a
Syrian priest to Rome to be put above the statue of Victory in the
Senate in anticipation of his arrival.

Jim segued in and out of his Penguin edition, assuring himself
that he would give the book a closer reading at home. He wondered
how Danny would like his platinum-blond hair, a characteristic he
had adopted in imitation of his subject. Jim reflected on how the
faculty of empathy had been a dominant trait in him since childhood. He had to his knowledge always possessed the gift of
dissolving boundaries and of being able to identify with his particular cast of heroes. This time it was Heliogabalus with whom he had
chosen to bond, and he wondered sometimes why he had taken up
with an obscure third-century Roman emperor, a man who had left
nothing behind but the record of exaggerated sensual depravities.
Someone who otherwise would have been forgotten for all time.

He was policing his thoughts, looking to freeze-frame a motive,
when Danny walked in. His head was shaved at the back and sides,
with a bleached forelock noodled on to his forehead. Dressed in a
white shirt, engineered jeans and an Agnès B jacket, Danny made a
habit of marrying casual with designer elegance. The son of
divorced tax accountant parents, raised by his mother in New Jersey,
Danny had chosen to escape his emotionally damaged upbringing
by doing post graduate studies at King's in London. Jim had met
him at First Out, the intimate café-bar in St Giles High Street
behind Centrepoint, and the fusing of their chemistries had been
almost instantaneous.

Danny came over to the table carrying a biffed briefcase wedged
with books. He discreetly kissed Jim on the mouth, momentarily
tweaking his lower lip before settling on to his chair. The catchlight
in his pupils twinkled like a constellation, but he appeared removed,
distracted in a way that Jim had not known before.

'Get caught in the shower?' Jim asked, noticing the beads of rain signalling from his friend's hair and studding the shoulders of his jacket.

'I walked over. The rain caught me along the Strand. Not that I mind. There's something compelling about London rain to a foreigner.'

Jim was about to switch conversation when a man he recognized from somewhere but could not place came over and asked if he could have a few words with Danny. He was on his way out, and Danny joined him as he was paying his bill. Jim was not suspicious but wondered why it was taking so long, and when his friend returned to the table he had a folded square of paper in his hand.

'Who was that?' Jim asked, feeling uneasy at the sight of the paper.

'That's Richard,' Danny was quick to reply. 'He wanted to know if you'd like to join us at the meeting tonight.'

'What meeting?' Jim asked, his suspicion returning.

'There's a group of us,' Danny said, doing his best to sound casual. 'We call ourselves the Night Watch, and meet at a top floor in St Anne's Court. It's not that I'm a regular, but I take it in sometimes.'

'I've heard about them. They're a bit weird, aren't they? I wouldn't have thought it was your scene.'

'I don't know how best to describe them. They're a sort of political cult, not so much activists as believers in a leader called Slut. Why don't you come along with me and see for yourself? Their beliefs link in with parts of your research.'

'You mean the thesis I'm writing on Heliogabalus?' Jim questioned, his uptake riding on a thermal of curiosity.

'Come and check it out for yourself later. There have even been Night Watch flyers out in the bars,' Danny volunteered, clearly trying to make the cult appear more acceptable. 'And how are you doing with Heliogabalus?' he added as a footnote, his eye helicoptering over Jim's downturned Penguin Classic.

'It's the facelessness of my subject that baffles me. If we go back to Heliogabalus' beginnings in Emesa we encounter a blank. Nobody has told us anything of his birth or education, and not one of his biographers has described his physical appearance. It's almost like the historians have conspired to wipe him from memory.'

'Didn't you tell me that a bust of him has survived?'

'Yes, in so far as we know it's him. The face is of the androgynous kind you would expect. I find myself writing a defence of an emperor who has to all purposes become a fiction. To my mind his so called depravities were little different to those of Caligula, Nero or Commodus, all of whom are praised for their better qualities by the historians. For some reason Heliogabalus was never given a chance.'

'Weren't they all crazy?' Danny laughed.

'Up to a point,' Jim replied, glad of the chance to grow eloquent on his subject. 'The way I see it is that they all correspond to a type in which obsessive behaviour replaced any notion of a selfless concern with government.'

Jim could feel himself getting wired by his own intense enthusiasms as the adrenalin started to fire. For the past year Heliogabalus had occupied a central place in his life. He thought of his book as like a drug to metabolism. Its stimulus came up for short concentrated bursts, and then the effects declined as the rush of excitement left the system. He had his doubts that Danny was interested in the subject and suspected him more of being polite than sincere in his questions.

'Didn't you once tell me that Heliogabalus worshipped some form of phallic stone?' Danny said, with deliberate pointedness. 'Our cult have adopted Slut as their icon. He's the patron saint of faggots.'

Jim laughed, then almost immediately grew serious. 'Yes,' he said in answer to Danny's question and feeling his knowledge come through. 'Heliogabalus worshipped some sort of black meteorite that was said to have dropped out of the sky. He had the fetish taken to Rome in a chariot and housed it in an Eastern-style temple on the outskirts of the city. He was a Syrian priest, a sun-god who gave himself the title "Sacerdos Dei Soli". But, tell me, who is Slut?'

'If you come tonight you'll find out for yourself. I don't want to spoil things for you. If I'm honest, I should tell you that I'm more involved with this cult than I've let on. It's not serious on my part, but I've been to a number of the St Anne's Court meetings.'

'You never told me,' Jim said, surprised to discover the hidden underside to his lover's actions. He had not ever had cause to reflect on the possibility of there being another side to Danny: a duplicitous one.

'It was just curiosity,' Danny replied with throwaway nonchalance. 'I met Richard in the street one night and he persuaded me to go along.'

Jim was uncertain as to whether or not he should let the matter drop. He did not want to blow it up out of proportion or appear unduly suspicious, but he was unnerved by the fact that Danny clearly had a secret life. Feeling the first jabs of disquiet infiltrate his thoughts, he was determined to find out more about Slut before dropping the issue.

'I'd rather you told me something about Slut before I agree to come tonight,' Jim said, the slight quaver in his voice indicating a degree of unease.

'You never get to see his face,' Danny replied, then stopped dead, realizing that he was committing himself deeper to the subject. 'He's blindfolded throughout the ceremony.'

'You're not answering my question,' Jim persisted, his imagination filling in the blanks with a series of visually distorted images to account for Danny's faceless mentor.

'He's supposed to represent risk,' Danny said reluctantly. 'Someone who has martyred himself to numbers on Hampstead Heath and been resilient enough to survive. I suppose you could call him a miracle of resistant immunology. He's from south London, I'm told, and considers himself a saint.'

'There's no end to the weird people who inhabit this city,' Jim conceded. 'But they're not half as bizarre as Heliogabalus must have appeared to his contemporaries.'

'I'm not sure about that,' Danny countered. 'This man has had arrows shot into his shoulder blades, he's fire-walked, carried his own cross through the Hampstead woods. You name it.'

Danny's sudden willingness to open up on the subject did nothing to allay Jim's fears. Something told him that Danny's knowledge of the S&M scene on the Heath may have been derived as much from personal experience as from stories told him of the eponymous Slut. It clearly went deeper than he cared to disclose, and Jim felt painfully on the alert.

'I don't think they come weirder than Heliogabalus. He was denied a sex-change, married his boyfriend Hierocles, colour-coded his dinners according to a particular theme, cruised the bathhouses for men endowed with big cocks and generally fagged it up in the Senate.'

'I'm not suggesting that Slut is his counterpart,' Danny insisted, 'but there's a resemblance in the way that psychological types recur over the centuries.'

'I'll grant you that,' Jim said, 'but enough of comparisons. I'd rather go out for a walk if you're up to it.'

Together, they went outside to a packed Old Compton Street. Walking was a pleasure they shared in common, and over the months they had developed a private itinerary that took them on a slow trawl of the West End in the direction of Embankment and the river's citified haul between Waterloo and Charing Cross. Their predominantly sidestreeted route had become a mutually exclusive map, a way of familiarizing the city so that it formed a miniature grid of reference between them. It was their London, and associations of place resonated in their speech as though the city had grown to be the physical extension of themselves.

Big clouds with blank faces still jostled across a bleached denim-blue sky. Jim hoped the rain would come on when they were down by the river, so that its green surface would appear pixellated from the downpour. He remembered how, when the two of them had visited the wasteland shore adjacent to Shad Thames, they had, on impulse, made love under cover of a deserted pier. The slap of dead water with its chemical tang came back to him as they headed in the direction of Wardour Street. Part of their circuitous journey involved taking in the Soho boundaries. The pheromonal buzz transmitted by a gay-friendly microcosm never failed to fire up

Jim's chemistry. All along the street a territory had been staked out and politicized by a once marginalized faction, to a degree that allowed in parts for a same-sex ecosystem.

At the top of the street they took in Camisa & Son, the Italian delicatessen that attracted customers from all over the city on account of its cheese and pasta selection. The usual compound whiff of garlic, salami, mature cheeses and spicy olives breezed effusively from its open door. They filed through the alley telescoped between Wardour and Rupert Streets, with its constellation of dealers rayed out in waiting, and made their way into Brewer Street. The recessed quiet provided by the village always gave Jim the impression they had stepped into a timeless precinct. The end of Brewer Street before it branched left into Sherwood Street was established as the terminating point of their Soho itinerary. Overlapping it, the monolithic façade of the Regent's Palace Hotel gave on to Piccadilly Circus, with its atomized, fragmented tourist trade creating a distinct separation of energies.

They browsed the length of the street, stopping to pick up herbal teas in Fresh and Wild, and turned back on themselves. A Rasta bolted down the road pursued by a policeman imparting urgent messages into a radio. The young man's body as he segued by had reverted to a state of primal fear. Jim could sense the turbo-rhythm of his flight-or-fight mechanism as he endeavoured to overtake himself in a mad burn-up for freedom.

When they got back to Wardour Street clouds were building to a frothy stack of indigo cumulus. The light appeared to have been squeezed out of the precinct. The first tingling berry-sized drops of rain hit them in Rupert Street as precursors of the imminent shower. Neither cared to stand out the rain in a doorway; instead they continued down the street, where a walnut-faced Jamaican crack dealer approached them before derealizing into the crowd. The rain was still holding off, the penumbral cloud-blocks building to a smoky density over central London. Jim felt they were deliberately walking into the storm and risking its violence as an issue that had to do with themselves and the nature of their relationship.

They cut through Chinatown, on their way to the Charing Cross

Road bookshops in which they browsed, the Photographer's Gallery where they would sometimes meet and take in an exhibition and, veering right from Great Newport Street, the theatre strip along St Martin's Lane. The sky had now turned inky black, and rain was imminent. To Jim Danny seemed unnaturally distant and to be out there on his own trip.

Jim took it for granted that they were headed for the river. They had done this so often before, been drawn there and pulled into a magnetic field. They walked on in silence as lightning dramatically flashed through them like photocopier light. There was a brief flurry of rain, then the shower stopped as abruptly as it had started, sending two girls toppling on spike heels clattering down the street for cover. The air was charged and flickery, like someone was playing with a light-switch.

'We're heading for a storm,' Jim said, breaking a silence that had lasted for much of their journey across town. When he looked up he realized they were making direct for its bruise-coloured eye.

People were jostling for the Underground, pouring out of Villiers Street to enter its network. Jim laid a reassuring hand on Danny's shoulder as they turned into the Victoria Embankment Gardens but met with no response on his lover's part. He was hit by the profusion of pink cherry blossom crowding into view. The flowers always reminded him of Japanese poems: fragile haiku professing a single ideogrammatic season.

They walked fast, their pace picking up on the storm's live-wire energies. He could smell the river now, its brackish churn turning over unbiodegradable pollutants. The tide was rising, tracking down from Blackfriars, and he could see the rapid current take on the colour of old rope as it picked up speed under Waterloo Bridge.

The rain had started up again, this time with steady persistence, but they ignored it in the interests of speed. He noted how Danny's forelock had been dislodged by the rain and split into a trail of disparate strands and that his eyes were lit with a sexual charge which seemed to be sorting the area for a suitable location.

They hurried past the Savoy with its imposing Art Deco canopy and broke into a run as the downpour exploded across the gardens.

Jim had the impression that with each stride they were running up against a series of glass shower-screens, each one superimposed on the other in an endless illusory sequence. They were being car-washed by the chemical London rain. They bolted in the direction of the underpass and the cover provided by the concrete stairwell under Waterloo Bridge. Vagrants lived and slept in its graffiti-slashed corridor, and there were always ruined mattresses to be found there, together with the residual vestiges of their survival kits littering the floor.

By now the storm had centred itself and rain was coming down in palpable columns, its driving architecture imposing a disposable liquid city on the one it was in the process of temporarily erasing. They came under cover breathless, clothes moulded to their bodies, the raw animal scent exuding from the stairs increasing their sexual hunger. Jim could hear rain sheeting from overhangs in agitated torrents and its force redoubled on the flyover above.

There was a wrecked mattress and a slew of discoloured blan-kets on the ferro-concrete floor but no sign of their faceless owner. Jim could feel the sexual tension coming up in him with the same powerful impetus as the storm outside. Some weird impulse had brought them here, and the danger only increased the excitement. Without saying a word Danny cracked open the zip on Jim's jeans and went down on him, and he gave himself up completely to his lover's urgency. He could feel a primitive mambo beating in his blood. All of his mistrust of Danny, his obsessive preoccupation with the boy-emperor Heliogabalus and the more pressingly imme-diate events in his life were being displaced by the cyclonic pressure in his groin. The incipient climax rooted in him like a volcanic core began to grow more urgent. He cradled Danny's damp head to him as traffic thundered under the bridge. Their energies were meshed with the city's as he pushed back against the concrete wall. He could feel London's giant modem connected to his brain. Venture capitalists, rainmakers, stockbrokers, accountants, their whole col-lective thrust was being converted by him into sexual data. He could feel black cabs and the whole shunting metallica of the city's traffic highways laning through his arteries. As Danny increased his rhythm he knew himself the agonized extension of the Waterloo complex, his penis constituting another office tower on the asymmetrical skyline. Sensing his urgency Danny took him in deeper, initiating him into an underworld rite. He could hear the rain slamming down on the flyover as he started to come, the molten aggression of the act rising from a core in him so deep it hurt.

He stood there, shaking from exhaustion and intense pleasure, his heart racing to explode. In the afterglow of his crisis he had a vision, and it was of Heliogabalus. He could see him as a youth, dyed hair turned damp on a foggy day by the Tiber, the whole assault of life in his nerves at that moment. A body floated by as he stood watching, and Heliogabalus lifted it out by the hair and kissed its slack mouth . . .

He was jolted out of his vision by the force of Danny's hot tongue wedged into his mouth, and his desire working convulsively against his body. It was Jim's turn to go down, and he pressed the fluted weight of Danny's cock against his lower lip in an act of measured calibration before sculpting it to his tongue. Giving what he had already received increased his need to communicate pleasure. He could empathize with each resonance highwayed through his lover's body. He came down on him as thunder reverberated over the South Bank, its nosediving bass-line stomping west in a series of dull sonic collisions. He could feel each successive crash rip through his chemistry. The storm was inside him as it was in Danny's percussive libido. He took as much of Danny into him as his mouth would allow and rooted for the life-force driven along those veins.

The thunder returned directly overhead as Jim picked up on the first signs of Danny's orgasm. It began with a throatily strangled cry, an instantly suppressed exhortation that sank back into the primal dark to be replaced by a rush of pelvic energies. Danny came in a state of ecstatic frenzy, a contorted shamanic dance that worked from the limbic area of the brain to his sex, via all the interconnecting gateways in his nerves.

He got up from his kneeling position on the cold floor and looked into Danny's dazed eyes. He wondered for a moment what had brought them here to have sex in a pedestrian corridor slung over the river. He thought of the way gay men identified themselves with public places and of their secret map as it existed all over London, like a network of territorial zones. The kick in it for him was the little nick in time that the fugitive left behind: a scratch on the social fabric, visible to other outlaws, like the red and blue inks of a sailor's tattoo.

They stood and kissed, but without warmth, as the expended storm gave over to persistent but lighter rain. Jim knew it in himself that even if someone had mounted the stairwell during the time they were having sex he wouldn't have backed off. He would have continued impervious to the intruder and without a sense of shame. He would have reinforced their rites by celebrating an act based on the mutual recognition of danger.

Reconnecting with reality was the hard part. They had created their own space in their urgent need for sex, and now it was necessary to go back to the city on different terms. He had decided to accompany Danny to the St Anne's Court meeting that evening and to find out for himself what went on there. What they had just done in a corridor used by so many tourists on their way to the South Bank was a complicitous secret to be stored in their privately zip-coded memories.

Soaked through, and for the sake of convenience, they headed to Embankment and tubed it over to Danny's apartment at Bedford Mansions for a change of clothes. As Jim stood in the spacious blue-carpeted living-room of the flat paid for by Danny's mother, he imagined the security that must come from living at a solid address. Reality dissolved behind these walls, and there was no notion of the noise coming from the incessant hard-core traffic as it thundered up Tottenham Court Road. The city was backdropped into a remotely ambient surf. He was glad of the glass of red wine that Danny had poured and settled to its flinty warmth as a pick-up after having been beaten by the violent rains. He could feel the wired tension in his muscles begin to slacken. By the time he had finished a second glass his mood had lifted.

Although the intense, almost violent nature of the sex they had performed had brought them closer, Jim still felt uneasy about Danny's recent movements. For the past month he had seemed detached, preoccupied and unwilling to be close. At first he had attributed it to study pressures – Danny had got behind with his work – but over the weeks a certain callousness of manner, and at times a deliberate desire to hurt, had left him feeling cautious of his partner. Danny had refused outright his suggestion that they should live together, and while wishing to remain independent had appeared perfectly natural to Jim he suspected Danny of having extracurricular affairs.

The disquiet he felt at his friend's elusively flexible laws within the relationship was suddenly confirmed by Danny reappearing from the bedroom dressed in leather. He had never seen him outside of a smart dress code of designer jackets worn with jeans or trousers, and it came as a shock to realize that his partner evidently had a double life. He had never imagined Danny adopting the ubiquitous butch image of the Old Compton Street bars. It seemed out of character with his natural gravitation to style.

Danny made no attempt to explain his dramatic transition from Agnès B to used leathers. He seemed absolutely sure of his identity as he massaged cushions back into shape and made minor revisions in the interests of tidiness before going out.

Outside the air was tonic after the recent storm. They made their way towards Soho Square, its broody custodial plane trees bringing nature alive in a rectangle brokered by media corporates. There were men picking up in the gardens, and Jim looked hard at a sweet-scented viburnum making headlines with its pronounced but slightly dumbed-down April fragrance.

Soho's night people were starting to come on as they cut through Bateman Street in the direction of St Anne's Court. So much of London's congested nightlife happened here in the clubs, bars and restaurants compacted into its recontextualized village. He wondered if anything as ordinary as a birth or death occurred in its residential lofts. He thought of William Blake parished here in boxy rooms in Poland Street and of the angels who had visited him there, like telepresent guardians of the archetypal kingdoms.

His head was full of this as they crossed over Dean Street to St Anne's Court. For Jim the alley was rich with associations, chiefly in respect to its having been the home of the old Marc Almond fan club, Gutterhearts, which had been run from a flat there in the 1980s. He remembered the entourage of Almond look-alikes hanging around the entrance to Trident studios in the hope of catching up with their idol.

They stopped outside a door painted air force-grey, and Danny pressed the buzzer to the top-floor flat. There was no name on the flat indicator, and the other floors appeared deserted. Jim was aware of the sound of rainwater pouring from a defective overhang into the alley.

After what seemed an interminable wait a voice on the intercom said, 'Number?'

Danny replied instantly, 'Thirteen/zero plus guest.'

'Come up,' the voice replied.

Jim's suspicions that the building was otherwise deserted were confirmed by the dilapidated state of the entrance and the visible state of disrepair into which the building had fallen. There was no indication of life on any of the lower floors as he followed Danny up a tall, unreliably lit staircase.

'Look out for the gap on the bend,' Danny warned, with the authority of someone familiar with the house.

He followed him up to the fourth floor and threw his head up at the sight of a blue slab of night sky blocked into a skylight. The sudden unexpected contact with rock-littered space brought an involuntary smile to his lips. The idea of all that planetary glitter arriving and receding according to the mega-impacted rhythms of Big Bang never failed to excite him.

The man waiting for them at the top of the stairs was wearing a leather-peaked cap and had a lozenge-shaped scar under one eye. Jim disliked him on sight. He could have been a superannuated leather queen, but there was something cold and inscrutable about his grey eyes. The man nodded at Danny, while largely ignoring Jim.

Jim followed Danny into a low-lit room screened off from the buildings opposite by black-out blinds. A circle of men uniformly dressed in leather and sitting on floor cushions appeared to be meditating their way into a different space. He noticed that they all wore uniform gold crosses in their ears and from what he could see had the signature of a black snake tattooed on the left wrist as some form of cult identity. The airless room only served to enforce the closed feelings generated by the circle. He felt an intruder in their company as Danny instructed him to sit cross-legged on one of the cushions provided.

As Jim looked around the room he discovered the word SLUT written on the walls in a number of typographical variants. The word had been disassembled into scrambled orthography, was spelled backwards, with letters inverted dyslexically or written up large in a pink graffiti typeface. There was an air of suspense pervading the room that told him the company was waiting on somebody.

Jim closed his eyes to centre himself and tried to imagine life without Danny. If his lover really was duplicitous and was mixed up with a leather cult devoted to the worship of a Heath martyr, then he was no longer the person he had taken into his trust. He wondered why there was always a blind side to love, like the stone existing in a peach. He had naïvely assumed that he had found security in Danny, only to discover their relationship was fundamentally flawed. He played with the idea of being free again in the city's bewilderingly anonymous millions. He would be another solitary man sitting in a bar waiting for the perfect stranger to walk through the door. He would be alone again with his work of recreating a post-biological afterlife for Heliogabalus.

Jim was shaken out of his slipstream of imaginings by the group beginning to chant. Somebody was busy setting up a mambo rhythm by the use of marimbas. He found it difficult to interpret the words written into what sounded like an incantation and heard Danny's voice taking up, fluent with the rhythm. Any doubts he may have had about the strength of his friend's ties with the group were dispersed on hearing how directly he entered into proceedings. Instinct told him to get up and leave, but he stayed on out of curiosity. The primitive hoodoo worked like a hypnotic, the malediction cooking in the chant. He tried to free himself from the spellbinding rhythm and its qualifying sexual motif before finally letting it take over.

The percussion steadily increased, the beat underlining the voices as they established harmony. He kept his eyes closed so as to shut out the reality of the situation. He knew instinctually that the chant was an invocation to Slut and that at some stage he would materialize in the room. When he opened his eyes briefly he could see Danny completely given over to the music. He appeared to be in a blissed-out state, completely oblivious to anything but the insistent rhythm.

Jim remained too tense to let go of his senses. His consciousness shifted in and out of the music, got caught up in it, then resisted. When he looked around again the lights had been put on dimmers and the room had darkened. He heard the door open and caught sight of the man he assumed to be Slut entering the room. The emaciated but defined figure was, as Danny had warned him, blind-folded. His naked torso was tattooed with interlocking serpents, and he wore jeans slashed to threadbare ruins. His shaved head showed a blue grizzle of hair-roots around the ears, and his multiple lip and nipple piercings enforced his evident masochistic traits. Jim backed off from any idea of becoming associated with such a cult. If, as Danny had led him to believe on their way over, Slut was peri-odically crucified on Hampstead Heath, then he looked the living image of his legendary status. Jim found him repulsive and fought again with the impulse to get up and go. He found it hard to believe that this primitive ceremony was taking place above a pedestrian Soho alley. The whole thing was so out of context with his own life that he wanted nothing to do with it.

When the music stopped Slut began intoning his own mantra. Jim kept his eyes open and watched the whole circle now focused on their leader. Slut was contorted into some form of expositive dance, like an urban shaman attempting contact with tribal spirits. He held an arrow in one hand and appeared to be working the point into his chest in imitation of St Sebastian. Danny and his circle looked on enthralled as the arrow went home, leaving a residual trickle of blood. The first arrow secured, Jim watched horrified as the man began working a second and third into his torso. He showed no sign of pain as he continued with his ritual of self-inflicted torture.

Jim had little doubt that the ceremony would culminate in an orgy, and he wanted to avoid the possibility at all costs. The room was becoming suffocating, and bad vibes fizzed in his head. He got up abruptly from his cushion and made for the door. The group were so concentrated on their leader that not even Danny turned his head to watch him go.

Jim found himself back outside on the badly lit stairs. The doorman looked at him menacingly but made no attempt to have him stay. He simply fixed him with the same inscrutable expression, the same glacial blank.

Jim ran down the three flights of stairs, opened the heavy security door and hurried out into the alley. He didn't stop running until he was safely back in the pedestrian flux of Dean Street. When he slowed up he was glad only of his freedom and continued for a while walking in a state of directionless shock. He found himself back in Old Compton Street, its hologrammed bars swimming up at him like the tropical tanks in an aquarium. Men were pressed up against the windows, staring dumbly out at the night crowds, engaged in watching a reality movie. He felt himself for a moment to be part of the same footage. He needed to be alone in the night and decided to walk it back to his studio flat in Paddington Street and use the exercise as a means of offsetting the effects of shock.

He knew without doubt that he had to break with Danny. Even the panic triggered by the prospect of being alone again seemed preferable to the option of continuing a relationship under these circumstances. He flexed his mind to take in the idea of loss and the inevitable carve-up to his nerves that would come from the split. Already he could sense the damage like broken piano-strings in the pit of his stomach. He wondered how many times he could stand up to being radically deconstructed by partners. He walked briskly, fooling himself as he went along that he was aimed for a new purposeful future. He had his doctoral work as pivotal support for the ruptured days ahead, and he might, he promised himself, take a short break in Rome and sniff out some vestiges of his enigmatic

46

subject's posthumous legacy. For some reason he found himself linking Heliogabalus with Passolini as he walked into the night. He reminded himself that both had been murdered in public toilets and that both had survived as metaphors for a distinct archetype in the gay world.

He kept up with his thoughts, and instinct guided him in the direction of home. It was starting to rain again, bittily, but without persistence. He hurried on, taking in nothing and seeing nobody, elated by the night air and in his mind determined to be free.

3

Rome was everything Heliogabalus had anticipated it would be. After the long haul through violently changing seasons and countries he was welcomed at the capital by shocked crowds who threw flowers. He had arrived, flexing the muscle on the way of six white horses which conveying the image of his god and was given an ecstatic reception. He had dismounted to pick up a rose coloured a particularly deep burgundy and had held it out to a youth who had caught his eye by reason of his perfect looks. The boy's archly camp expression and dyed hair had him assume he was rent or else the adopted heir to an older benefactor. He was determined to find out more and mentally put the youth's image on file.

With his minders looking on apprehensively, he had repeated the gesture, again stopping to present a flower to a boy made up like a butch cabaret artist. He could sense the suspicion on the part of the spectators who observed the incident. They were clearly passing judgement on his sexual preferences and categorizing him as a fag.

The sun was starting to break through a low-cloud ceiling, spotlighting him in his moment of triumph. His only thought was for his mother and that she should be appointed his principal adviser. It was she who had guided him all along and prepared him stage by stage for the role of emperor. All the preliminaries of his education in rhetoric, the part he had played in the Emesan priesthood, the tangy introduction to hedonism that she had encouraged, her choice of tutor, all of it had formed the baseline to her plan to see him rule over the Roman Empire. The whole thing seemed unreal as the city crowded in on him with its mad celebrations. He could feel the sun on his face, and he thrilled at the prospect of coralling pretty boys from all over the city. It occurred to him that, of course, he would be forced to go through the pretence of marriage, but he knew as he stood there picking out faces in the crowd that a woman could never offer him the intense emotional high that came of a same-sex union. He knew this from his chemistry and from the encouragement given him by his mother, who had pointed him towards liaisons with his own sex.

Already in his mind, as he confronted the excitement of the crowd, he had decided to build a high-rise temple to his god on the south-eastern edge of the city, in what were the lowlife suburbs. The building would face the rising sun and attract solar energies to its heliocentric god. He had planned it after having seen maps of the city while *en route*, and now he gave his attention over to the musicians who were accompanying the procession. The band played a variety of instruments ranging from castanets to barrel-shaped drums called tambours, to Egyptian rattles used in the worship of Isis, to silver trumpets known as hasosra, as well as the kind of large harp known as nebels. He worked with the music, its rhythm building in him to the pitch of frenzy. He was fizzy on deci-bel-clusters and engagement with the beat. He knew that even on first sight he was a scandal to the people, not only because he had the audacity to wear jewels on his shoes but because he appeared openly to celebrate a marriage with death. He may only have been sixteen, but his upbringing had distanced him from everyday life. He knew the score only too well. He was a weirdo. A shaman. A ritualist. A religio-maniac. A magician. A pretty boy. A mythomaniac. A quasi-eunuch. But he was emperor.

He had also been told by his advisers that there was the belief common amongst the people that Nero would return and that, no matter the murdered emperor's abuse of power and his atrocious crimes, he still remained an idol to the masses, who remembered him by placing roses on his grave. There was some hazy notion amongst the collective that Heliogabalus, as the newly appointed caesar, was in fact Nero's reincarnation.

The palace, as he had been instructed on the road, was surrounded by a dense area of cultivated parkland. As they came within sight of the grounds he could see how a profusion of blossom had turned the park into a cerise blizzard of bitty petals. He felt himself caught up in the pink choreography of spring, as if nature's regenerative energies were also his own. He insisted on stopping under an arrangement of cherry trees, and for a brief moment Julian's image returned so blindingly it was as if he had hallucinated him back into existence. He remembered Julian's warning that he would come to nothing and die young. It came back to him now like a hex frying in his blood. For a second he was afraid before he let the reminder go.

As the procession approached Nero's restored Golden House his mood brightened again. That he was to occupy a palace built proportionally to house a mad emperor's ego was an impossible reminder of his chosen destiny. He knew from reading Suetonius that Nero, prior to torching Rome, had announced, 'While I yet live, may fire consume the earth.' And that written all over the city's walls at the time were the graffiti pronouncement: Alcmaeon, Orestes, and Nero are brothers. Why? Because all of them murdered their mothers.

As he stepped into the entrance hall of the palace, originally built to accommodate a 120-foot statue of the emperor, he felt the full ferocity of Nero's mania rush at his throat. He started to choke in a sudden paroxysm, which he explained away as a tendency to asthma. But the incident had come as a shock. No matter the emperors who had walked its blood-stained floors, something of Nero's hysterical presence remained in the achingly empty rooms, spread out like the vast complex of an abandoned hotel. He took it as a sign and one that he would submit to his temple priests.

He knew from his reading that the place had been built with the illegal gains Nero had fisted out of his subjects, promising in return the security of newly discovered gold from Ethiopia. Some of the walls were still studded with jewels, and most of the rooms were done out in red and gold, with the added detail of black marble floors. The kitsch, the hieratic, the looted and the mindlessly exotic were all scrambled together by generations of bad blood, who had fed in turn on the equally corrupt exploits of venture-capitalists.

As he journeyed deeper into the palace he noticed that the dining-rooms had fretted ivory ceilings and that the main dining-hall was circular, its ceiling revolving slowly, day and night, to match the movement of the earth's tilt. There was a sophisticated ventilation system that dispensed hot or cold air and a library stocked with Greek and Latin works as the core of modern knowledge.

He resisted the impulse to be tempted by too much too soon. It was as if he had been offered a box of candies the size of a swimming-pool and been asked to choose. Inwardly he wanted the lot, but he professed a lack of interest so as to conceal his inordinate need for kicks. He would like to have been left alone with his mother to enjoy the freedom of the place without being under the close scrutiny of an officious entourage. He was forced to conceal his nervous irritability. The exhaustion of having been on the road for almost a year was starting to tell. He had lived without a home ever since leaving Syria, and no matter the luxury of the villas he had used for short-lived stays he felt time-lagged from lack of a place to call his own. He had also been seriously ill and had come close to sweating out his life *en route* to Rome as doctors worked around the clock to lower his fever. He had hallucinated violent endings in his delirium and still remembered the fire that had ripped through his dreams like the fins of a torched city.

His body was road-mapped by the ups and downs of life. Getting to Rome had involved a transcontinental journey, so debilitating in its wear and tear that ruling the Roman Empire would seem small by comparison. That Nero had never left the popular imagination fitted well with his intentions. From his first infatuation with the idea of becoming emperor, he had taken aspects of Nero's biography as the role-model for his future lifestyle. It was the decadent and sensational in Nero, rather than the vicious and homicidal, with which he empathized. It was the Nero who had gone through a marriage ceremony with the boy Sporus, liquidated the economy in the interests of self-indulgence, been the dedicatee of Seneca's work 'On Mercy' and whose religious sympathies were also directed towards a Syrian cult who continued to colour his imagination. Again, as Heliogabalus stood looking at the suite of rooms he was personally to occupy he could feel Nero's presence invade his system. It was like an interference with the electric noise in his body. He wondered if others could detect the disturbance when it came up in him and was careful to conceal his thoughts. Nero, he knew, had worshipped the Syrian goddess Atargatis, until a fit of temper had him urinate on her image as a means of expressing his superiority. Nero's inflation of ego was something of which he knew himself incapable. He made a silent promise, as he stood looking at his reflection in the marble floor, that he would never outgrow the influence of his god. If the union he celebrated of the divine pair Ishtar-Tammuz was to him a way of life, then he was determined to maintain the distinction between the divine and human.

Already, despite his exhaustion, he was beleaguered by requests, sycophantic compliments, bitchy asides and the naked intrigue of those hoping to gain office. He despised them for their scheming. He was only too aware that the empire he was inheriting was itself responding to a tropism of decay, a sort of ideological AIDS in which a pernicious retro-virus policed a declining organism. The problem, as he had been briefed on his circuitous journey to Rome, lay chiefly in the uneven distribution of wealth. He had learned of how both Tiberius and Caligula had attempted to solve the problem of big estates and dispossessed peasantry by a radical redistribution of land, but both had been frustrated in their attempts by the oligarchs, and the senatorial class had resumed its sway. He had been told that the wealth of the empire rested on looting, on slavery in the plantations and on provincial labour and that the contrast between the hedonistic pursuits of the aristocratic landowners and the abject misery of an institution of slaves was at its most acute. Living largely from a wealth derived from the land, the senatorial class were the opponents of any economic expansion which challenged its own position.

He had been warned that his hands would be tied from the start, and he had agreed to announce an amnesty for all the slanderous things said about both Caracalla and himself by every division of society.

People kept coming at him until he felt he had been put through a juicer. He disliked them all and intended to stick with his own. He would rather appoint rent boys from the docks to positions of power than the unscrupulous individuals who queued for his ear. He wondered, anyhow, what they thought of him choosing to wear a

Persian tiara and makeup for his entrance to Rome. He felt sure that no other Roman emperor had ever presented himself in this way, and that word would soon be out all over town about him being a pretty boy.

Although he considered state affairs of secondary importance to religion, he knew himself to be suitably well informed of the problems facing Rome to hold his own with his advisers. The damage done to the empire was largely irreversible, and he could see it in the people and smell it in the air. The city was imploding like a quasar. History had told him that the great plague of 167 had made permanent inroads on productivity, and this, combined with Commodus' extravagance, the ambitious enterprises of Severus and Caracalla's desperate liberality to the Army, had radically depleted the economy. Macrinus had exacerbated the issue by way of his unsuccessful war with the Parthians. Unable to defeat the enemy, he had burdened the state with the double expense of maintaining an offensive as well as buying peace from the enemy. The impostor who he had defeated had done further irreparable damage by abolishing the taxes which Caracalla had imposed on inheritances and manumissions and so had further depleted resources. Heliogabalus felt like he was the principal performer in a burning theatre and that he would be lucky to escape the flames. Emperors, he knew, were always in the spotlight. The power invested in being caesar carried with it the downside of being vulnerable to the assassin's mark.

All he wanted to do was to withdraw into the privacy of his rooms and discuss the day's events with his mother and intimate circle. He felt a victim of overexposure to the crowds. Reading Seneca had taught him in advance of his years that everything had been said before and done before and that all human aspirations were cut short by death. Mortality provided no re-entry routes, only a very clearly lit exit sign. He understood that being in his teens differed little in terms of absolute values from the problems common to every age in life. He had dared to take himself on to a stage where the price of survival was usually paid for by murder.

Complaining of exhaustion, he eventually won the right to withdraw. There was a naked youth, lying face down on the couch, but he wasn't in the mood, and he threw the boy out, telling him to come back later. His head felt like it was about to explode.

Symiamira, he noted, was delighting in the attention given her by a train of hangers-on. She was being looked over by women and by boys half her age. Food had been prepared in abundance, and a bronze donkey stood on the sideboard holding panniers of green and black olives. There were delicacies, such as dormice rolled in honey and poppy seed and supported on little bridges soldered to the plate; there were hot sausages laid on a silver grill and under the grill damsons and pomegranate seeds.

He amused himself with the chichi *hors d'œuvres*, preferring to look rather than taste. He was attended by servants and a personal valet who fussed over his needs. The sheer volume of food presented seemed sufficient to feed an entire tenement in the suburbs. He found it like tasting the concept of empire: an addictively ruinous obsession.

When the second entrée arrived, its novelty quickly won his attention. A round plate was carried in with the twelve signs of the zodiac set in order, and on each one the artist had laid food proper to the symbol. Over the Ram, ram's head pease, a slab of beef on the Bull, kidneys over the Twins, seafood over the Crab, African figs over the Lion, a sow's paunch over Virgo, muffins and cakes in Libra's scales, sea fish over Scorpio, a bull's eye over Sagittarius, lobsters over Capricorn, a goose over Aquarius and grey mullet over Pisces. It had all been prepared with loving attention to detail for his eye. Never before had he been presented with such an inexhaustible variety. He went for the fish in blue sauce, preferring, ever since he had read the teachings of Pythagoras and his disciple Apollonius of Tyana, to avoid meat. It was something he used in sacrifice but abstained from eating. But more interesting by far than the food laid on was his valet. The young man was tall, well defined, possibly Ethiopian and without a doubt gay. His eyes were attentively kind and seemed without the capacity to be duplicitous. There was a sensitivity in his manner that set him apart from the other servants, most of whom seemed downright obsequious. He could see that the man was artistically inclined but probably lacked the education to promote his talents or simply was denied the encouragement that Heliogabalus himself could supply.

He picked at the food like a seasoned gourmet. The mélange continued to excite and reminded him of much that he had learned from Apicius in his book *De Re Coquinaria*. Reading the celebrated author on the subject of food had been the trigger to cultivating his own culinary tastes. At home he had learned to cook and was, despite being warned away, a regular in the kitchen. There was no occupation too feminine for him, and he intended to continue with his love of cooking, even if he was emperor.

Wines from Marseilles and the Vatican were served between courses, as well as a Falernian with a label stating the vintage. Given his exhaustion, he felt drunk by the time the roasts were carried in. The well of the dish contained peacocks and sows' bellies and in the middle was a hare given wings to look like Pegasus. Fish done in a blue, spiced sauce created an overlapping fringe. He was unusually slim amongst a company used to gorging on multi-decked courses and was determined to keep his figure. Already guests who were physically exhausted from cramming down an overload of food were being conducted to red-hot baths or to chill-out rooms where they continued drinking.

He sat there conscious of his isolation in the room. Nobody expressed interest in him as a person or seemed the least curious about his opinions. He realized that what he had brought with him from Syria was a condition of acute loneliness and that, rather than diminish on arrival at Rome, it would in all probability grow worse. He wondered if it was his appearance put people off or the more obvious reason that he was a foreigner and lacked connections in the capital. He was quickly learning that people were almost wholly self-interested and that the Roman aristocracy excluded even an emperor thought to lack patrician blood.

After the roasts had been demolished, the chef sent in the dessert. The confectioner had made a figure in the form of Priapus, holding up every kind of fruits and grapes in his wide apron. The colour-coding was an achievement in itself, and Heliogabalus was shocked by the rapacity with which the arrangement was so quickly shredded. There was not the slightest observance of the chef's meticulously constructed *objet d'art*, only the greed of the privileged stoppering their mouths to excess. Most of the women invited into his company had quickly realized he was gay and had given up any attempts at attracting his attention. Instead, they had regrouped into a gossipy, competitive list of rivalries, concerned with their hair and the line of an expensive gown.

All he wanted to do was sleep and to bury the memory of his illness and the year-long journey. He was also anxious to wipe out the faces of the anonymous lovers he had known at every stop of the journey. The memories when they returned were too painful and hallucinatory. The awareness that he would never encounter any of these boys again rooted in him with a deep sense of loss. And there was the undiagnosed virus he had caught, which his doctors suspected was sexually transmitted. It still recurred some nights in the form of high fever, with lumps occurring in the lymphatic region under his arms. He had heard it rumoured that gay people all over the empire were going down with a form of plague said to have come out of North Africa. He hoped he was free of it but couldn't be sure.

When he fought free of the last of his minders he was grateful of the chance to be alone. A big wind had risen outside, and he could hear it thrashing through the trees, like trampling elephants.

He slept as if he was on the high seas, the current of his dreams washing him with turbulent rhythm. He woke once to find his mother trying to fit herself to his body, and it took real force on his part to kick her out of his bed.

He awoke to discover that the wind had died out, and the view from his windows was one of spectacular blossom. For all the pink and white cushioning of the trees, he could sense the manic graft of the city on the other side, and all the crazy night-and-day excitement it offered. The first thought in his mind was that he would have attendants search the bath-houses and gymnasiums for youths who were well hung. He intended to make it clear from the start that his preference was for solid genital muscle. It meant nothing to him that his obsession might be frowned on by the prejudiced.

But before the day began he was to be visited by his personal hairdresser, whose job it was to layer and curl his hair in the style originally adopted by Nero. The day's busy agenda was also to include an introduction to the Senate, the body politic he despised without ever having met.

After he had washed he was dressed by his Ethiopian servant. The man, who gave his name as Antony, was anxious to please without being in the least subservient. Sensitive to a degree that palpably flinched from the possibilities of being hurt, his manner combined tact with genuine concern. Heliogabalus assumed the man was in his mid-twenties and had probably been raised as a servant. He had mint-green eyes, and his body was slim to the point of self-conscious definition. But what made Antony so particularly special was the selfless, self-deprecating way in which his desire to please was without the expectation of gain. It was a quality absent from the servants he had known at home and one he had not counted on finding in Rome.

For a moment he wondered what it would feel like to fall in love with him. He let his eye track the curved rondure of the man's buttocks before taking up with the shapely outline of his thighs. The compact tightness of his body contrasted with the soft expression in his eyes, creating the exact combination of masculine and feminine energies he found irresistible. He felt a catch in his heart as Antony attended to his personal needs, and was at the same time acutely aware that society would refuse him the right to love this man, no matter the truth of his feelings.

He listened as Antony told him of the large number of public readings currently on in Rome. Poets and philosophers used recitations not only as a means of propagating their work but also as a valuable form of income. There was to be a series of readings that afternoon at the Athenaeum, its auditorium having been converted into a platform for the city's revolutionary poets. According to Antony, most of them performed to backing bands, the music working in tandem with the lyrics.

He took time in putting on his jewellery. He eventually settled for a number of pins in his hair and a selection of glitzy sparklers on his knuckles. The Senate was unlikely to approve, but that was half the fun. Defiance and the refusal to conform were coded into him like a blood type.

Antony's eyes bumped up at the sight of the rings, his slightly arched eyebrow signalling that they were a little too *outré*, while his silent amusement was a clear indicator that he had given them his personal approval.

Heliogabalus still felt road-lagged and secretly dreaded having to attend the Colisseum later in the day to witness the gladiator shows put on in the amphitheatre as part of the celebrations. The barbaric blood-letting cruelty of the displays were renowned for their savagery. He had heard that animals and humans were carved up like meat in the arena. It wasn't something he relished seeing, and the enthusiasm expected of him would have to be faked in the interests of pleasing the crowd.

When Antony came up close to make a final check on his appearance he traced a finger lightly along the small of his back and met with no resistance. There was no sudden tensing or movement away on his part. The naturalness of his response told him that there were no obstacles in the way of their having sex later that night. Already he could feel the fit of their perfectly matched bodies.

He picked at a fruit bowl before wandering out to the sunlit terrace. His strappy sandals were bound to cause a sensation, but he didn't care. The Roman light was clear, busy and atomized with charge. The whole scented parkland rose to his nostrils. When his mother came out to join him he could read in her dissolute features the years of heavy drinking and sex to which she was addicted. She ran a finger playfully along his smoothly shaved jaw, reminding him at the same time of the necessity for him to continue with his education. He was to resume studies with Serge and was to be taught etiquette, history and some law as a means of consolidating his position.

He was full of his own immediate plans to build a temple to his god and told Symiamira of his intention to visit the Senate in a carriage drawn by naked youths. The gesture would shock, but it was all part of his image. He had come to Rome to subvert the existing hierarchy and intended to do so with style. He was determined within a month to call a convention of all the city's prostitutes, male and female, and to preside over the meeting in a warehouse on the docks. He had planned the whole thing during his time on the road; and now it was simply a matter of feeding it into his agenda.

Downtown he found the streets infested with people. They stopped in their tracks to watch him pass, and already he could see the look of disapproval in their faces. While the youths who carried him looked festively camp and wore ostrich feathers around their necks and waists, the message was nevertheless clear. He could hear laughter and disparagement interspersed with the general popularity his presence excited. Rome was alive, and its cosmopolitan inhabitants were all purposefully headed for their groove in the city. Part of his pleasure lay in sighting faces that he considered attractive. They came from every nationality, although it was the distinctive Roman boys to whom he paid attention. Making a note of the local boys was important, for he intended to have sex with as many of them as his energies permitted.

His eye picked out a florist's stall under one of the arches, and the youth selling flowers was just his type. He was busy grouping blue irises for a customer, but for some reason he looked up when Heliogabalus was passing, and their eyes met. It was his first direct eye-conquest of the day, and he would ask Antony's advice about how best to win the boy over. He was excited now, and the thrill of it all had him put the meeting with the Senate out of his mind. He had little or no interest in government, and it was primarily for sexual kicks that he had come to Rome. Here everything awaited him, and his excitement was uncontainable.

There were girls, too, who caught his eye, hair piled up in elaborate constructs, bodies made off-limits by the hauteur with which they screened out the invasive spectator. They walked in a way quite different from the Syrians, who were lazier in their indolent emphasis on the hips. He liked the pretty blondes with their inscrutable green eyes and hieratic gestures.

The way to Senate House was his first real taste of the city. He could sight the up and down sides of the chaotic metropolis and longed to be left alone to explore the slums and dockside areas. It was there that he knew he would find the rent boys for whom he was looking. He wanted real life in the form of sailors, thieves and those who had invented themselves according to the mythic terms of the underworld.

The exact and rigid system that comprised the senatorial order was of the sort he inwardly despised. The élitist landowners fed off the food chain of slave labour. They were the fat cats who sat on top of the social pyramid. While it was within his power to appoint a senator to act as legate or proconsul in most of the important provinces, to administer the chief services of the city or to hold the higher posts in the priesthood, he was aware that his powers of appointment were limited. He disliked them for the stranglehold they had on all dissenting factions. Their networking was responsible in his mind for the likes of Antony being subjugated to the role of servant. He objected immediately to their imperiousness and absurd sense of self-importance. By contrast, he felt grateful to Serge for having always reminded him of the need for humility as a check on ambition.

He could tell straight away that the Senate were suspicious of his motives and the strategies he had prepared. His announcement that he was to build an Eastern-style temple to his god in the suburbs rather than the capital, and that his own religion was to take precedence over Mithraism, was greeted with a note of silent disapproval. Worse was to follow, and he had deliberately saved his lemon-squeezer effect until last: his demand that women should be permitted to enter the Senate was greeted with open hostility. He proposed setting up a women's senate, on the Quirinal Hill, to be presided over by his mother. It was the chance for which he had been waiting, and the effects were devastating. Most of the assembly rose to their feet in protest, except for one who remained seated and applauding his proposal. He wondered who this was who dared entertain the courage to differ from his opinionated colleagues. He decided then and there that he had most probably found a friend and would reward the individual by asking him to dinner at a later date.

Having scored a spectacular personal victory with these innovative and unpopular measures he decided to appease the Senate's anger by promising to make gifts to the public. He made it clear that he was to open a public baths in the palace and to make the baths of Plautianus available to the people. He was to have coins minted and distributed to his subjects as well as reprieving criminals tried under Macrinus. These were the general measures expected of him, and on this score he was anxious not to offend.

He was high for having acquitted himself so well and felt that despite his vulnerability he hadn't faltered. He had always trusted in real personal conviction having the edge on those who lived by received opinions. It was the force of his beliefs that had carried the day. The rest of the proceedings were given over to judicial trivia in which he took no interest.

His business over, he asked for a detour to be made on the route back to the palace. He wanted to explore the dockside complex and sniff out his future territory. The river's ropy smell had left him fascinated. It came up in the air with the pungent scent of pollution. He longed to see its vertebrae uncoil and the great force of it run with the sky on its back.

The youths carrying him set off in good humour. Once again there were crowds lining the pavements, staring out with the flat faces of tourists confused by the difference between what they had anticipated and what they were actually seeing. Most of them appeared fazed by his pop-star appearance. He had the impression that he moved through the crowds like a hallucination. He was the purple and gold image responsible for distorting their visual field. Unable to contain him, he knew they would invent a language to describe him, and this in turn would have a knock-on effect in creating the legend he intended to become.

They left the city centre with its congested traffic and negotiated a passage through a grid of bulky warehouses. There were workers everywhere shouldering sacks and crates, most of them stripped to the waist in the blond April sunlight. He could smell the fusion of spices and river sewage now, and it was direct in his face. The sensory input was raw and abrasive, and the information carried to his groin.

He could hear stevedores shouting out instructions as they

unloaded a red-hulled cargo ship in from the East. He knew that the cargo would contain, amongst other things, spices, perfumes, dyes, slaves and thick black Indian hair used in the making of wigs. He was excited by the feeling of risk generated by being in the precinct. The maleness, the foreigners, the cutting-edge sense of danger, they all came together in his blood like a drug. Then there was the river, and his first proper sighting of its pythonic coils and muddy undertow dragged out of the hills. There was a wind frisking a blue finish to the mud-whisked surface. There were a number of ships moored to the nearside dock: big, alien and alarming as extra-terrestrial visitors. They looked to him like craft arrived from the near planets as a prelude to a take-over. Gulls harassed the rigging and dived in hysterical forays for offal. He hadn't heard or seen these birds before and was suspicious of their yellow-eyed aggression and their querulously guttural diction. They were like a mob without camaraderie as they fought over whatever *disjecta membra* the current turned up.

Surveying the territory, he asked to be taken into a yard behind a restructured warehouse. After the continuous spotlight he had faced at the Senate, he felt the need to dissolve into shadows. He asked for only one minder to accompany him in his mapping out of sexual territory. He knew the madness and danger involved in such an enterprise but couldn't help himself. He could be killed on the spot or subjected to humiliating ridicule by a gang of workers, but he didn't care. He couldn't cure himself of the habit, and that was his kick. He should have been back in the comfort and security of his quarters, instead of exploring the oily-dark underbelly of a dockside warehouse.

He kept with a gold stripe of sunlight that advanced like a probe into the building. From where he stood he could make out the crouched figure of a docker sitting resting on top of a packing crate. The man seemed contracted into himself like a closed accordion. He could hear him breathing, his naked torso polished with sweat in the grainy dark. Even in the half-light he could see that the man was dark-skinned and perfectly proportioned.

He continued going forward, the risk firing his heart, its beat so loud it was like amplified bass. The place was stocked with grain-sacks packed tight with their cereal contents. He was glad the light went in all the way to the interior. He had half a mind to turn back, before it was too late. He felt unable to breathe. His chest was knotted. The dark was suffocating, and for a moment he associated the laser-beam of sunlight with his own life-force. He had the terror that if one went out the other would follow.

The man had sensed him now and was defensive of his territory. He was clearly skiving and frightened of being found out and flogged. He had all the instinctual alertness of an animal surprised in its lair. He sat up rigid, clearly prepared to jump off the chest and run.

Heliogabalus didn't falter. It was too late now. He kept his eyes fixed on the man and dropped his shoulders low as a sign that he intended no hostility. He wondered what the response would be when the man saw him dressed as emperor. And, excited as he was, he had already decided to put aside the idea of sex. Venturing into the dark and coming on to the man was sufficient. He knew that if he took it a step further and the man resisted then his minder might run him through. He didn't want the man to die in this way. The two had formed an almost complicitous pact in the dark, scenting each other out and sharing the apprehension of the act. He wanted to leave it at that and back out while there was still time. He drew out whatever money he had on him and threw it in the direction of the stranger. There was the muffled sound of coins pinking on the stone floor in a series of dispersed ricochets.

He turned around immediately and made for the open door, imagining he was going back into the light after having participated in one of the mystery cults. He felt stronger for the encounter, no matter his sense of sexual disappointment. Rome, he knew, offered him everything, but his first attraction had been to an unknown docker taking time out in a corporate-owned warehouse.

Outside he was glad of the zingy river air. Only one person had witnessed his frustrated attempt to make a conquest of rough trade, and he wasn't bothered. If the man wasn't anyway similarly inclined, then it was unlikely he would dare talk. So intense was the experience that he felt he had entered a pocket of missing time and was coming back to a different sort of reality.

They went back through the city in the late afternoon light, its mix of pink and gold pointing up the buildings. Their progress was deliberately slow, and when they got back it was early evening. An abrupt hailstorm seethed across the park, the atomized ice hitting target like miniature ping-pong balls. The shower seemed to come out of nowhere, with all the blustery assault of April weather.

Back in his palatial suite he settled to a deep scented soak, but not before he had requested a dinner based on dishes made popular by Apicius. He knew that he would hardly touch the food, but the aesthetic was important. He ordered sows' breasts with Lybian truffles, peacock's tongues flavoured with cinnamon, oysters stewed in garum, sturgeons from Rhodes, fig-peckers from Samos and African snails. The variety was like creating a menu from the various components of his empire. He would pick at it and order that the rest should go to his staff.

The hot water reached him everywhere a lover should. He abandoned himself to weightlessness and the juniper scouring-oil. The scent got right into him and stayed there like a tonic. It had him long to explore Italy's forests and to go deep into the Bacchic mysteries, with their emphasis on sexual frenzy.

After a while he called for Antony to bring towels into the room. He fought with the idea of telling him about his experience at the docks earlier in the day, imagining he would find a sympathetic ear. Even if he had been instructed by his mother never to confide in servants, he knew there was always the exception. He felt the necessity of having someone in whom to confide, and Antony seemed that person.

When he came into the room he knew he had chosen right. Antony didn't appear in the least disturbed by his nudity, and his green eyes took in everything with tact and sympathy. Heliogabalus flopped lazily, his chin appearing to rest on the surface. His body felt elastic and his mind fine-tuned. He basked in the pleasure of being alone in his own space and one that he was prepared to share only with his valet. He felt like a fish scrubbed of its scales, the filigree bones hidden by a soft membrane of skin. He had journeyed across rivers, streams and oceans to arrive on the banks of the Tiber, exhausted but alive, his colours still vibrant, the mud washed off his body.

Antony's attentiveness touched him in places he had never expected. His readiness to understand and to dissolve all hard edges made confession easy. Heliogabalus told Antony of the crazy impulse that had overcome him on his way back from the Senate and how he had gone looking for sex on the piers. He asked him about the dangers of cruising and laughed at how he had outraged his seniors by insisting that women should play a part in government. He had run the risk of blowing it all on the first day and still wasn't sure how he would live down the scandal. He was encouraged to make light of his problems by Antony's habit of arching his eyebrows in response. Their rapport was buzzy and spontaneous, without violating the nature of their relationship.

When Heliogabalus got out of the bath he was rock hard. His penis in its tapering reminded him of a closed iris bud. Antony wrapped him in a large violet towel and dried him with assiduous fingertips, taking care to avoid all contact with his genitals. His understanding of the body was an example of authoritative discretion.

Heliogabalus could hardly bear it. His whole being rooted to make contact with Antony. He felt like a tree in a wind-break waiting to throw itself into the arms of another tree. Desire came on with deafening force in his arteries. This time he abandoned himself to the sensation. He led with his tongue as the prehensile feeler searching for contact. Antony accepted the probe with astonishment and passion. As his tongue intermeshed with Antony's Heliogabalus was conscious of being sucked into a place every bit as large and exciting as Rome. He let himself go, the towel slipping from him like a shed skin, and dragged Antony back with him into the tangy, simmering bath.

4

The telephone rang at three in the morning, but Jim let it go. He knew instinctually that it was Danny, but he wasn't prepared to get involved at this hour. Experience had taught him that most excuses were preconceived and that lovers in the wrong usually attempted to justify themselves by lies. Much to Jim's annoyance Danny tried again twice in the next half-hour before giving up.

When Jim awoke to a foggy grey sky roofing the West End he immediately felt the pain of loss. He had the sinking feeling in the pit of his stomach that reminded him of vertiginous Boeing drops *en route* from London to New York. He had the sensation that he had been bounced from a great height and still hadn't managed to find his feet. But he was absolutely clear in his decision. He would, of course, miss Danny, but he didn't want him back. He realized he only knew half the man, and the rest was something he didn't like. Duplicity reminded him of a knot that could never be untied. You straightened out one kink only to be presented with another and another. There were millions of Dannys all over the city, living out double or multiple lives. Jim had encountered this pattern before, and he was determined to put a stop to it before it became a stranglehold. Even if Danny came looking for him he would refuse him entry. He was quite clear about it in his mind. He also needed to work single-mindedly on his dissertation and broker the way to a clearer interpretation of Heliogabalus' commentators.

He made himself breakfast. Tea and toast. A smoky lapsang souchong and rye bread oodled with Frank Cooper's Vintage Marmalade. The pop on the radio was tinny with smudged lipstick songs, floaty hooks that spoke of broken hearts and the vocabulary of teen hang-ups. None of it stuck with him, and instead he busied his mind with ideas about Heliogabalus to sound against his tutor. When his mobile went off, perversely he let it go, suspecting that his voicemail would confirm that it was Danny.

As he sat with his tea he tried hard to wipe the image of Slut from his mind. The picture of the blindfold, wounded sex-god kept coming back to him like a plague carrier. He didn't want the man anywhere in his life and felt nothing but abhorrence for his values. The idea of taking a short break in Rome occurred to him, both as a means of distancing himself from Danny and of visiting the city in which Heliogabalus had ruled.

From his window he could see a magnolia toppling in the nearby gardens. The pink conical flowers had been burned by the unseasonal cold or mashed to a rot by the continuous rain. He tried to imagine Heliogabalus looking out on his grounds all those centuries ago and perhaps also noting a drift of pink petals catching with the wind. That life comprised a series of optimal moments, always recollectable but often eluding analysis, was, he knew, the key to understanding psychological history and the part played by the individual in its recurring patterns. His way into his subject's life was through the multiple gateways leading to the psyche. The rest of history as he knew it had derealized.

Pouring himself more tea, he asked himself the fundamental question, one that was sure to come up: why Heliogabalus? According to Dion, the duration of the reign, which terminated on 11 March 222, was three years, nine months and twenty-eight days, although the figures applied only to the time that Heliogabalus was in Rome. That Heliogabalus had managed in such a short time to stamp his individual signature on history, given that no facts were recorded of his life prior to his becoming emperor, was what had drawn Jim to his subject. Heliogabalus lived on as an image coded into the collective, a pre-pop icon who seemed somehow to have been committed to film. And the way the film rolled, scratches and all, from century to century, its contents continuing to come up, was what he found fascinating. By rights Heliogabalus should have disappeared in the food chain of forgotten characters over the centuries, but he was still there, demanding attention.

He knew his choice was an unusual one, and his tutor had remarked on the relatively limited sources available for research. It was the fact that Heliogabalus was a poet rather than a politician in his behaviour and that he had tried to transform government into theatre that held Jim captive. There was also a loose theory of his that found affinities between the youthful emperor and the subversive life and work of the schoolboy poet Arthur Rimbaud. He had drawn attention to the fact that Heliogabalus' term of office corresponded in years to the formative state in youth, fourteen to eighteen, in which Rimbaud had attempted in a series of hallucinatory poems to recreate the universe according to his imagination. It mattered to Jim to make the connection, no matter how tenuous. He believed that both had acted out of a similar visionary impulse.

The rebel in him also identified with Heliogabalus' policy of degrading governmental posts. As a means of undermining the self-importance of most officials, the emperor had put unqualified people into senior jobs. A dancer had been appointed prefecture of the guard; Gordius a charioteer, prefect of the watch; Claudius, a barber, had taken over the Ministry of Agriculture; and rent boys were pushed into the Senate. Jim regarded these anarchic gestures as belonging to the theatre of the absurd, as well as examples of the emperor applying favouritism to some of the lowlife he had met through sexual encounters.

As Jim understood it, Heliogabalus had attempted to overthrow the system. He was an emperor who had substituted the heterodox with the unorthodox, the heterosexual ideal with its homosexual counterpart and the regenerate with the degenerate. His actions had mirrored the cultural entropy at work within the empire itself and as such were symptomatic of the times. He had exposed the sugar-rot at work in the Senate and found it to be a form of ideological diabetes. Jim laughed to think that the same corruption was at work today. He was only too well aware that nothing created a stronger sense of moral self-vindication than an establishment able to divert attention from its inconsistencies by pointing up the shortcomings of the opposition.

Jim let another incoming call go, as he reflected on the inveterately negative core at the heart of all politics. This time the caller had left a message, and he punched in digits to retrieve his voicemail. As he had suspected, it was Danny, but there was no sense of apology or attempt at reconciliation in his tone. The message was cold and brief. 'Slut's looking for you. Watch out.'

Jim felt a ripple of fear go through him like a guitar chord, and the riff ran up and down his spine before subsiding. He played the message once again and saved it for reference. He had anticipated hearing a marginally contrite Danny but instead had encountered a voice loaded with threat. The contempt in it stayed buried in him like a knife.

He went back to his place at the kitchen table and looked out at the splashy April clouds. Even if Danny intended to scare him as a joke, the undertones were clearly malicious. The image of Slut that he had tried so hard to suppress swam back into view, the wounds on his body reopening as the perverse stigmata of the sexual outlaw. He saw the image so intensely that it was like the man was standing in front of him in the kitchen, the blindfold in place, the damage cut into his skin.

Rather fantastically he began to wonder if he wasn't the recipient of some sort of voodoo hex put on him by Slut's cult. The hallucinated quality of what he was seeing lived like fire in his mind. He tried to dissociate from the image each time it came up, but without success. Slut was in his head, securely locked in there like a zoo creature in its cage.

In the effort to free himself Jim tried to concentrate on his work. He looked out of the window where blue windy patches had opened up in the sky again in between toppling constructs of cumulus. He thought of calling a friend but knew it was too early to talk about his break-up and the weird goings on he had witnessed last night.

He worked his way back to the idea of Heliogabalus and the nature of biography as fiction. That the emperor was the victim of bad press and had become the subject of largely apocryphal anecdotes went without saying, but the question remained as to why Heliogabalus' conduct should have appeared so scandalous to a generically decadent society. Even if his search for the man behind the fiction was frustrated by historians writing to gain favour at the time, the level of acrimony was still disproportionate to the vehicle at which it was directed. He had no doubt that Heliogabalus had been the victim of a homophobic assassination. The atrocities committed on his dead body – which had been chopped up, placed into a sewer and finally thrown into the river – were undoubtedly the actions of vindictive gay-bashers. That he had been denied a burial and in effect fed to the fish, despite his being popular with the people, was further confirmation of the ephemeral place he occupied in history.

Jim decided to stay with this theme of the absent body as one to present to his tutor. What additionally puzzled him was the way Heliogabalus had been denied any form of psychological motivation by his biographers. He had been factored to a formulaic set of sensations, in which there was no subtext to account for his actions. But to Jim's mind what distinguished him from the likes of Commodus, Caligula and Nero seemed to be not only the mystery surrounding his life but also the relative lack of violence in his character. Unlike Nero, whom he emulated in terms of spending the state fortune on himself, he was without the pathology that had made Nero into a serial killer. He had read in Suetonius that Nero, after having killed his mother, put her naked body on display, so that he and his friends could comment on the shape of her legs, the curve of her bottom and the size of her breasts. If Nero was a psychopath, then Heliogabalus was a benign ruler who was known to have put only one person to death during his reign, despite a series of rebellions aimed at deposing him.

Jim put this down to gender and Heliogabalus' acceptance of his homosexuality. While Commodus, Caligula and Nero had all openly engaged in same-sex relations, they had done so with a vicious edge of misogyny quite different to Heliogabalus' unashamed pursuit of his own sex. Gender, then, was a definite angle to his thesis and one that would provide a controversial focus to the subject of men marrying men. There was also the confusion created by Heliogabalus having reputedly married three women, two of them old enough to have been his mother and the third one of the Vestal Virgins, who were part of a religious order responsible for guarding Rome's sacred fire. The complexity of the emperor's emotional life, which combined incest with bisexual tendencies, was a complete psychological study in itself. What he aimed to do was to rehabilitate Heliogabalus in contemporary terms. Nobody to his mind could relate to a past that wasn't in some way linked to the present. His own work was being done in a small West End flat, the windows grilled by pollution, and the whole sonic overdrive of the city collecting as noise in his head. He was conscious, in writing terms, that his subject was directly involved in the variables of his biochemistry and in the fluctuations of energy he brought to the work, together with their opposite – periods of disillusionment in which the work was temporarily abandoned. He had got Heliogabalus in his blood, and he liked it that way. He was confident, too, that he would coerce his supervisor into seeing things from his point of view.

Still feeling unnerved by the night's proceedings and the subsequent threat he had received from Danny, he decided to call in and see his friend Masako on his way to college. Like many Japanese girls based in London Masako was sold on fashion and pop. With her fringe dyed pink and blue and her clothes comprising Topshop-retro and bottled Miss Sixty jeans, Masako had joined the hundreds of thousands of young Japanese who had chosen to make London their home. Still wired from the cyber-ethos of Tokyo Masako had found in London a basis from which to free herself of the inherited traditions of Japanese family life. Here she was free to explore the pop capital and date Western men as a welcome antithesis to their Japanese counterparts. Her fashion degree at St Martin's was going well, and she lived in a studio in Frith Street, a space loaned to her by a friend who had returned to Tokyo for a year.

Jim called in advance to say he would be stopping by and headed off on foot across the city. With the tube network in a state of chronic dysfunction, he preferred to avoid the Underground and had taken to walking almost everywhere. London was on the way to becoming a Yardie-infested war-zone, its tensions throbbing in the conflict between an outmoded capitalism and a populace who had taken to arming themselves. Shootings had become a regular occurrence, and the Prime Minister's armour-plated Jaguar with its shatterproof black glass – a state-of-the-art vehicle that was able spray oil slicks and throw out smokescreens to shake off pursuing attackers – symbolized the fortress security needed to protect a discredited autocrat from warring factions. The PM had often eluded assassination by having a dummy substituted for him.

Jim hurried into the continuous pour of the London streets. He had quickly discovered on coming here that London provided more stimulus in an hour than a year spent elsewhere. Above him the clouds seemed to interface the buildings, their massive skyscrapers forming a city above a city in endlessly agglomerated suburbs that continued as far as the eye could see.

He made his way along a traffic-blasted Euston Road in the direction of Cleveland Street, its constricted artery still carrying undertones of the nineteenth-century gay scandal that had shocked society to its bleached roots. He imagined, as he walked down that road, the Victorian glitterati leaving their cabs waiting outside in the street as they ducked out of the brown rain into the discreetly sign-posted male brothel. He thought of Prince Eddy, screened by a UFO-shaped umbrella, giving the entrance code to the boy on the door.

He continued across Fitzrovia, connecting up with Charlotte Street and aiming to cross over Oxford Street into Soho. London was characteristically spacy with its offloaded commuters coming out of the Underground. He didn't know why, but an acute feeling of vulnerability came over him as he walked down Charlotte Street. He had the unnerving suspicion that something bad was about to happen. Most of the restaurants were still closed and, apart from a courier having difficulties in finding in an address, the street remained relatively quiet. There was a couple sitting huddled in their coats outside a café, the girl appearing affronted by something her partner had said.

Jim was half-way down the street when he froze. Coming towards him, looking like they had stepped out of a doorway, were two clones whom he recognized from the St Anne's Court gathering. Dressed in their uniform leather and denim, and with conspicuous nose, eyebrow and lip piercings, they stood out by way of their trans-species ugliness. Jim didn't have time to cross over, and the two men, forming a solid resistance, refused to let him pass. He found himself face up against the opposition, which parted only after one of the men had bitten his ear.

It had all happened so fast that Jim reeled from the pain and shock. He instinctually put his hand to his ear and, although the bite had been a superficial one, a trickle of blood ran in thin branchlines across his fingers. When he turned around the two men had disappeared down a sidestreet.

He stayed rooted there, paralysed by fear. He felt powerless to act and at the same time angry with himself for having been so passive. A part of him wanted to give chase and confront his antagonists, but he knew without doubt that he would come off worst and might even get seriously injured. Nobody had witnessed the attack, and it had been done with a speed that was breathtaking. He knew for the first time how it felt to be the victim of assault. There was no help at hand and nobody to whom he could turn. There was just the terrifying realization that he was all alone in the big uncaring city. Being jumped was something he had always dreaded, and now tasting the raw reality of it he felt he had let himself down. He told himself he should have seen it coming and got out of the way. Even more excruciating was the realization he had been set on by his own kind. Luckily the wound appeared to be shallow and the blood loss minimal. He played briefly with the idea of checking into casualty, before deciding against it. He had received a tetanus injection a year back, and if the risk was HIV then there was nothing he could do about testing at this stage.

With the fear of infection needling his mind, he crossed over Oxford Street into Soho. He was in a hurry to get to Masako's and tell her his story. His whole life seemed to depend on getting there without delay. He had never before been so conscious of the separation of mind and body. In his head he was already there. It was the physical that let him down and the sheer impossible size of the city.

The Soho streets were already busy, as he cut through Bateman's Buildings on his way to Frith Street. He had picked up in these alleys at night and was surprised at how different they looked by day and how demythicized of their sexual contents.

He arrived at Masako's flat to find her only just emerged from

73

the bath. She was dressed in a black T-shirt and predamaged blue Levis slashed over the knees. Her hair was still wet and, always the observer of cute details, he noted that her toenails were painted turquoise.

Seeing he was in a state she had him sit down and went into the kitchen to make tea. Jim settled on two cloud-shaped shocking-pink cushions in his usual place under the skylight. Looking up at the grey sky gave him a little hit of calm before Masako came in with two mugs of herbal tea.

Now that he could relax for the first time since the incident had taken place, he realized he was still in shock. He was shaking inside and he could feel an involuntary twitch under his left eye. More frightening was the feeling he had been cut off from language. The words he needed wouldn't come up in his brain.

Masako, who was all sensitivity, let him be. She, too, stared up silently at the spun-sugar vocabulary of clouds moving in a convoy across the sky. To Jim the skylight was like a meditation-point, and the more he stayed with it the calmer he grew. He sensed words slowly coming back as a communications tool. A switch had been thrown, reactivating patterns.

'I got bitten on the way over here,' he said, hurrying his speech. 'Two men blocked my way in Charlotte Street, and one of them bit my ear. I can hardly believe what I'm telling you.'

'You mean now, on the way here?' Masako gasped, incredulous.

'Don't worry. I'm not badly hurt. It's more the shock,' he managed to say.

'But who are these guys?'

'I don't know. But I should probably tell you about what happened last night.'

'Mmm,' Masako encouraged, her jeans revealing her bare midriff and the little turquoise chip in her belly-button.

'What I'm going to tell you sounds weird, but it's true. Last night Danny persuaded me to go with him to a place in Soho, where a group of adepts – for want of a better word – were meeting. Well, I had no idea that Danny was a part of all this, but I'll come to that later.'

'Go on.'

'The worst part of it was when a man called Slut was introduced into the room. He's some sort of numbers freak from Hampstead Heath. I don't want to shock you, but men go there at night to take part in anonymous sex. Slut sees himself as a hero to a cult who engage in numbers.'

'I hope Danny's not into that.'

'I think he is, and I've left him. But let me go back to last night. The two men who attacked me a short while ago were there, and they must have recognized me.'

'Are you sure?'

'I clearly intruded on something secret last night,' Jim said, 'and when I saw that Danny was so much a part of the cult I walked out. This morning he left me a threatening message, telling me that Slut was looking for me and that I'd better watch out.'

'Mmm, kinda scary,' Masako said.

'I'm not going to be intimidated,' he defended himself, 'but I wonder if I shouldn't go away for a while. I was thinking of Rome, as a visit there would be helpful with my research.'

'I'm not sure if you shouldn't go to the police. Do you want me to look at your ear and see if it needs dressing?'

'I'm fine,' he pretended. 'It's only a scratch. I'd rather avoid contact with the police at this stage.' Inwardly he felt his reserves collapsing, and wondered why he remained so rigidly defensive. The fear in him was beginning to map out its territory and settle to a nervy alert. He visualized it as an animal on guard.

'You can stay here for a while,' Masako said, 'if you need a place for a few days.'

Jim considered her offer before replying, 'No, I'll be all right, really. I've got my work at home, and I don't want to blow the thing out of proportion.'

Again he found himself acting contrary to his needs, by allowing an innate sense of perversity to go against his best interests. He knew he should take up Masako's offer of a temporary refuge and stay undercover until things blew over. It would be by far the best solution. But instead he was once again making himself vulnerable by refusing help.

75

'I've got to see my supervisor later this morning,' he said. 'It's an important meeting, as I've got to justify the angle I'm taking on the subject.'

Masako suddenly pointed up at a black cloud that was filling in the skylight with its density as it dragged over. To Jim it looked like Africa being stretched across the sky. One of the little games they shared was to find similarities between the shapes of clouds and geography. It was something they had done all one autumn afternoon, when the cloud arena was constantly changing and being driven by a tail-wind.

'Looks like China,' he said.

'Mmm,' Masako concurred. 'But it could be America. Let's see what follows it.'

Jim momentarily lost himself in the game, as he let his mind dissolve into the cloud masses. For a brief time it seemed as though Danny had never existed. The moment was closed to all other associations but those of the game.

'You sure you don't want to come back tonight?' Masako asked.

Jim continued to think on the idea and of the complex set of emotions he felt for Masako. That they were friends had never ruled out the possibilities of a deeper involvement, and he was sufficiently flexible to know that being gay didn't mean he could only have relationships with men. He enjoyed the romantic undertones to the friendship they shared and the excitement implied by the fact that anything could still happen. Masako was pretty, boyish and possessed the sort of aesthetic sensibility he found so attractive in Japanese girls. A combination of inherited and adopted values, the mix providing a refreshingly new take on life, particularly in a city as historically present as London. It would be easy for him to become involved with Masako, and he had every reason to believe that she would be sympathetic to his continuing relations with men.

As Masako busied herself with making more tea for them, he had a serious think about coming to stay. A change of address would, he hoped, put Slut and his associates off his trail. He still couldn't for the life of him think why he should be of any importance to the group. He had witnessed only the preliminaries to the

76

night and had nothing on the participants. There appeared no reason why he should be singled out in this way, unless, of course, it was Danny's doing. The shock that his ex could be behind this hit him hard. Although Danny had been cold of late there had been no hint of a break in their relationship.

When Masako came back into the room, he said, 'I've changed my mind. I'd like to stay here for a few days. It would do me good and help take my mind off things.'

Masako settled to a mauve cushion on the floor and smiled in her usual taciturn manner. It was a gesture as protective as it was well-meaning. He knew that from habit and was glad in himself that he'd made the decision. He liked her ambience and the delicate signature she had impressed on the studio. There were parrot tulips arranged in a vase on the table, beside a number of books and fashion glossies, the black beret she wore out in the rain and a glass bowl full of Shiseido lipsticks and other items of makeup. Her CD collection was racked in the far corner of the room, and the dynamic generated a feng-shui sensitivity to arrangement and comfort.

It was raining again in fast sequences. The skylight sounded like someone was bunching tissue paper. April in all its blotchy unpredictability had moved into the city, muddying the river and stripping the parks of blossom. Jim could never find the same comfort in spring rain as he did in its autumn counterpart. There wasn't the sense of settling in that October rains brought but more a feeling of skittish electric surprise.

The hot tea was a comfort, while he faced the prospect of having to go out soon to meet his supervisor. A quick fifteen-minute dash through the rain would get him there, before the business began of arguing his case. Despite the set-back he had suffered he still felt sufficiently fired up to win his cause.

Masako had to be out and about in town that day and told Jim that she would be back at around five o'clock. She gave him the spare set of keys to her flat and promised to cook for him on her return.

He braced himself to face the downpour and, feeling a lot more secure in himself, hurried out into the Soho streets in the direction of Bloomsbury. He made rapid progress. A black cab thugged its way through segueing traffic towards Centre Point. There were young people tented in sleeping-bags on the pavement. An out-patient manifesting delusional symptoms was conducting a run-in with himself outside the Dominion Theatre. The man's aggressive body language complemented the distraught emotional arena he was in the process of addressing. Jim gave him a wide berth and headed up Oxford Street. A gang of youths wearing obligatory baseball caps were busy hassling an innocent bystander and he decided for safety's sake to make a detour down a sidestreet. London with its warring interzonal factions had become the least tolerant of all major cities. Yob culture with its accompanying street crimes had spread like a pathogen through the city's dangerously mismultiply-ing cells. Jim thought of London as an urban jungle, its populace only a fraction away from exploding into organized warfare.

He made his way by detours into Gower Street, the rain giving over again and being replaced by a watery blue sky. The air was fried all along the main concourse by traffic pollution. A truck driver was leaning out of his cabin haranguing a young woman behind the wheel of a scarlet BMW. Their road-rage dialogue ripped across the dual-lane traffic before the woman sped away at the lights.

Jim arrived at college to find his supervisor waiting for him in his room. Martin King was a fortysomething academic, sometimes pedantic but more often laid-back and wonderfully unconventional in his approach to history. While trying to steer Jim away from too psychological a take on his subject, he was none the less committed to treating history in part as fiction. While his business wasn't to authorize Jim to write a novel about Heliogabalus, he was sympa-thetic to blurring the boundaries between history and imagination.

Martin was casually dressed in a charcoal lambswool V-neck and lived-in jeans. His particular clothes fetish was the wearing of impeccable leather shoes, polished like a car to a waxed gloss. Jim checked for the reassuring characteristic in his supervisor; a man who was so consistently private that he had never succeeded once in penetrating his defences. They had never drunk together or met each other off campus.

Jim was still nervous from the morning's events and kept on feeling his mind go blank. He was terrified of losing his natural eloquence at a time when he most needed it. He didn't want to concede territory to Martin and knew that he had it in him to hold his own. He was starting to experience the hot flushes he dreaded, and for a moment the room seemed to up-end like it had somersaulted.

Martin seemed not to have noticed. He was busy switching attention from the database he had been surfing and confronted Jim with the fazed look of someone going through the motions of returning to real time.

'How's Heliogabalus?' Martin asked, telescoping Jim and his subject into one character. 'It's the first time in my experience anyone has chosen to write about him. I'm looking forward to your dissertation.'

'I'm still struggling with the concept of separating fact from fiction,' Jim said, conscious as he spoke of the selective faculty he brought to language when addressing his tutor.

'I think we have in part to dispense with the reliability of sources in your case,' Martin said. 'Whether, for instance, the *Augustan History* was the work of a single writer or a number of biographers is more the subject of bibliography. Much of the controversy surrounding Heliogabalus' life comes from faked documents anyhow.'

'That's my problem,' Jim said. 'I need you to tell me what licence I have to recreate Heliogabalus in contemporary terms. What matters to me is making him live now. My sources are too sketchy for me to lean on historical fact.'

'I've no objection to your partially inventing history,' Martin replied. 'I'm all for students being original. What I don't want is a purely psychological thesis. One that uses Heliogabalus as the baseline for a case history.'

'Part of my work will, of course, be gender-based,' Jim said. 'There seems little doubt that his enemies were provoked by the fact that he was so openly gay.'

Martin laughed. 'No objections. If we're to believe Lampridius, then Heliogabalus was the first – probably the only – Roman emperor openly to discuss the possibilty having a sex-change. This opens up a fascinating area of study that I hope you'll explore. I think you'll find Nero had similar tendencies, or at least he transferred them to his male lovers.'

'Yes, to Sporus, wasn't it? I'm glad you see this as a rich area of research. Although I think I'm right in saying there's a pathology attached to Nero, which is not the case with Heliogabalus.'

'I think so, most certainly,' Martin replied. 'Nero turned by degrees into a psychopath, committing one crime to cover for another. There's certainly no evidence that Heliogabalus shared this tendency. But I'm still curious as to why you should choose such an obscure emperor as the subject for your dissertation.'

'Empathy,' Jim laughed. 'But also the desire to rehabilitate him to history. He's in many ways the emperor who has gone missing. It's like he's been sucked into a hole in the middle of the galaxy.'

'There's also the question of ritual,' Martin added. 'What for instance did his cult worship, other than the sun? Nobody's ever made it clear, at least not in the way that we know about constituents of Mithraism or the rites conducted as part of the Elysian mysteries. I'd like you to tell me something about the cult of Elagabal. Allusions to it are few, but it shouldn't be too hard to reconstruct.'

'What we do know', Jim said, feeling his assertiveness return, 'is that he sacrificed animals in his temple and also underwent the *taurobolium*. There's also an allusion to him having celebrated the rites of Salambo and if I recall correctly a reference somewhere to him throwing animals off a high tower as part of some ritual.'

'Good,' Martin said. 'I'm sure if you follow your sources you'll hit on the right trail. It's an area in which I'm particularly interested. And what about his three marriages? They were surely organized around motives of religion –'

'Perhaps, but there were other reasons. I think his first marriage to Julia Paula was undoubtedly dominated by the feeling he should marry into the Roman aristocracy. It seems to have been an attempt on his part to infiltrate the patrician classes.'

'You mean because he himself was a foreigner?'

'Precisely. He had no kudos in Rome other than a tenuous claim to be an Antonine.'

'But his second marriage, though, to the Vestal Aquilia Severa, was undoubtedly an attempt to superimpose his own god on Rome's existing one,' Martin said.

'Without question. Although his perversity was such that the idea of violating an off-limits woman was probably an additional incentive.'

'I see you've got his psychology well sewn up,' Martin approved. 'And the third marriage? The motives behind this have always seemed obscure to me.'

'Anna Faustina was, of course, an aristocrat. She was the great-granddaughter of the emperor Marcus Aurelius through his fourth daughter Arria Fadilla. We know little about her, although she seems to have been implicated in a plot involving two senators aimed at deposing the emperor. That she wasn't executed again points to Heliogabalus' benign nature.'

'Weren't all these women middle-aged if I remember correctly? And none of them particularly attractive?'

'So we're led to believe. They all seem to have been in their mid-forties and long past the age of producing an heir. I imagine they were a cover for his sexuality.'

'It would seem so,' Martin said. 'It's hard to get away from gender when considering Heliogabalus. He was clearly looking to marry mother figures, I suppose.'

'A not unreasonable conclusion,' Jim said, with inflected irony. He could sense that he had more than held his own and displayed his knowledge to reasonable effect. He judged from Martin's tone they were nearing an end to the meeting, something enforced by his supervisor's habit of studying his snakeskin loafers as a preliminary to winding down.

'I'd like to see some more work from you in about eight weeks,' Martin said. 'Perhaps with some of the ideas we've discussed today incorporated into the thesis. It's shaping up well.'

When Martin stood up Jim felt relieved he had acquitted himself commendably. The feelings were almost compensatory, given the bad things that had happened earlier. He walked out of the room feeling elated, the hole in his nerves momentarily stitched, as he briefly forgot Danny and his invidious threat.

As a reward Jim decided to go and do some reading in a little café in Monmouth Street.

The staff never bothered him there and left him free to work at his table for as long as he wished. He was still reading the Penguin edition of *The Lives of the Later Caesars* and using the book as an overview on the often mad, depraved and perversely inhuman personalities who ruled over the declining empire. In most cases their pathologies were inseparable from their actions, and he found himself fascinated by the belief common amongst them that they were gods. The drive towards self-divinization, a recognition conferred on the emperor by the Senate, was at the roots of the megalomania so often displayed by the tyrannical individuals written up in the *Augustan History*. Although Jim didn't see madness as belonging to a hereditary genotype, he was none the less fascinated by the irregularities of behaviour attributed not only to the later caesars but also to their prototypes such as Caligula and Nero.

Jim occupied himself with this network of thoughts as he headed off in the direction of the café. Decadence, he reminded himself, involved a total preoccupation with the moment. To live as Heliogabalus had, fast and recklessly, meant addressing the moment without concern for an illusory future. By magnifying the instant and living within its register, Heliogabalus had succeeded in maximizing immediate sensation. Immediacy, Jim realized, was also the counterthrust to an acute awareness of threatened mortality.

When he looked around him at faces in the street, bleached from long hours of sitting in front of terminals, he was aware they were working for a future they would probably never meet. All the rewards offered for their corporate lifestyles were conditional on service. It was a system he despised. He was determined to be free at all costs.

Walking always allowed him to think in sustained sequences. It was for him the best method of booting up ideas programmed in his unconscious. He ignored the red buses blasting their way down Gower Street towards an irate gridlock at the lights. Unable as yet to contemplate life without Danny, he took advantage of the high that came with the thought of beginning a new life. He felt a brief-lived but intense excitement at the prospect of being without commitments, a rush that almost immediately gave way to feelings of vulnerability and isolation. Looking for comfort it was Masako to whom he turned. He was suddenly glad he had taken up her offer to stay. The thought of going back to her flat later was a welcome one and an incentive to work hard throughout the afternoon.

He carried on walking, his mind full of his thesis. It was odd, he reflected, to be out in London with a little-known emperor in his head and to be preoccupied with restructuring his life. It was the business of imagination to recreate history, and he got off on the thought of feeding this outrageous third-century Syrian youth some of his own intransigent ideas about the nature of the individual in contemporary society. He saw the two of them bonded by a conspiratorial pact. They were subversives, and their weird hyperlink was maintained by a sort of cyber-telepathy.

He had just got into Monmouth Street when he stopped dead in his tracks. Something made him look across the road to the entrance to Neal's Yard. The bare-footed emaciated person emerging from the yard was none other than Slut. Dressed in leather and denim, and seemingly impervious to the wet streets, he had a carrier of groceries in one hand. Jim backed up against the wall, quite certain he hadn't been seen, and watched Slut go off down the street towards St Martin's Lane. The man carried a bad aura and kept his eyes turned down to the pavement.

Jim watched him go with the certain knowledge that he meant evil. There was something about his debasement lived on his skin. The almost colourless eyes and ravaged features were a pointer to the twisted emotions that undoubtedly governed his thinking. He took a last look at Slut disappearing into the crowd before slipping into his café. He felt safe there in its bohemian ambience and in the unpretentious atmosphere that it offered. Things were basic but perfectly acceptable. He sat down at a table by the window and thought of Masako. Her image lived in him today like a single carnation in a vase. He looked out at the revisiting shower, then quickly lost himself in his work.

5

He wished he'd never married Julia, and she'd quickly driven him to drink. As he lay in bed with the early morning haze fuzzing the park, he could think of nothing but Hierocles. They had met only yesterday in the steamy fog of one of the more notorious bath-houses, but one thing had led to another and now he was obsessed.

It was cold for early summer. The great shock of burgundy roses arranged in a vase by his bed were at odds with the sea-chill that hung over Rome. The smoky morning sky was flecked with pointillistic drizzle. He needed a drink and didn't care that he allowed for no resting point in his intake.

He realized he would have to put an end to this marriage, which anyhow had been little more than a political move on his part. In marrying Julia he hadn't anticipated encountering so formal a partner. Her lack of humour, the correctness instilled in her by her father and her refusal to experiment sexually left him feeling cold in her company. Nothing about her turned him on, least of all the possessiveness that came from her insecurity. Alone with her, she wouldn't let him be but endlessly questioned him as to his friends, whereabouts and the amount of time he spent downtown.

At first he had put it down to the fact that she was at least twice his age. She was not unattractive but evidently still carrying the scars of an earlier marriage, and their chemistries hadn't gelled. More tedious was the fact that she had taken to having him followed. He was aware that she knew all about his visits to the public bath-houses and the dockside area of the river and that her inquisitiveness gave him grounds to annul the marriage. While he wished her no harm he wanted her out of his life.

He felt too young to be restrained by her class-bound consciousness and her beliefs in strict monogamy. The structured life she wanted for them was the exact opposite to his idea of freedom.

What the drink couldn't erase in him was the knowledge of his mortality. The taste of it was so acute at times that he longed to die in order to be free of the apprehension. When the awareness of death peaked in him then the sensation was like sex. He surfed it ecstatically in the process.

It was with good cause that he recollected Seneca's writings, and they were always a source of comfort to his solitary thoughts. As he lay in bed, he remembered a line about the transience of all things in the essay 'On the Shortness of Life'. It came to him now: 'Your speed in using time must compete with time's own rapid pace.'

He slept apart from Julia, not only because he brought boys to his bed but out of a need to reflect in the quiet hours on his destiny. He remembered that at some time in the night Antony had visited him, just for the warmth and symmetry their bodies created. Their relationship was an easy one and free of all tensions. When his life was too crowded, turning to Antony was like jumping from a high building to land safely on warm sand.

He wasn't in the mood for business with the Senate today. They disapproved of the temple he had built to his god in which he worshipped and sacrificed. They would rather the money had been spent on the military or a new office tower and challenged him over the funding. It would soon be procession time, and he intended to lead the rites in having his god conducted across the city from one temple to another. It was to be an extravaganza like no other and a ceremony in which Eastern rites were dubbed on to a Western aesthetic.

But, for the moment, his mind was occupied with thoughts of Hierocles. He was young, darkly attractive, considered, as a performer, *déclassé* and had undoubtedly at some time or other been somebody's favourite. He had assured Heliogabalus that he was no longer kept – and whether it had been said to please him or not he felt sure he had found his match.

He called Antony to his room, although he knew it was still an unsociably early hour. He wanted to tell him about his meeting with Hierocles and ask him to assist with the ceremonies tomorrow. No matter the hour, he knew Antony never objected or lost his consistent sense of cool. The homeostasis of his mood seemed untouched by the irregularities that affected the majority of people.

When Antony came in, already dressed and carrying a bowl of grapes that seemed to have been polished to a shine, Heliogabalus felt free to abandon himself to camp. He lay across the bed in the exaggerated pose of a fallen angel, hamming it up as a diva whose tempers left him shredded by passion. He knew that Antony would soothe his head, massage his shoulders and generally play mother.

'I met somebody in one of the baths yesterday,' he announced, determined to keep Antony in suspense. 'A real pretty boy but one with an edge. Could be dangerous. About my age, drives in the arena sometimes, big green eyes and a mischievous sense of humour. No education and a bit rough but . . .'

He caught himself out describing a particular type for the hundredth time and laughed. He knew he was incorrigible and Antony shared his laughter.

'Sounds like the right one for you and the wrong one for Caesar,' Antony commented, the smile upgrading itself from his lips to his eyes.

'I want him for always,' Heliogabalus said, aware as he spoke that he was allowing his extreme youth to colour his feelings. He wanted Hierocles in the way his obsession wouldn't rest until he had acted on his desire. It was always the same, his urgency made subordinate to every other consideration. And sometimes his mania got out of control when the object of his desire was the sun, the harbour, a particular street, the billions of gallons of air over a mountain or an idea that could find no external correlative.

'I'll have him here waiting for you when you return from business,' Antony promised him in his usual reassuring way.

'I've so much on my mind, and need your help with the preparations for tomorrow. The streets have to be cordoned off, the Praetorian Guards are needed for back-up to the procession, there have to be police out to suppress potential riots . . . The list is endless. Plus it's also the time when an assassin could strike. Being emperor makes me the most wanted person alive.'

It was still early, and a burnt-orange sun was beginning to show through the mist. He didn't want to wake Julia up at this hour with the news that their marriage was over, but he had decided that he could no longer continue with the pretence and that she should be sent back to her father with some sort of annuity. He would leave that up to his lawyers. He had it in mind that to make his own religion popular with the people he should marry Aquilia Severa, one of the Vestals who officiated over the Palladium in the temple. The marriage of Elagabal with the earth goddess Vesta would, on a symbolic level, bring about the ideal union of East and West.

He toyed with the idea, while Antony massaged his shoulders with juniper oil. Of course, a marriage as controversial as the one he intended with Aquilia might also explode in his face. Marriage with a Vestal Virgin would be considered, by anyone's standards, a violation of taboo, but the mystic in him argued for a union in which the bond would be spiritual rather than physical. The knowledge that vestals found guilty of having sex were traditionally buried alive worked in his interest. If, as he hoped, Hierocles was about to become his lover, then Aquilia would prove the ideal mental partner.

His head was busy with the audit as Antony worked along his spine. What he secretly had planned was to remove the image of the goddess Vesta to his own temple. He was fascinated by the idea of the inextinguishable fire kept burning in honour of the goddess. Aquilia was part of the order devoted to never letting that fire go out and by appropriating the practice for his own cult he intended to take on that power and have his name become a metaphor for the city itself. Its commerce would be reflected in the activity of his neurons, its sex-drive in his hormones and its spirituality in the dance he performed inside his temple.

He amused himself with these thoughts as Antony, having finished on his back, wrapped him in a heated towel and left the room, coming back in again minutes later carrying a tray, on which there was bread and halva topped with yoghurt and honey. There were fresh figs and a selection of little cheeses that had been sun-dried on rush mats.

Now that he'd had a drink Heliogabalus felt better able to face the light meal prepared for him. The preparation of food interested him more than its taste, and he had himself the previous night prepared a dish of pumpkin with a seseli, asafoetida, dried mint, vinegar and liquamen dressing. He would never grow fat like the Circus Maximus gladiators of the vomitarium, the liverish *commissationes* who collapsed under repeat gourmand courses and who could tell at the first taste whether an oyster had been bred at Circeii or on the Lucrine rocks.

Equally he couldn't help himself sexually. Despite his busy agenda, he was obsessed with only one thing, and that was going back to the same bath-house in the hope that Hierocles would show up again. The place where the action happened was the bath-house built by Titus beside the ancient Domus Aurea, with its external portico facing the Colosseum. The place was notorious for its gay clientele, and almost anything could be had in the recreation rooms. He liked the steamy hothouse effect of the place and the abundance of naked bodies from which he could take his pick. And when the sun beat through the rotunda at noon he had the feeling his body was being solarized by its rays.

Although he imagined it would be meaningless to him, Heliogabalus was anxious for Hierocles to witness the procession he would lead tomorrow. He was determined to leave the city stunned by his performance as part of the rites. The musicians had been instructed to lay down a beat that would translate itself into crowd frenzy.

Acting against his own best interests, he decided to go to the baths by the Colosseum. Preparations were going on all over town for the festivities the next day. Streets were already being cordoned off and people were starting to set up stalls. Rome was still dusted in haze, and he looked out at a cemetery used by prostitutes, its marble statuary defaced by graffiti and eroded by time. Seneca was right, he told himself; we must live in the knowledge of certain death.

Leaving his minders to mix freely with the other bathers he went into one of the dressing-rooms. The place was all black-and-white marble with mosaic inserts and statues of the gods commissioned by Titus. Even though he made light of his identity and adopted a series of disguises, word had got out that he was emperor. It was known that he had a liking for *onobeli* or big cocks. That he had used up the talent available at the baths of Plautianus was also common knowledge and explained why he had chosen to patronize this place.

A number of youths were in the process of getting undressed. Everyone swam naked, and the boys here were mostly rent or belonged to theatre. What he liked was the way in which his sexuality dissolved barriers. Even though he was emperor his predilections made him as much an outsider as the fraternity who came here to have open sex in the recreation rooms. Nobody seemed suspicious of his motives or grew inhibited by his presence. Rather, he was amused to hear, via Antony, that he had been given the nickname 'Patron Saint of Rent Boys'.

He was in no hurry to pair off and disappear into one of the private cubicles. He had only one thought on his mind and that was finding Hierocles. He was nervous with apprehension. Elation and fear collided in his nerves. He kept seeing Hierocles' face everywhere, as though hallucinating him into existence. He saw him in every face that looked in at the dressing-room. His own need was so great that it was being answered by multiple variants of his obsession. Several times he was about to call out 'Hierocles' when, at the last moment, he realized his mistake. He ended up engaged in a long kiss as a result of misidentifying a dark youth with the hots. The kiss seemed to go on for ever and tasted of the sulphur traces in the water. Normally he would have followed this through to sex, but realizing his error he backed off. He didn't want Hierocles to find him going down on a possible rival.

Jealous without any reason, he imagined Hierocles involved in an orgy in one of the vaulted back rooms. He saw him engaged in a noodle dish of naked bodies glued to each other by positioning. He blanked the thought and went out to the pool with its turquoise floor shimmering through the rippling steam.

He dived in, searching for himself at the bottom. The water closed over him like a protective skin. For the moment his world seemed without boundaries. He gave himself up to weightlessness in an arc that took him effortlessly to the blue-tiled floor and up again in a fluent trajectory to the surface.

He surfaced, gasping, and looked around at the other swimmers lolling on the surface. The boy next to him had his curls collapsed like a bunch of black grapes over his face. People hung motionless in the water like bottles or made lazy circles with indolent breast-stroke. All around the pool naked youths sat displaying their bodies or paired off and disappeared into the recreation rooms. Those looking out and those looking in the pool had come here for the same purpose, and Heliogabalus felt safe in their company.

He made a slow round of the pool, scanning each cluster of faces. He was about to dive under again when he saw Hierocles coming out of one of the dressing-rooms. He accidentally swal-lowed water and felt his heart turn over. He was so nervous that his first impulse was to dive under and come up on the opposite side of the pool. He wanted to dematerialize on the spot and pretend the whole thing hadn't happened.

Instead he stayed dead centre of the pool, marginally obscured from view by a tangle of playful swimmers who were busy diving each other. He could see Hierocles looking around to acknowledge friends with a smile or a wave. He must have known he was being watched, for he went and stood by himself against a marble pillar and presented a moody profile to the pool.

Heliogabalus pretended not to notice and flipped over on his back so that he could stare up at the changing sky through the rotunda. The clouds had returned the grouping of a dense aerial forest. He lay there, lost in his reflection, hoping that by now Hierocles had joined a group or friends or had jumped into the pool. Without daring to look he began to create the lazy backstroke designed to get him back to the edge of the pool. He wished he'd never come here, and his only thought was to get out of the place fast.

He propelled himself back to the rim of the pool and was helped out by his minders. He looked across and saw that Hierocles had disappeared from view and was both relieved and terrified that he had gone off with someone else. He sat there, oblivious to the youths competing to catch his eye, his mind preoccupied with nothing but the thought of winning Hierocles. As the minutes passed, he grew more despondent at having missed his chance. He decided to punish Hierocles by slipping out through the back and leaving him to rot. Nobody in his world was going to play that hard to get.

With the intention of following his plan through, he stormed off towards the dressing-rooms. He brushed aside attendants and masseurs offering to dry him and, still wet, changed into his clothes. His mood had radically changed, and he could feel the blues driving out the optimism with which he had started the day. Suddenly nothing seemed important, not even the prospect of the festivities tomorrow.

He sulked as he dressed, his mouth down-turned like his mood. He wanted to stay and he didn't, and neither option pleased him. He took his time in preparing to leave, assembling his clothes without interest and avoiding eye contact with everyone.

When he got back outside he saw Hierocles waiting on the other side of the street. He was standing with his arms crossed, looking directly at him. Their eyes met in a freeze-framed moment that seemed to eliminate his entire past.

He didn't care that his minders were watching but instead hurried straight across the road. Hierocles looked nervous in a streetwise, bashful sort of way. Although the boy clearly lacked refinement, Heliogabalus was fascinated by the dodgy world Hierocles represented. There was something of an underworld shadow in his face, a sort of smokiness that suggested he had lived fast and wild.

Heliogabalus didn't wish to draw attention to himself, so he simply said, 'I'll have someone pick you up outside here at eight o'clock. They'll drive you to the palace.'

Hierocles nodded, and without wasting time Heliogabalus hurried back, his heart turning somersaults as he ran.

The day had suddenly picked up speed, and he was glad of the pearl-coloured sky that continued to shut out the sun. It added to the city's mystery and the sensation he had of the whole place being a fractal illusion that changed according to his vision. Perhaps because he was new there he felt he never encountered the same city twice. Rome seemed to be endlessly in the process of constructing and deconstructing itself.

He had cancelled his day's appointments and instead insisted on being taken to his temple to be with the god he was preparing to celebrate. Elagabal lived in him like a river sunk into a deep groove. He was his source and the reason for his good fortune in being emperor. It was imperative he honoured him at all times and made his phallic symbol into Rome's chief signature. Sacrifice was needed and, by way of showing his dislike of the military, he had transferred the duties of some of the leading generals to those of attending his temple. Their job was to officiate over the slaughter of animals and to prepare parts for sacrifice. The high-ranking military involved deeply resented their downgrading of office and the withdrawal of privileges that went with it.

What Heliogabalus did within the temple was guarded with such secrecy that the rites were known only to himself, his mother and the priests. He was aware of the rumours that he engaged in human sacrifice, selecting boys from the best families for this purpose and divining from their entrails a prognosis for the future. The idea amused him as much as it annoyed. It owed its origins to the malicious gossip of the military leaders he had demoted. Infanticide played no part in his scheme, nor did the abduction of youths from Italy's finest families.

He was driven across the city to his temple on the Palatine Hill. The huge colonnaded structure within a rectangular porticoed enclosure was surrounded today by a filigree mist. The place was to be his starting point tomorrow, and from there the procession would cross the city to his other temple in the suburbs. He liked the fact that a slow fog was rolling in and obscuring the city's high-rise buildings.

Insisting on being left at the entrance, he went inside to a temple lit only by a fire at the altar. Only last week it had been reported that he regularly fed human genitals to lions as part of his rites and that he castrated his lovers for this purpose.

A priest wearing a long Phoenician tunic with a single purple stripe running down the middle came to meet him as he approached the altar. Together they knelt before the black phallic oracle surrounded by offerings. He led the way as they chanted an incantation to his god that repeated a magical formula, and one that he was sworn never to divulge. The vibration set up by the chant deepened to a drone. Time ceased to exist as the mantra created its own autonomous rhythm. He was conscious only of the conversion of breath into a sound so charged it established a vibration round the walls. It was the old dynamic in which he lost himself to a higher plane of consciousness.

He continued chanting until the rite was through and his head felt spacy. Sacrificial sheep and cattle were to be killed at dawn as an offering to Elagabal before the procession began. He was keyed up at the prospect of leading the extravaganza and of being in the spotlight before the crowds. The exhibitionist in him was planning to excel as never before. His costume was already arranged, and the streets were to be sanded with gold dust.

Back at the palace he remained impatient for Hierocles to arrive. Unlike the selfless passage of time in the temple, the hours now seemed to have got stuck together. The waiting was interminable. He could find nothing to take his mind off Hierocles, except a visit to the kitchens to assist with the preparation of dinner. He had requested that the food should be colour-coded bright blue and that the various courses should be themed around this colour. Everything from the canapés to the vegetables to the multi-decked desserts were to be dyed a uniform shade of blue.

He enjoyed introducing an element of camp into the kitchen and having the chefs sing along with him in choral falsetto. Not that they needed much encouragement in their predominantly feminine pursuits. They were also responsible for preparing speciality dishes for his animals. He fed goose liver to his dogs, grapes from Apamea to his horses, parrots and pheasants to his leopards. The whole staff would sing the refrain 'Big cat, fat cat, boss cat, rank cat, alley cat', adding a castrati flourish to the signature.

He added spices to the sauce as it simmered in a pan. He felt completely at home in the kitchen and was accepted by the staff as one of them.

Satisfied by what he had tasted, he left them to it and went back to his quarters. To his amazement he found Hierocles waiting. He had arrived early and was sitting on a couch drinking wine. Again he noticed the butchness about this youth, the rough-diamond quality of somebody used to living by their wits. Enamoured as he was, he felt instinctually wary of the streetwise manner written all over Hierocles' expression. He didn't seem at all nervous about being in Caesar's apartment or in the least apologetic that he had arrived early.

Heliogabalus put his thoughts briefly through a search engine but was quickly won over by the youth's looks. He noticed a prominent scar above Hierocles' lip and wondered if it had come from a fight. He imagined him getting beaten in some alley brawl down on the docks.

He didn't hesitate. He walked over to Hierocles and kissed him full on the mouth, only to find the lips wouldn't let him go but drew him into an aching vortex. The response was so charged that he felt shaken. When he pulled away he felt his senses had been stretched across a line.

He needed a drink and badly. He knew it was all crazy and that what he was doing would earn him the animosity of the people. His impulses were so ballistic that he was almost flying. He could feel his emotions on collision course and his hormones creating overdrive in his shook-up system. He made no attempt to disengage from Hierocles, even when servants carrying dishes came into the room. He didn't care if they gossiped. They would have to get used to the fact that he was uncompromisingly gay.

Hierocles was suspicious of the food at first and couldn't understand why it was dyed blue. The grilled mullet was not to his taste, nor were any of the culinary embellishments designed to please the eye. He appeared interested only in the wines and drank with the self-destructive pace of someone out to blind himself. Heliogabalus couldn't keep up. He was starting to lose his grip on the conversation and to hear a stranger talking in his place. Hierocles was trying to tell him that he had worked in the theatre and the circus and that he had driven cars on the race track. The whole thing had started to take on a montage effect, with no clear boundaries being observed.

94

They began kissing again, before entering a hot bath prepared for the purpose of aiding the digestion. They tumbled in together, legs kicking like frogs, arms working like flippers to secure a hold on the marble rim. The heat had them instantly erect, but Heliogabalus was determined to hold back. He didn't want to treat Hierocles like rent and so repeat a common pattern in the youth's life. By resisting he hoped to show him that he thought more of him than his previous lovers.

He must have passed out at some stage, for when he came to Antony was standing over him, and he found himself not in the bathroom but laid out on his bed. The morning light was streaming through the window in a blond halo of impacted photons. It seemed only seconds ago that he had been lying in the bath, and he couldn't account for the block of time that had gone missing.

'I rescued you last night,' Antony smiled. 'You blacked out in the bath. I sent Hierocles home and put you to bed. You probably don't remember anything.'

'Nothing,' Heliogabalus said, feeling the dent in his heart at mention of Hierocles' name.

'He'll be back, don't worry. He's left you his details.'

Heliogabalus sat bolt upright at the realization that it was his day. The fog had lifted above the city and light transmitted by millennia of burnt-out stars hurried into the room. He felt the catch of excitement in his stomach, knowing his whole life had prepared him for the events to come. His head was amazingly clear, given what he had drunk last night.

He sat up and the light hit him direct. He was out of bed immediately, while Antony prepared his clothes and breakfast. Today the ritual took on special significance, and there was no holding him back as he went out to the terrace naked and saluted the sun. It was red and blue and orange behind his eyes, the molecular components of light busying their way into his consciousness.

Back inside he dressed in the clothes applicable to his priesthood. He wore a long gold and mauve tunic and had his hair styled like Nero. When the procession crossed the city he wanted the crowds to assume he was the reincarnation of an emperor who had written his name in fire on the night sky.

He had his schedule carefully planned. He was to meet the musicians at ten o'clock, attend the sacrifices and take it from there. The prefect of police had orders to give the procession maximum back-up, and there was to be a massive fireworks display over the river later that night.

He went inside to have an assistant fix his makeup. He knew that Hierocles would be in the crowd, and half his pleasure came from this thought. Already he could hear an insistent heart-beat drum establishing a rhythm for the march as it alerted the city to its beat.

Summer had broken over Rome like gold highlights. His mother, who was to play a prominent part in the day's events, came and spoke to him about her place in the procession. She had a new lover, this time an Eastern woman called Natasha, and wasn't sure about being seen with her at the festival. Natasha hung on her arm with all the fizz of a new flavour. Together they looked like women evaluating their lives through each other, pitching their past experience with men against the benefits of the relationship they had discovered.

Accepting Antony's council, he advised them not to provoke the crowds by openly displaying their affection in public. It was important to him that the day should be treated as a religious occasion and that the crowds should respect his god.

He had himself driven over to the Palatine Hill to meet up with the extravaganza's start. Six white horses had been groomed for the occasion and were already hitched to the chariot on which the black stone was placed. His own cult were largely assembled and ready to march. They were mostly carrying flowers and were in the mood to get blissed out on drugs and the music. The beat was already stitched inside them as noise in their heads. Some had begun to dance on the temple steps in the sexually explicit way of youth.

He had a word with the leader of the Praetorian Guard, and was assured of their protection. The disdainful way in which the man addressed him, hardly bothering to suppress his contempt for the activities, gave Heliogabalus an indication of just how unpopular he was with the Army. The man had the leathery features of a seasoned campaigner and the outright machismo of a thug. His hands were large and weathered like his face and looked like they could crack a wooden beam. He smelled of drink and something raw like turpentine. He was used to butchering men across continents, trampling natives into the marshes, pursuing the enemy through rolling dust-clouds, but clearly none of this was as objectionable as taking orders from a made-up emperor. The man stamped back to his guard, dismissively leaving Heliogabalus to take up with his own.

He spoke to the musicians and the priests who were to take leading roles in the march. The sky was seamless except for a few clouds drifting like floaters across vision. He saw the clearness of the day as a sign after the weeks of summer rain. It was all part of the exhilarating atmosphere created by his god.

They set off at ten o'clock across the network of straight roads blasted through Rome and continuing out to the suburbs. At first he was aware of his vulnerability, but after a time his self-consciousness disappeared and he entered so fully into the music that he became the rhythm.

His band were playing primitive beats with rattles, castanets, maracas and drums. The expression communicated to his head, heart and groin. People were throwing flowers at him, and again, as when he first entered Rome, he stopped to pick up the best and acknowledge the well-wisher. Half-way across town he began to feel exhausted, but he leaned on the music to help keep him going. He could feel his individuality breaking down and morphing into the collective. The dance had got under his skin and he was suddenly hundreds rather than one, the city rather than the street, the god rather than himself. He was stoned on noise and excitement. Somebody threw a stone against the chariot and it struck a wheel. This was followed by a succession of missiles aimed at himself and the fetish he worshipped. There was a brief skirmish in the crowd, and a number of dissidents were dragged off by his bodyguards. He didn't lose step for a moment but continued backwards on the points of his toes, shaken by the experience but determined not to show it. The crowds were packed six and ten deep all along the way, straining against the cordons. He scented that things could turn nasty but was determined not to lose his cool. Another stone pursued a sharp trajectory over his head and found a casualty in the crowd. A man dropped down and was trampled and the sea closed again. A moment later a red rose hit him between the eyes, and the beat dramatically picked up tempo. He was too involved in the dynamic to falter, too spaced out by the high of performing to take note of the danger.

The heat was starting to grow intolerable. He was light-headed from working so hard with the music and decided to mount one of the horses and sit in reverse saddle facing his god. To his surprise he managed to do this first time and to position himself without startling the horses. He had dreaded fluffing it and earning the rebuke of the crowd. Instead, he held his own and kept a hold above the animal's trembling musculature, its house-sized heart beating time in its interior.

They were moving slower now, and the crowds were growing voluble as curiosity increasingly gave way to abuse. He took comfort in the fact that the Praetorian Guard were his support, although his mind was cut across by the fear they would defect and turn on him and his supporters. He knew that if the worst happened he wouldn't stand a chance. The crowd would lend its support and he would be liquidated within minutes.

He did his best to keep his nerve and present an imperturbable face to the public. He concentrated on the music again, and here and there in the crowd there were gay boys saluting him with pink banners. He recognized some of them from the baths, while others had clearly chosen the occasion to come out. Each time he caught sight of them he felt a reciprocal sense of sharing and a pride that they should dare to go public. He hoped that their sexuality would persuade them to join his religion and consolidate its premises in Rome.

He thought he could hear dry thunder rock the sky. There was no sign of the densely packed crowds thinning. All the way out to the graffiti-slashed suburbs people had gathered under the monitoring eye of strategically placed troops. The buildings grew uglier, as warehouses and tenements jostled for space. The sky was clouding over, and he could feel a storm twitching on the horizon.

He quickly dismounted, having decided to dance the remaining distance to the temple. People stared at him and his entourage and either remained silent out of respect for him as emperor or loudly voiced their disapproval. The music came on again as he started to dance, the full Dionysian assault of instruments lashing the crowd. He knew they were starting to turn the situation around and hold their own. The risk he had taken in declaring both his sexuality and religion was finding payback in the way they performed. The more he danced the more he realized the energy protected him and his group. It was the dynamic that made them invulnerable. He knew that if they lost the rhythm the crowd would move in for the kill.

He estimated they had less than half a mile to go. Suddenly, to his left, he saw Hierocles pushed right up against the barrier, watching the procession with a blank face. When their eyes met he smiled but in a way that lacked commitment. He looked marginally furtive, and the sassy youth leaning against him told the story.

For a moment he doubted it was Hierocles, and when he looked back his sight was obscured by the moving wall of people. He couldn't find him in the angular slab of bodies and tried to push the idea from his mind. He had to keep on moving or go under. Jealousy fired him to new heights of exhibitionism. He caught the flowers being thrown and used them to beat time on his body. He was in a state of orgiastic frenzy. He wanted Rome to feel his heartbeat throbbing in its arteries. Drops of warm rain were starting to splash his skin as the cloud ceiling lowered. He almost welcomed the rain after the oppressive heat. There was a rumbling detonation like a building had collapsed, and when he threw his eyes up to the sky he saw it scissor-kicked by white lightning. The crowds, too, had scented rain and people were breaking for cover. Unable to free themselves from the wedge they began to kick out at the obstruction. He could see fights breaking out in the crowd as the rain started to get heavy. The storm had broken in answer to the music, and the drums competed with the thunder's reverberating bass.

They were almost there when he saw the man leap the barrier

blade in hand. Instinct had him throw himself to the right as the man was brutally cut down by a guard. Again, he didn't falter, as the man's dead body was booted back under the barrier in an act of merciless efficiency. The killing-machine had stepped in to save him but couldn't take away any of the shock of attempted homicide.

The music continued to push him on like current feeding his energies. There was no give in the tension. He was gasping from shock and the elemental rawness of the storm, but they were almost there. The rain was so hard that Rome seemed to have dissolved like confectionery in front of his eyes. What he couldn't erase, though, was the image of the blade pointed directly at him, the man's hair matted by rain and his body punching the air before the guard struck.

When they got to the temple, he relaxed in the shared spirit of the group. If the music had encouraged the incident of his near assassination, then he was unrepentant. There were no boundaries to his dance, and if there were he had exceeded them all.

He embraced the dark interior like skin. The priests had been chanting all day and the vibration was a solid hum. The crowds, the storm, Rome's incessantly morphing perspectives, they were all shut out by the temple's voluminous interior. Here his true life began, the one in which he connected to a source so powerful that if he was to attempt to contain it he knew he would be burned alive.

He took his place before the fire at the altar. The power was in him now, and he felt its energy climb his spinal column like a snake. He was himself again, as he had been as a child in the temple at Emesa. The chant massaged the altered state he was experiencing. The attendants were preparing to offer sacrifice. It was his moment. He waited in the dark for his cue, while the thunder broke overhead, then went forward, trembling, expectant and surfing the music's unbreakable beat.

6

When Jim let himself into Masako's building, he was still unnerved from his close encounter with Slut. The man's image kept showing up on repeat, and walking back he had found himself periodically turning around to see if he was being followed.

He found Masako studying a book of Helmut Newton's, her attention focused on a photo of a nude woman in tomato-red stilettos lying on fallen leaves in a park. When he joined her in looking at the photo he could see the partially obscured, dark-suited man's hand on the model's left buttock and the way her head was supported by the white cuff of his other arm. The two were interlocked in front of the wheels of a parked Citroën carrying the registration plate 8461 DK 92. To Jim the shot seemed extraordinary for its juxtaposition of the woman's audacious shoes with the car's black ultra-glossy panelling. One was translated into the other in the symbiotic union of flesh and metal and in a way that dissolved the barriers between human and commodity.

Jim looked at the cold marriage of opposites so brilliantly realized in the photograph and at the shadow thrown on the page by Masako's spiky fringe. He crouched down beside her as she turned the pages for them both. Newton's celebration of nudes in spike heels and fetish wear or designer-dressed on the streets of Paris, Berlin and New York came up as a genre obsessed with glamour and its self-regarding importance to the wearer. That the models combined an archetypal curviness with the stern character traits of a dominatrix made them in Jim's eyes appear sexless.

Masako spent a long time looking at a model with her right leg in plaster standing beneath a huge rain-dropped chandelier in a hotel room. For some reason the image fascinated her and she was reluctant to let it go.

They breezed through endless *Vogue* shots of girls wearing leopard-skin, black silk stockings, face-nets, stylized hats and the trademark

Newton red lipstick and high heels. As glamour statements transformed into figurative art, the photographs were unparalleled documents of obsessively observed fetishism. Jim thought of them as one man's continuous attempt to reshape the world according to a visual aesthetic.

'You hungry?' Masako asked, breaking the spell imposed by the book. She was wearing a black lipstick in contrast to her pale features.

Jim hadn't eaten since the morning and only now became aware of the fact he was really hungry.

'I'm starving,' he said, feeling the roll of his stomach juices. 'I haven't eaten all day, and guess what? I almost bumped into Slut in Monmouth Street. He didn't see me, thankfully. He was coming out of Neal's Yard, bare feet in the rain. He's a real weirdo.'

'You mean you've seen him again?' Masako said quietly, trying to stay calm.

'It's almost like I've been hexed,' Jim replied, his laughter failing to suppress a deeper note of anxiety.

'Mmm, it's odd. You talk to me while I start cooking. There's some wine out if you'd like to open the bottle.'

Feeling the need for a drink, Jim poured out two glasses and felt the Bordeaux nettle his tongue before catching on his empty stomach. He liked the light-headed rocky feeling of the sugar kicking in and the immediate relaxant it proved. His nerves were bad, and he quickly poured a second glass.

Masako was busy chopping vegetables for a stir-fry, her glass still untouched, and when she finally returned and took a sip it was with a delicacy that savoured the tang before swallowing. Her lip-signature left a black tattoo on the glass, and Jim found himself preoccupied by the detail to the exclusion of all else.

He went and stood at the entrance to the tiny kitchen while she chopped mushrooms and peppers, adding tofu to the bean-sprouts and noodles in the pan. He knew all about Masako's strict vegetarianism and how she had never been won over to the junk-food regime of her Japanese friends in London. Like him, she was conscious of what she ate, and was highly selective about what she put into her body.

He found himself drinking fast and getting off on the effect. He was on his third glass and knew he would have to go out for a second bottle but for the moment preferred to stay talking to Masako.

'Everything all right with your tutor, Jim?' she asked.

'Yes, fine,' he laughed. 'He's endorsed quite a few of the unorthodox approaches I intend to bring to my subject. Heliogabalus is bizarre even in the world of crazy emperors. You're probably tired of my telling stories about him.'

'No, go on,' Masako said, the black T-bar of her G-string showing above her jeans as she bent to retrieve a runaway onion.

'Today, I'm sure he would have hair like yours,' he said, inflecting the compliment with humour. 'What can I tell you that I haven't already? That he was a drama queen, that he liked to surround himself with Chaldean magicians, that he ordered a pyramid of snow to be constructed in his orchard in July, that he had the villas in which he stayed torched on leaving, that he insisted on depilating his genitals and that he got married on five occasions – three of them to women and two to men.'

'Mmm. Makes Japanese pop stars seem very ordinary.'

'The reason he's survived is, of course, because he was so extraordinary,' Jim said, powering up to his theme. 'He's still so relevant today. I suppose in part it's the sexual ambiguity surrounding his name that's helped. He's the ideal subject for the politics of gender. Nothing fascinates people more than dubious sexuality.'

'Mmm, you're right,' Masako said, tooling a mosaic of chopped vegetables into the wok.

'I suppose his intentions were to undermine the whole principles on which empires are built, and that gives him the appeal of a rebel. He even outspent Nero and managed to get rid of the equivalent today of about four hundred million in three years.'

'That's good going,' Masako said, adding soy sauce to the packed ingredients.

'Well, he certainly needed it to organize his lifestyle,' Jim replied. 'He would arrange dinners at which ten thousand mice were served, or ten thousand weasels, and in which fish had been expressly brought frozen from Egypt, Africa or the Adriatic. He was also a zoolatrist and accumulated snakes, crocodiles, rhinoceros and hippopotami for his own amusement. His pet lions were let loose in the palace.'

'Leopards, too, I suppose,' Masako said, as she continued to apply sauce like graffiti.

'They were a favourite with all the later emperors. While you're cooking, I think I'll go out and get us another bottle of wine. I've almost killed this one off.'

'Wine's a good relaxant,' Masako said. 'But don't be long. The food'll be ready soon. You need to eat.'

Jim hurried downstairs and out into the night air. It was almost dark, and Frith Street was coming alive with Sohoites. There was a spill of people sitting outside Bar Italia, as well as the cappuccino bar on the corner next to Jimmy's.

Although he could have picked up the wine in Old Compton Street, he decided to match it by going to Nicolas in Berwick Street. Lit up by the drink, he was more confident than ever that he had his dissertation on the right track and looked forward to supplying Masako with more colourful details about Heliogabalus on his return. There was so much to relate, and he welcomed the security that staying with her for a number of days would bring.

Old Compton Street was packed with clones on both sides of the street. It was the usual jostling, hustling crowd, interspersed with the inquisitive and the curious. He had used most of the gay bars in the precinct and was perfectly at home in the sympathetic milieu.

He walked the short distance up to Dean Street. There was a rainy aftershine to the neighbourhood, and he could see lumbering white clouds going over in the dark-blue sky. It hadn't occurred to him that at Masako's he was only minutes away from St Anne's Court, and he tried to block the thought out of his mind. The reminder pushed buttons, and for a moment he almost turned back.

Zapping his momentary indecisiveness, he turned left into Meard Street, its smart Queen Anne houses facelifted and repointed after decades of having been run down and used as brothels. Long before the media and the shirtmaker John Pearse had moved in Jim remembered the street as an unlit alley in which girls materialized out of the dark.

Sanitized under Thatcher as desirable conversions, the properties now stood disinherited from their underworld connections. The street was empty, and there were sloshy puddles underfoot as he decided to cut through to Wardour Street. He walked quickly and was almost through when he noticed someone standing with his back to the wall on the corner. There was a black car parked up in a strictly no-parking zone, but he didn't give it much attention. He didn't like the vibe of the character waiting there. It was only a feeling, but he was tempted to turn back, as much as he resented living in fear of his shadow. This person could have been waiting for anyone, and he tried not to be concerned.

He kept on his way determined not to make eye contact with the man. He was almost through to the other side when the man came at him from behind. He felt his arms pinioned and the bite of metal locking on to one wrist and then the other. He thought it must be a case of mistaken identity and that he was being wrongly arrested. He was waiting for the words 'You're under arrest' but instead found himself being speedily bundled into a car door opened from the inside. His appeals for help were silenced by a hand placed over his mouth. The driver took off at high speed, flooring the accelerator in the direction of Oxford Street. Jim felt himself projected into a parallel universe, and his first thought was how panicked Masako would be at his disappearance. As the hand was removed from his mouth he recognized the two men he was sandwiched between as members of Slut's cult. One of them had accosted him earlier in the day in Charlotte Street and the other he remembered by the indigo-coloured bat tattooed on his neck and the severity of a pierced, angular chin.

He thought again, as the car tailored itself to traffic and negotiated an erratic course to the lights, of how anxious Masako would be growing. She would doubtless be listening for the click of his key in the lock, impatient for his return.

Jim had no idea where they were headed, and attempts to ask

met with no reply. The driver skewed the car into Tottenham Court Road, tucking in behind a red bus before overtaking on the straight. Clearly not wishing to draw attention to himself, he drove within limits and without the reckless flourishes characteristic of a getaway car. He followed up and went all the way through on the Hampstead Road towards Camden. It was fully dark now, and a shower opened up tinnily on the roof with a popcorn crackle.

Jim could do nothing and felt it better to offer no resistance. One of the men advised the driver to keep straight on as he killed the car at the lights. Jim had a hunch that they were heading for Hampstead Heath and, given the cult's association with the place, he wondered if he was being taken there to witness their nocturnal rites. The rain came and went again in abrupt flurries. Jim was amazed they hadn't searched him for his cell-phone, which remained secure in his inside pocket.

The road was clear all the way up to Mornington Crescent. He kept appealing that it was a case of mistaken identity, and would they please let him out of the car. Camden was busy with ordinary people going about their lives, and he looked out at an excerpted High Street with its speed-trap cameras and rebranded chains. Freedom had suddenly become the most valuable thing in the world to him, as he recognized how all of his life he had taken it for granted. He would have given anything to have had it back, as the driver handled the black Toyota effortlessly with a light touch of the wheel.

'Follow the road all the way up,' the man next to him instructed. 'Keep going until I tell you to turn off.'

Jim once again insisted that they let him out, but his words met with a blank. That he had been abducted and was unlawfully being driven towards an unknown destination communicated barcodes of panic to his system. He had read about big city kidnaps but had never thought that he might experience one. He imagined Masako now growing frantic over his failure to return, and he clung to the idea that she would almost certainly notify the police. That someone knew he was missing was his one hope, as the car burned up the largely open road. That his kidnappers were gay made the situation additionally confusing, and he could only think that the whole thing had been engineered by Slut.

As the Toyota came up parallel with a number 168 bus at the Pond Street intersection, the man with the bat tattooed on his neck winked at him in a manner that seemed to say 'It's all right.' Jim looked out at the free world and saw a blonde reading at the near-side window of the bus. There was no chance of him making eye contact with her, and anyhow he existed in a parallel universe.

They took off up Rosslyn Hill, past the police station on the corner of Downshire Hill and into a mini-tailback of red brake lights. The rain had given over and the moon trained a white spotlight on the city. Jim felt even more certain now that they were headed for the Heath with its busy nocturnal scene.

His suspicions were confirmed as the driver took the right-hand turn at the top of the High Street and accelerated up the hill towards the landmark of Jack Straw's Castle, the pub's imposing white façade pointing the entrance to the East Heath's deep oak-woods.

They pulled up in the pub's car-park, and Jim was told that he was to accompany the men on to the Heath. 'We want you to meet someone,' he was told by the man on his right. 'We'll take the handcuffs off here, but it's not in your interest to try and escape.'

Jim felt instant relief as the constraining metal was removed from his wrists. He flexed a hand, aware as he did so of increased circulation. He followed the men out of the car and down a track that led to a dense cluster of trees. The moon had come clear with the quality of substitute daylight, giving to the immediate landscape the look of a reversed negative. As they struck down the track he could see a light glowing in the wood, as though posted there to signpost the way.

Jim could just make out figures going in and out of the trees and realized they were the undercover cult who occupied the woods after dark. He had never visited the place before at night and had heard of its legendary status only from those who got high on the dangers implicit in anonymous sex. His vulnerability would never have allowed him to come here in the dark and risk being compromised or even attacked.

As they drew nearer the wood he could see that the light came from what looked like a number of lamps placed on one particular tree. Somebody stepped out of the dark in front of them, looked in their direction and was instantly swallowed up by leaf cover. He could hear somebody else wading through bushes before the silence flooded back. The landscape appeared to be alive with fugitives dissolved into their places of concealment as black on black.

A froth of rainy foliage exploded in his face as they ducked in under overhanging branches. The man in front knew precisely where he was going as he led the way into an alcove where the trees formed a roof over a clearing. Jim could make out a circle of men grouped around the light, obviously convened there for some sort of ritual. They had lit a fire from branches, and a busy orange flame had started to draw, the smoke snuffling from wet undergrowth. He was certain he could see Danny in the group, a peaked cap pulled well down over his eyes, his leather jacket twinkling with studs.

Jim stood there, still unable to believe that what he was seeing was real. He avoided looking at Danny and kept thinking that if he closed his eyes the whole thing would disappear.

'This is Jim who was with us last night,' the tattooed man said to the group. 'He's the one we thought needed to find out more.'

Jim was about to protest his innocence but decided against it, realizing he was up against the group. The faces concentrated around the light were ones he recognized from St Anne's Court: the same shaved clones, metalled with studs and rings and singularly focused into a perverse phallocentric culture. The shadow they projected seemed more intense here and to be an extension of the surrounding night.

Jim was told to sit, and he took up his place by the blood-orange fire. He could hear rain tapping the leaves on the outside and pitting drops into the flames. A tall cross, fashioned out of branches, had been thrust into the burning, and he assumed this was part of the ritual. Some of the group were chanting a mantra, the low vocal grumble sounding like a bee was being passed from lip to lip. The vibration was contagiously hypnotic, and without knowing it he felt compelled to join in. Something was speaking through him and casting a spell.

The chant stayed unwaveringly level, once it had established its own autonomous volume. He experienced it as a sort of molecular energy, something almost palpably alive in the dark.

He didn't know how long he had been chanting, only that the fire had caught to a sharp blaze and the acrid smoke prickled his nostrils. Somebody was in the process of building up the flames, and the chant had dropped to a barely audible hum, like it was shortly about to end.

The group remained sitting, and Jim opened his eyes to catch the circle in a state of meditative repose. He could hear nothing now, but a branch lifted by the wind and the accompanying volley of raindrops. They could have been seated in deep countryside rather than in an area of woodland tracked by officious police, the place seemed so remote.

As Jim continued to stare at the flames he became aware of a noise in the bushes that sounded like someone coming towards them dragging a chain over the ground. He immediately thought of Slut. It was the sound he had heard the previous night when Slut had entered the room, the jangle of a masochist's self-chosen instruments of punishment, this time forcing a way through undergrowth.

The sound grew closer, the indiscriminate snapping of branches suggesting the person was wading through obstructive growth without concern for safety. The crackle sounded like fire as it travelled steadily towards them with its snappy commentary. When Jim opened his eyes he could see Slut standing there in the reflected light. His torso was naked, with chains roped around his jeans at the waist. He looked every bit the self-professed martyr, body strafed by the lacerating whiplash of branches. He stood with his face turned to the ground, as though self-debasement was something that set him apart from humans. He carried the same air of perverse distinction that Jim remembered from last night, only now Slut was there as a nocturnal journeyer, someone who belonged to this wooded precinct and who had evolved from its indigenous culture. He half expected to see leaves sprouting from his skin and hair, his identification with the Heath was so complete.

Jim rose with the others as they stood to form a circle around the fire. Slut made a deferential sign that they were to resume sitting, and Jim selected a dry spot at the bole of a silver birch. He could hear the rain coming and going in short-lived attacks, the sudden ripple of it in the leaves sounding like small stones pinged at glass.

Slut stooped over the fire, warming his emaciated body, and put his hands out to the flames. He could have been someone partially screened by dry-ice on a low-lit stage, as his spare gestures asserted their usual hypnotic fascination. His body language clearly substituted for words, and he continued to use the fire to advantage, moving in and out of the light to stage his drama. He went through the contortions of what looked like a shamanic dance, arms thrown out to the trees, his wasted body showing its ribcage and the taut stretch of tattooed skin over bone. The firelight threw now orange, now blue choreographed patterns of light over him. Jim thought of Slut as a demented fire-eater, someone swallowing his cult and their orgy-tree in a series of omnivorous gulps.

Without warning, or it may have been a trick of the light, he appeared to walk straight through the fire, but it happened so quickly that he couldn't be sure if he hadn't imagined the whole thing. The smoke was growing cloudier and transmitting dense blue clusters that worked themselves upwards through the trees. The whole scene was like a chiaroscuro painting, and Jim followed Slut's movements in and out of the light with polarized concentration. He had forgotten even his sense of resentment at being brought here against his will and of the danger in which he was placed.

One of the circle got up, moved towards Slut and placed an ivy wreath over his head. It was clearly, Jim observed, part of the ritual, and Slut responded by engaging in a jerky, animalistic dance around the flames. When the smoke cleared he could make out Slut's body posted against a tree-trunk.

The group now rose and formed a circle around their leader. They were chanting again, but this time in a manner that incited frenzy. Slut had adopted a crucifixional pose against his tree and had thrown his arms out horizontally, so that he appeared to be an integral part of the rough bark. Although the group seemed to have forgotten about him, Jim followed, feeling totally absorbed by the action.

The dance had begun, and he felt too stunned by events to stand back from them and too engaged in the ritual to think. As people joined hands in their celebratory romp, he had the feeling that the whole wood had come alive and that the trees were also participants in the ritual. Someone had fed the flames with a swatch of branches, and the fire busied itself with renewed energies. Jim was breathless as the tempo continued to quicken, the momentum sustained by group impulse. He felt hot, dazed and on the point of dropping, only to be forced around on the muscular circuit that kept Slut at its core. Just when he felt like giving up, his lungs full of smoke, a new jab of current would inject him back into the dance.

They were trampling the undergrowth flat as they pursued a groove around the orgy-tree. The whole wood crackled with their animalistic stamping out of a territory in a manner that was defiantly unlawful. The heat was turned up, and Jim felt the circle start to contract as it narrowed in on its victim. The pace had slackened, but the chanting continued to assert a powerful, rhythmic hold. It was the force managing them as they closed in on Slut.

Jim watched as one of the group broke rank and pulled a torch from the flames and brandished it at the night sky. People were growing increasingly reckless as they narrowed in on their target. The excitement raced through Jim's blood, propelling him forward. He was beyond exhaustion and impelled to live out the experience to its end. He wondered what Masako would think if she could see him now, transformed into a horned creature ravaging through heathland with a group of sexual outlaws.

They moved in closer on Slut, who remained motionless, head thrown back in what looked like a state of ecstatic trance. He was fascinated by the man's ectomorphic body and how his skin was a road-map of grainy scars. He could see clearly now that Slut had ropes attached to his wrists and was probably waiting to be lifted and tied to the tree.

Jim felt himself choking as the smoke thickened like fur inside his throat. He noticed how the wind pushed the full assault of it in Slut's face and how he never once flinched from the billowing irritant. He remained rooted in the position he had adopted, like he had grown into the tree's body and had taken on its punished and twisted anatomy.

When the chanting stopped the circle came to an abrupt halt. The man carrying the torch held it up as a fisted salute, its signal raging in the solid dark.

Jim watched as two of the group climbed to an overhanging branch and, assisted by those below, managed to lift Slut up and tie his hands as two horizontals to the branch. With his feet lifted off the ground his ankles were fastened to the tree by rope secured around the trunk. Slut's identity as the wounded god had been achieved with a facility that shocked Jim, so quickly had it been managed.

He squinted through the diffused smoke at Slut who had thrown his head to one side, looking like a giant lizard slung across the warped bark. The man holding the torch continued to thrust it up vertical towards Slut's face, so that the light crawled over him in an orange flickery shimmer.

The group set up a slow liturgical chant that hung on the air. The torch-carrier now stood directly beneath Slut's raised body, and Jim could sense the sexual expectancy shared by the group. He, too, felt the excitement rush to his groin, as the measure of an experience that both thrilled and terrified him. The wind dragged bushy clusters of smoke back at them, and he temporarily lost sight of Slut through the dense, curling clouds. Suddenly he froze, as a voice like a bird's cry issued from the tree, inhuman, raspingly pitched and shredding the silence. He knew instinctively that the sound was coming from Slut and that it was the cry of the wounded man strung up on the orgy-tree.

It happened a second and a third time, as the note of a shaman communicating with his tribe through the pitch black. The group responded with similar bird-like cries, having Jim think they had been transformed by the rite into ground-hopping owls. He could see that the two men nearest the tree were in the process of stripping off their jeans and that the anticipated orgy was about to begin.

There was rain again slashing through the foliage, cracking the leaves like the sound of nuts being shelled. It was coming on harder now and drumming the flames with an insistent sputter.

Jim lost his footing for a moment and fell back into bracken exhausted, his face exposed to the cold night rain. He lay there gasping, up-ended and unwilling to rise. As he sat up he heard shouts coming from the bushes, followed by a piercing succession of whistles. There were lights moving through the trees, and he knew without doubt it was the police.

He got up and listened to the sound of people crashing through the wood, flashlights advancing ahead of them in crazily shifting radials of light. He guessed immediately the Heath Police had been alerted by the blue rollers of smoke surfing above the tree-tops.

They were coming closer, and he stood there confused, uncertain whether to stay or run. He looked towards the orgy-tree at Slut's immobile body grafted to the bark and heard someone shout, 'Quick. Get out of here. It's the police.'

He didn't waste a second. Without knowing where he was he took off into the dark, forcing his way through the wood in the opposite direction to the fire. He ran with his hands stretched out in front of him for protection, terrified that he was being pursued. He could hear shouts behind him and guessed that the police had discovered Slut roped to the tree and were rounding up whoever had remained behind.

He continued running, tripped over on his face, got up again and zigzagged his way across a clearing. The rain was coming on hard, and he was soaked through, but he was off again, this time in a different direction, the whistles cutting in behind him and the shower steadily increasing.

He thought of the warmth and safety of Masako's studio and of his need to get back there. He cursed Danny for the trouble he had landed him in and kept on running. He had never before realized the effects of darkness and the way it came up as a tangible wall to impede his progress. It felt solid as it opposed his body, like he was up against a resistant mass of grainy energies. Whenever he advanced, he felt immediately displaced and thrown back on himself, his tracks reversed. His hands were cut by brambles and his clothes torn by snagging branches.

He made a sudden detour and reasoned that if he continued in one direction he was sure to meet up with the road. He went left again, up steep ground overhung by hawthorns, and made out lights in the distance. He didn't know at first if they were headlights from passing cars or windows sunk in houses, only he needed to reach them and fast. He slowed his pace now that he knew he wasn't being pursued and longed only to be out of the night and the blinding rain.

The ground was slippery under foot, but he was determined to find his way and get his bearings. He wondered if Danny had stayed behind with Slut and been taken off by the Heath Police to the station. He didn't care, and the night's proceedings confirmed his belief that Danny was into a dangerous scene.

Jim reckoned he must be up high, probably behind Squire's Mount, and hit in the direction of the road ahead. He came down a side path into a quiet street and guessed from the landmarks that he was somewhere in Frognal, up above the High Street. He stood under a streetlight's halo and read the name Branch Hill posted on a wall. His clothes were dripping, and he thought of himself as someone who had swum across one of the ponds and emerged as a night-chilled amphibian trailing a slimy signature across a residential precinct. His trousers looked like fatigues, and there was a long tear incised in the left sleeve of his jacket. His normally elegant appearance had been trashed by his encounter with the Heath, and he shuddered from what he recognized as a travesty of himself. The shower had lifted, its massive chandelier had been drawn up into the sky, and he took advantage of the break in the downpour to organize his thoughts.

He needed to find a taxi and get out of the district. His middle-class values ruled out the possibility of taking the tube in such wrecked clothes. He had no intention of being viewed in this disordered state and made whatever repairs he could to his appearance, while sloshing a defeated trail down the hill.

He was confused, too, as to how much he should tell Masako about what had happened. It all sounded so improbable, the idea of him having been kidnapped and taken to the Hampstead woods to witness a crucifixion. It would be almost too much to ask of her to believe that such bizarre practices took place at night in London. Besides, he felt guilty about his involvement in the ritual and knew that he had only just narrowly missed being arrested. He had let himself go and wasn't sure where in the proceedings he would have stopped. He knew he had let himself down, and the rain doubling again provided a fitting soundscape to his mood. His sense of dejection was acute as he stood in Heath Street looking to left and right for a taxi. He could have let Masako know he was all right by using his mobile, but he decided not to, preferring instead to tell her the edited highlights in person.

Jim cursed the misfortune that had brought him to this and blamed Danny for his involvement with the group. To console himself, Jim thought of taking Masako with him to Rome and of getting away from it all. Going there, he hoped, would be like cleaning his blood and making a new start.

He stood outside the tube station and waited disconsolately for a taxi to show. He no longer cared about the downpour, he was too destroyed by the night's experience, too shredded by the whole thing. He thought of going back to his own flat to clean up, but the idea of being alone was intolerable.

He could hardly believe his luck when a taxi strolled down the hill, its amber light swimming through the rain. He threw up his hand just in time, and without consulting the driver jumped into the rear.

'You looked half drowned, mate,' the cabby joked, before taking Jim's instructions to head for Soho.

7

Against all advice, he had gone ahead and married Hierocles. That Rome had taken the matter seriously bit into his sleep as he sat up in the empty dawn hours, listening to a subdued roar surf over the city.

Sometimes, when he awoke before daybreak, a nerve resonating in his unconscious told him he had gone too far. While he couldn't locate the exact source of his unrest, he knew it existed somewhere within the modalities of his confused gender. He had risked a same-sex marriage, despite it being regarded as a violation of taboo by almost everyone, including the Army. And that he had insisted his bride dress as a woman had been considered detrimentally faggy even by the gay community.

Hierocles had taken to going out at night and sometimes not coming back for two or three days at a time. Heliogabalus had grown to despise Hierocles for his reckless hedonism, and propped up on a couch, counting his thoughts, he wished him dead.

He thought of Nero, who had been terrified to go to sleep for fear of encountering those he had murdered in his dreams, and now insomnia had overtaken him, but for different reasons. He had committed no atrocities in his reign, but pacifism and a refusal to become involved in political issues had turned the Senate against him. The one war he could have staged – against the Marcomanni – he had refused to initiate on the grounds that Commodus had sub-dued this state by Chaldean magic and it was dangerous to risk lifting the spell. He stood by his decision, proud of having avoided a bloody offensive.

Giving up all attempts at sleep, he took himself out to the terrace and looked up at the shattered stars exploded across the galaxy. It would be light soon, and his thoughts were busy with the coming day's agenda. He reminded himself that he was due to address a convention of rent boys later in the day and that he was to be given first choice from a priceless cargo of silks recently arrived from China.

He was drinking already, but he didn't care. His mind raced with buzzy data. Finance, he assured himself, was stable. Under him the government had increased its volume of credit by depreciating the standard of the currency. Gold was still relatively pure, and he had succeeded in keeping the weight of the aureus at 6.55 grams, no mean feat given its significant reduction under Caracalla.

He was about to go inside and fetch another bottle when he felt Hierocles' hand on his shoulder. He could smell the alcohol on his breath as an undeclared roster of drunken nights. He knew the procedure backwards now, his lover's appeals for forgiveness, followed by the usual vicious recriminations that he was being used and forced to live in the emperor's shadow.

This time Hierocles looked ravaged by the scene. He was losing weight and the story of his nights was written in his face. Heliogabalus didn't like the look of this waste: it seemed to cut to the bone like the inroads of plague. He turned away as Hierocles searched for the obligatory drink and went inside to collect a bottle, seething with a catalogue of hidden reproaches he felt bound to contain. He realized their relationship lacked the contrast of opposites, that it was one fired by an attraction to each other's shadow. They had no shared culture, no proper meeting-point, and the conflict of their interests struck a succession of ugly chords.

He came back to the terrace carrying a bottle black as storm. Hierocles had thrown himself on a couch and looked bruised by the orange rift of light that had broken over the eastern suburbs. The cloud-break looked like an orange being peeled slowly, and Heliogabalus searched the horizon for his temple, which dominated a cluster of multiplexes.

This time he was determined to avoid a scene. He promised himself he wouldn't get involved in arguments even if Hierocles wound him up. He would play dumb and let it go.

They drank in silence for a while, and he could feel all his worry rubbed to attention by Hierocles' wasted presence. If he missed anything, it was home, despite the opportunities that Rome provided.

He was emperor of everything and nothing. Time, he knew, lived in his arteries and was self-limiting. When he told himself that, the world disappeared, together with his power. It was a subject he couldn't discuss with Hierocles without things getting nasty.

Without warning Hierocles turned on him with one of his recurrent accusations. 'They'll kill me, too,' he drawled. 'When they come for you, I'll be hacked to pieces. Do you realize what you've done? You've set me up, you shit.'

Heliogabalus let it go. The bitterness of the complaint contained a truth that stung him with its force. He had no answer to the charge and no defences.

'You'll be the death of me,' Hierocles continued. 'You trapped me in this rotten marriage. We'll both die like dogs as a consequence.'

Again Heliogabalus refused to get involved. He knew that if he set his anger off he would explode with all the weight of frustration, displacement and political pressure to which he was subjected. Instead, he looked up at the canyons of mauve and pink clouds as they flooded through with light. In his head he ran over the blueprint of what he intended to say to the assembled rent boys and let Hierocles continue to sink himself with drink. They were both alcoholics, only he made a better job of concealing it.

'I've been with Paul,' Hierocles got out. This confession, intended to provoke, was also aimed at giving him kudos in his lover's eyes. 'You're a blond faggot,' he cut at Heliogabalus. 'You're too much of a girl for my liking. Give me them rough . . .'

Heliogabalus bit his lip, thinking that focusing on the pain would help screen him from the insult. He worked his teeth in deeper and felt the probe draw blood. However hard he tried he couldn't free himself of a bond in which hate was inextricably tied to love. Being the recipient of hatred, he realized, was in a way like depriving the bee of its sting. He knew from habit that it was only a matter of time before Hierocles started the usual tirade about being straight and how he had been corrupted by his partner.

The arguments always followed the same pattern and never found a satisfactory resolution. Sometimes the woman in him needed to be hurt, but this time he wasn't prepared to give Hierocles the advantage. He looked on cautiously as the alcohol, far from knocking his lover out, seemed to have shifted his consciousness to a trickier plane. He could sense the whole dodgy arrhythmia of his friend's thoughts, the impulses looping instead of creating an established beat. He wanted to be free to sit with the generous morning light before going to worship, rather than face the trouble Hierocles had dragged in from the night.

He could have got up and walked away, but guilt kept him rooted to the spot. What held him there was the fear that if he made a move to leave he might return later to find Hierocles gone for good. It was a terror he lived with and one that ruled his life.

So far his plan of non-retaliation was working. He knew Hierocles was regularly unfaithful but, even so, reminders of it hurt. He couldn't care less about Paul or the hundreds of others and had come to accept that same-sex relations rarely observed a code of fidelity, but what he had hoped to experience with his partner was the sensation of moments lived together, bright, tangy and polished as a lemon. Instead, their relationship had devolved into a series of psychological manœuvres, in which each tried to make the other dependant through jealousy.

He watched Hierocles attempt to stand up then collapse back on the couch. Reading his thoughts, he went back inside and fetched another bottle, hoping that this time the wine would take effect. He dreaded Hierocles throwing still another scene that would be heard all over the building. Their rows had become proverbial for their epic proportions and for the hailstorm of broken glass and terracotta that accompanied them.

As he opened the bottle he told himself he had to clean up his life. Already there had been attempts to depose him and, while these had been instantly suppressed, he knew he wouldn't always be so lucky. His policy of selling government positions to opportunists, and of pushing his own god at the Roman people, had made him enemies. He reflected on this, glad of the brief respite from his lover, and felt the invisible wound he knew to be the assassin's mark open in his jugular vein. He didn't know where the idea came from, but he had the premonition he would be hit there.

He went back outside and poured with a shaky hand. The city was visible now beyond the grounds, its architecture appearing to have been assembled overnight like a filmset. He could never get over the magic of the experience each day, watching the urban skyline swim back into place through the mist, while he sat on the balcony arrested by the thrill of it all. It was so special that sometimes he imagined he was dreaming with his eyes open and that if he closed them the vision would fade.

Hierocles was operating on automatic. Something within his consciousness wouldn't quite shut down but kept reconnecting like a faulty lead. Heliogabalus watched him feel for words like someone searching for keys, and with the same scrambled effects.

'You'll be the death of me,' he managed to say, directing a red-eyed stare at his lover.

This time Heliogabalus poured himself a drink. Given the options at his disposal, he wondered why he subjected himself to such an ugly relationship. It could only be love he reflected, for sex was available to him all the time. Something within him told him that he couldn't live without Hierocles. The idea of losing him was insupportable.

The sky had coloured a hectic strawberry-red, shot through with flocked blue, and he looked forward to a break in the stormy weather that had persisted without let up for days. Antony briefly appeared on the terrace, but he waved him away, preferring to deal with the situation alone. If glasses started to fly, he didn't want to put Antony at risk of being hit.

Hierocles drank with the fatality of a kamikaze. He made a fist at Heliogabalus but let it drop to a limp-wristed gesture. Something about his anger wouldn't finally subside but kept flickering on the surface. One more glass, and he finally collapsed, mouthing at Heliogabalus as he went, 'Faggot. We'll both die.'

Heliogabalus called for Antony to assist him in carrying his drunken lover to bed. He knew the pattern by now and how Hierocles would most likely crash for the next twelve hours and wake up in a sorry state, full of a drunk's churningly repetitive remorse.

Sensing the moment was right, his mother paid him a brief visit, full of her plans to issue decrees about who should have the right to wear jewels on their shoes, who should dress in certain colours, sit in a certain place in the Senate or drive a particular make of car. Symiamira's obsession with ritual usually left him exhausted, and today was no exception. His mind went into shut-down at mention of her exhaustive catalogue of observances. He knew very well that her demands irritated the people and made her unpopular. Word had got out that she had decorated her rooms like a brothel and that she regularly had prostitutes instruct her in bizarre sexual techniques. Still dressed in her négligé, he knew her to be even more radically out of touch with the people than himself. She lived for nothing but pleasure and whatever kinky permutations of sex she could add to her already expansive repertoire.

She wanted him to spend the morning with her so that she could tell him of her new conquests. Her inexhaustible need to narrate the intimacies of her promiscuity had once amused him, but now he found it tedious for the repetition it brought. Something of her shamelessness had begun to jar with him, and partly because it interfaced a characteristic he recognized in himself.

He left her on the terrace, with Antony catering for her gastronomic demands, such as lobster garnished with asparagus, goose liver and truffles for breakfast. Free of her, he was none the less reminded of the increasing pressure being put on him by the Senate to appoint his adopted cousin Alexander joint caesar. He had sensed the danger in such a move right from the start, for the boy was popular not only with the Senate itself but also with the equestrian order on account of his quiet, philosophical nature and the justice he argued for in all matters. Their contrasting natures provided fuel for Heliogabalus' critics to compare him unfavourably with his cousin, an equation he made little attempt to do anything about. But he couldn't disguise the fact that he was concerned. People had taken to whispering in his presence and sharing conspiratorial jokes at his expense. It was a practice that had spread to street corners, and he guessed the military were to blame. These days they made little attempt to conceal their disrespect and were doubtless feeling out the territory before plotting a *coup*.

Transport was, of course, waiting to whisk him downtown. He always travelled with one of his pet leopards sitting with him in the rear, as a token of the style for which he stood. Antony, who had managed to get free of Symiamira, joined him as they headed towards the unprecedented event of an emperor addressing a crowd of the city's rent boys.

The convention was to take place in a dockside bath-house, one notorious for its sexual practices and its popularity with sailors. The baths, shunned by most citizens, had earned the name Onobeli on account of the ready availability of sex there. Heliogabalus was used to visiting the place in disguise and making his identity known only to the most special of his conquests. As they crossed town he had a sudden flash as to how young he was to be doing an emperor's job. Most people his age were relatively carefree, whereas he had to think for an empire.

Crossing town was like connecting to the city's modem. They sped into the Via Sacra and Via Nova, which crossed the Forum, and arteried their way through a maze of narrow streets. Everywhere shop-owners were unloading crates of vegetables brought in from the surrounding countryside, and bulky carcasses of cattle and sheep were being offloaded into warehouses. The stench in the butcher's area was ammoniac and would increase with the heat of the day.

Visiting the river was always the high point of his routine. No matter that the city's sewers uniformly discharged into the Tiber's muddy undertow – the big Cloaca Maxima opening into the river at the level of the Ponte Rotto – he thrilled at the current's rip and the cosmopolitan tang to the district. It was here that he met real people rather than the arrogant despots who presided over government.

There was a building on fire as they approached one of the bridges, the smoke billowing into black cumuli before going off on the wind. The memory of the great fire in Nero's reign had left each successive generation afraid of a recurrence. It would take so little to reduce the city to base-line grit. Part of him didn't care. It would burn off the good and the bad, and the people would have to start out all over again. He had no reverence for history or the attempts of civilizations to outlive themselves.

He pressed Antony's hand, and they accelerated away through smoke that looked like fog scrolling dense spirals over the bridge. For a time they were enveloped in it and drove on through a massive grey cloud and out the other side to a shore littered by semi-derelict buildings and warehouses with faded industrial lettering. There were several baths in the district, all of them frowned on by the authorities and functioning in a run-down state for a gay clientele. This was the underworld he should have been cleaning up instead of granting it his personal seal of approval.

They drove around the back of a large disused warehouse and continued down an alley into a labyrinthine complex of streets. Even here he could smell smoke in the air, like the fire was spreading its news across the face of the sky. They parked up at the rear entrance to the bath-house, and he remained there checking his makeup in a mirror. If he had a reputation for making up in a way that shocked his contemporaries, then he was determined to capitalize on it today. He looked like a stage artist in white cake as he met his face in the compact. For an agonizing moment he didn't recognize himself in the split between what he hoped to see and the image with which he was confronted.

The bath-house, as he had anticipated, was already full to maximum. It looked like the majority of the city's rent boys had turned out for the occasion, each dressed according to his particular code. A stage draped in purple had been set up in what was once a small auditorium, and the huge audience was grouped around the speaker's lectern. Men hung out under the vast girth of cylindrical pipes or sat perched on the rim of the large bronze basin placed central to the bathing area. Others could be seen taking a quick dip in the pool, their bodies arching in and out of the wreathing cumuli of steam.

Heliogabalus moved through the crowd unafraid, safe in the knowledge he was amongst friends. He could see couples disappearing into back rooms, determined to miss no opportunity to practise their profession. A band had struck up a medley, the music meshing with the underworld aura that permeated the place. Some of the boys had naked torsos splashed with red tattoos in imitation of the Egyptian sailors to be found on the docks. These boys wore earrings and were proud of the erotic lexicons written on their skins in the form of a private vocabulary. Some had chosen flowers' others symbolic creatures such as the jackal, the eagle or the eye of Horus.

He was in no immediate hurry to begin and took his time in soaking up the atmosphere of the place. One of the small bronze basins had been used as a receptacle for his favourite red roses, and these formed a heady shock of colour in a space that had otherwise been left undecorated. He was inwardly glad of the lack of ceremony attached to his visit. He liked the run-down lawless impression the building created and wouldn't have wished its character changed for anything. He had lived out most of his sexual expressions here and intended to continue in this way.

The rotunda lighting the building was tarnished by a patina of grime. It looked as though it hadn't been cleaned for years, unlike the fastidious upkeep given his suite of rooms at the palace. To his amusement a group of dancers and performance artists began to put on a show to celebrate his arrival. Some of Rome's most prominent transvestites gave signature to a dance that was both provocative and tragic. At the end, the leader of the group lay down and simulated being stabbed, while roses were laid over his body.

There were fire-eaters, magicians, hermaphrodites and finally a singer whose theme was that of Nero's great fire, a subject that seemed ideally suited to the day given the earlier conflagration in the suburbs.

When Heliogabalus rose to speak he was greeted with a solid roar of applause. The bath erupted with the sort of welcome he received nowhere else these days.

He began his talk by commending the gathering on their chosen profession. 'Male prostitution', he said, 'requires an imagination superior to its female counterpart. Its risk implied a corresponding invention, for same-sex relations, lacking as they did an opposite, involved the recreation of the body as a mythic ideal.'

He went on to talk of how he regarded the gathering as a fraternity, each of them representing family. He spoke of the colour and difference they brought to Rome and of his delight that their calling offended the Senate. He was quick to add that 'deviation originates from within that which it perverts' and that the reaction to male prostitution was invariably conditioned by the normal being hung up on the perverse.

In his eccentric way he suggested they study books on sex, not just Ovid's *Amores* but a variety of ancient writers who discussed the priapic cult: Greek, Egyptian and Roman. Sex, he said, was a serious study, and the enhancement of pleasure could be brought about not only by experimentation but by knowledge.

He spoke of society's fear of the individual and of how he as emperor had refused to compromise, no matter the opposition from the government and Army. He encouraged them to remain true to their calling, in the knowledge that even if all civilizations ended in ruin the individual was the unit which counted. He said he knew this in spite of his years and that it was better to burn and die young than continue unfulfilled into old age. He called himself their patron and promised to reward them with pensions in difficult times. Each of them, he said, on leaving today would receive a substantial gift as well as his protection for as long as he was emperor.

His speech over, a guitar wailed from a recess in the building, all the collective pain of the assembly given voice in those bruised notes. Again and again the player sounded his wounded call as the dancers returned to the performance area. Treating Heliogabalus as a friend rather than emperor, each made a skittish run at him to present him with a rose before returning to a gestural mime in which they acted out the process of a number of rent boys competing to win a client's attention. Striking up various poses from coquettish, to butch, to provocative, to dismissive, one of them eventually succeeded in winning the client over by his sassy walk.

After the actors had gone off and music cut across the bathhouse, there was a run for the pool. People jumped into the water in a serious of vaporous explosions and were soon joined together in an aquatic orgy. Heliogabalus stood and looked on through the rolling clouds of steam at the geometry of bodies as complexly linked as a plate of spaghetti. The amazing configuration increased as he watched, the whole spectacular display being conducted for his benefit as he stood rooted in the auditorium.

When he and Antony walked back outside he felt an immense compassion for all those he had addressed today. Their lives were difficult, and they would always be society's outcasts.

As they headed back through the dockside complex Antony, who had been visited by a courier during the proceedings, told him that a man called Seius Carus had been arrested for trying to incite the Alban Legion to make Alexander emperor.

Heliogabalus took the news calmly, even though his murder had clearly been intended. Again he could feel the vulnerable point in his neck come alive. He suspected Antony of deliberately down-playing the incident, so that he wouldn't grow unduly alarmed. But the prospect of having to return to legislate over the culprit severely dented his mood. He resented state affairs making inroads into his life, and when he looked out at the city it was to superimpose a grey mood on a blue sky.

They drove back through a city that had suddenly come alive. The centre was congested, and someone, probably claiming to be a prophet or a messiah, had attracted a crowd who formed an atten-tive hub at the man's feet. Heliogabalus' own admiration for the miracle-worker Apollonius of Tyana, about whom he had read, made him sympathetic to all myth-makers providing they didn't challenge his rights as caesar.

Back at the palace he was immediately informed by the cen-turion responsible for the man's arrest of Carus' attempts to trigger a revolution. The Army wanted the man executed as an example of what happened to those who tried to subvert the emperor's rule. And, to make matters worse, Hierocles was up and about, insisting that his word was law when Caesar was absent.

Part of Heliogabalus resented the way the incident had been blown up out of all proportion, largely, he suspected, to satisfy the instincts of the morally vindictive. When he entered the hall where judgement was to take place, he could see a badly made-up Hierocles sitting in the place reserved for the emperor. He was sprawled in his seat in an undignified manner, his eyes looking blotchy and wasted.

It was a bad start to proceedings, and when Heliogabalus took his place next to Hierocles he could feel the silent disapproval of the soldiers burn him like a rash cobbled across his skin. His friend's presence and the embarrassment it caused placed him at an immediate disadvantage, and the undertow could be heard in a brief snatch of laughter that came from somewhere near the back of the hall. If it had been left up to him he would simply have had the criminal banished from Rome and sent to one of the islands. He despised capital punishment and the whole judicial machinery it set in progress. When he looked at Carus he could scent the man's fear coating him like a glaze on a pot. He assessed his age as about thirty; muscular build, long eyelashes for a man, coarse features, and his misfired cause suddenly gone dead in him. He wondered if Carus had ever really believed in his short-lived rebellion and how he would have benefited even if he had been successful in promoting Alexander's cause. When Heliogabalus hesitantly made eye contact with him there was a brief flickering attempt on Carus' part to keep his attention. He knew without doubt that the man was resting his entire appeal on the hope of the emperor's clemency.

The case was presented with a remorseless, clinical bias. A number of potential conspirators from the Alban Legion had been arrested for questioning, but all had denied playing any part in the scheme. The onus for the attempted assassination fell squarely and conclusively on Carus' shoulders. Any attempt to depose the emperor, the prosecution stated, was answerable by death.

When Heliogabalus glanced at the man again Carus was impertinent enough to return his look with a smile. The centurion next to him immediately slapped his face for daring to be insolent, and in that brief moment of violence he saw with restrained anger what it was like for one man to be humiliated by another's authority. When Hierocles made a brief protest, he stamped on his foot to silence him. He couldn't risk angering the Army by having his partner attempt to intervene on Carus' part. To interfere now would be to risk the reprisal of a military *coup*.

The evidence presented appeared irrefutable. When Carus was allowed to speak it was with the confused air of somebody who had already been spoken for. He looked shocked to have heard the contents of his mind described by a stranger. He had no defence other than that he had never intended the emperor's death and was being accused of a charge that couldn't be substantiated. He spoke like a man in the process of catching himself out lying, as he went off at a tangent that refused to add either conviction or eloquence to his case. That he had lost the plot was apparent in the way his source quickly dried up like a stream in a time of torrid drought. That he knew he wasn't being believed only added to his lack of belief in what he was saying.

Heliogabalus looked away. He wanted to dematerialize and leave them to their sordid business. Justice, he knew, was simply the code that suited the oppressor. The oppressed lived by different laws, equally pertinent to their cause but existing as the reverse values to a society rooted in received notions of justice.

Carus was shouting now, but his words lacked the adhesive to stick. They were being dragged out of a core threatened by extinction and lacked all context. Heliogabalus felt Hierocles take his hand as Carus began to lose dignity and break down. Every cell in the man's body was opposing the prospect of death with instinctual resistance. 'I am innocent of any crime,' he appealed, his voice resounding against the marble walls. 'I am a soldier, loyal to Caesar.'

The prosecution didn't waste any time. Heliogabalus could smell the acrid reek of wine on the lawyer's breath as he came up close and said, 'The crime is punishable by death. We await your sentence.'

Heliogabalus heard the assembly go silent, the way a town does when it snows. He hated the prosecution for conferring upon him the responsibility for Carus' death, knowing that if he declared him innocent then he was likely to spark an uprising. The contempt he felt for the whole affair showed in his indifference to proceedings. He looked away diffidently, pretending the matter was beneath him, and by the briefest nod signed away Carus' life to appease the military.

He had known since his earliest education with the monks at Emesa that the nature of reality is death. Only the theatrical world of high camp, with its extravagant attention to superfluous detail, had ever allowed him to escape from an awareness he had learned too young. He would like to have told all those present that their own deaths were as potentially imminent as Carus', only they were spared for the moment by reason of luck, health or political correctness.

Instead, he couldn't wait to get out of the hall and away from the reek of soldiers. He felt coated by issues concerning the right and wrong use of justice and the impossibility of ever making inroads into the existing system.

Hierocles followed him out and, accompanied by his minders, Heliogabalus made for the park with its shady avenues of junipers, pines, poplars, planes, ilexes, magnolias, hornbeams and oaks. He needed to be outside and in the presence of nature as a means of finding peace. If Carus wasn't already dead, then his execution was imminent. He tried to imagine what the exact moment of shutdown was like and if it was really true that the whole of one's past life was flash-forwarded for review. He thought of the purple cords braided with gold that he had ready in the event of having to hang himself and how at night he would run a hand reassuringly over the softened fibre, just to know his death-kit was ready and prepared. There was also his scarab ring, filled with sufficient poison to stop his heart within minutes. To live it was necessary to know how to die, and he had been instructed in the methods best suited to an emperor faced with the exigency of suicide.

He chose a spot of deep-blue shade in a concealed oak grove as a convenient place to take refuge from prying eyes. His attendants laid out cushions on which to sit and produced a range of chilled wines packed in ice-buckets. Two servants holding fans made out of peacock's feathers stood over him and batted the air into a liberating breeze. A salad was offered of squat lettuce sprinkled with mint and sliced eggs garnishing lizard-fish served with rue. There were beans, tender young sprouts and ham, but the afternoon's proceedings had left him without appetite. He needed above all to be alone, but his life rarely allowed him this luxury. Hierocles had started to drink again, presumably to sober himself up, and Heliogabalus dreaded the consequences of him growing progressively drunker. He felt he couldn't take any more hurt, any more abuse aimed at undermining his self-esteem. He wondered why his friend hated himself to such a degree that he felt compelled to turn it around on his lover. His vicious diatribes seemed like the irrepressible anger of someone consumed by self-loathing.

He closed his eyes so as to avoid being drawn into conversation and to re-establish contact with himself. As he lay back drowsing in the shade he had a vision. A huge black snake had emerged from its place of concealment in the undergrowth. As it pushed upwards, uncoiling like a rope, so the sun appeared to come closer, as if the two were attracted to each other, only the sun had turned black as it does at the moment of eclipse. He continued to look on as the two narrowed in distance. The snake had his colours, purple and gold for fangs, and triggered like a giant phallus to meet the sun's collision course. The whole thing was happening audio-visually, and he could hear the intense roar of the disorbited planet rushing through space. He felt like his brain was frying as the heat was turned up like the recreation of Big Bang. The snake and the sun continued to move in on each other with what seemed like equal speed. He could feel acute sexual tension firing in his groin and sensed he would never be able to survive the impact when they collided. The orgasm built towards detonation as the snake drove its fangs into the sun. To his amazement the sun, on swallowing the snake, changed into its streamlined shape and spat out the black, bullet-shaped meteorite he had recognized as his god in Emesa and brought with him all those miles to Rome. As the conical stone hurtled earthwards, so he came in a manner so explosive that he gasped at the excruciating intensity.

He was so overwhelmed by the experience that, ignoring Hierocles and his minders, he walked off by himself into the wood. A woodpecker broke free of cover and took off with low irregular flight for a place of deeper concealment. He followed it into the trees, the shade closing over him like a dark green sea. The right to be alone was what he wanted, although he suspected that Antony was sighting him from a discreet distance, watching out for him as was his way.

He could smell earth scents, and a deep litter of dried acorns crackled underfoot. All of nature's regenerative coding went on unobserved in its abundantly restorative way, right from the trumpet-shaped convolvulus that was strangleholding a sapling to the little red campion seeded by a bird. He stood communicating with the ecosystem at his feet and taking in the diversity of small lives that lived in this earth like pores in skin. It reminded him of the unnaturalness of his life, and while he couldn't strip himself down to anything like an instinctive response to nature he was none the less aware he was engaged in a learning process.

He stayed listening in the clearing, and this time the woodpecker emitted a cry that sounded like insane laughter. He had read somewhere in Pliny that its raucous package of notes was an early warning of rain to follow. He looked for the bird, but it was hidden from view.

He could feel the temperature had dropped. Coincidental with the woodpecker's shriek, a burst of white lightning showed through the trees, a zigzag of charged ions, the voltage of which left him stunned. He turned around abruptly in response to the sign and hurried back towards the company he had left picknicking in sunlight.

8

Jim hadn't found it necessary to tell Masako the worst of his ordeal. She seemed to know instinctively that he would tell her when the time was right, and he had been grateful to sit shaking on her floor, drinking the hot tea she had provided and slowly catching up with himself, rather than having to apologize for what happened.

Now in Rome together, he realized that her intuition spread a sensitive network through every aspect of his life. It wasn't just that she was by nature unintrusive, it was more that she appeared to assess her thoughts in a deep level before deciding to speak. It seemed to him that she possessed the faculty not only to tune into his mood but to make allowance for every nuance of its inconsistencies. Danny had always ruffled him in ways that causes friction. Masako, by way of contrast, disliked confrontation and had clearly erased the need for it within herself. There was a quiet shimmer to her emotions that pleased him, a vibration that kept count of the deeper things in life as well as the everyday.

Watching her now, sitting with her legs arched on the bed as she painted her toenails a vibrant red, he loved the boyishness of her thin shoulders and flat torso, the black flounce of her page-boy cut with its purple fringe and the convexity of her buttocks as they described a perfect width and proportion. He liked the fact that the masculine and feminine components of her body were each sharply identifiable, so that she formed an easily recognizable androgyne.

They had been fortunate to have a friend loan them the use of his apartment on the Via degli Avignonesi, a quiet back street that runs parallel to Via del Tritone. The single-bedroom flat was light and minimally furnished. Two dense eucalyptus trees shared their window on the city, their hard green leaves forming a link with nature in the urban, petrochemicalized landscape.

Jim, who still hadn't slept with Masako, turned his erotic focus on the bottle of vermilion Shiseido lacquer that she was using to paint her toes. It was the colour of geraniums and red peppers and autumns in New England. Without saying a word he knelt down and took her arched foot in his hand, its smallness fitting his palm, the three painted toenails in the process of drying an intense scarlet. Holding her foot in his left hand, he took the brush in his right and began texturing one of the unpainted toes with red gloss. He felt her thrill at the contact, as though he was manipulating a powerful erogenous zone. She closed her eyes and abandoned herself to the sensation, her foot coming alive as an instrument of pleasure. Jim deliberately took his time in applying a signature to each of the two toenails. He worked meticulously and slowly, keyboarding the foot from time to time with his left hand in response to the little cries bottled in Masako's throat.

Letting go her left foot, he took hold of her still unpainted right, the sole tensing on contact with his hand. He could feel the expectation run through her like a charge.

This time she lay back, completely given over to the esoteric vocabulary of pedic sex. Intuition taught him the routes to follow, and by the softest manipulation of the sole he was cupping he found himself able to attune Masako to pleasure. He continued all the time to paint her toenails the livid Matisse red, stopping only when her foot contracted from sensory overload and locked on the stimulus.

Glossing her big toe to a berry shine, he jabbed the brush back in the bottle's viscous contents and traced one finger the entire length of her sole, drawing from her the sound of a wounded viola. He had never conceived of the foot as a soundboard for erotic pleasure and felt challenged by discovering the potential in Masako to orgasm through this particular fetish.

He could hear a siren tracking through the city, its urgent signal parting traffic, as he returned to scrutinizing the complex map of highways written across Masako's sole. Her foot had the soft texture and colouring of a magnolia petal, the same purple veins dissolved into an ivory backdrop. It seemed to have a life of its own and to be sensitive to each exploratory tweak of his fingertips. He massaged it gently, learning by experiment to connect with the pleasure spots. He worked with the fineness and precision of a mapmaker at his task, extending his line across uncharted territory and backtracking where the response elicited was acute. He could see the dampness spreading through the black fan of Masako's hair and feel the orgasm coming up in her like a wave riding with inexorable momentum for shore. When it broke, she arched her body off the bed, convulsed by its sizzling delivery.

Jim let go of her foot and lay down beside her on the bed's terracotta-coloured linen cover. Her entire skin, he decided, was just like a magnolia flower, unblemished by the least scar or discoloration. Her foot, as an extension of this line, was a *tabula rasa* on which he had performed a cartographer's art, connecting the meridians to her sexual core.

They lay together silently, her depilated body resembling a young boy's, her blacked-out eyes casting shadows each time she blinked. The sonic roar from the city surfed into the room and meshed with the noise inside Jim's brain. Even though Masako had encouraged him to explore the gay scene in Rome he had stayed away, finding in her company sufficient interest to burn a hole through the busy days. Being in the city had generated an excitement in his nerves that kept him on a permanent high, both for its associations with Heliogabalus and because of the distance it put between him and Danny and his underworld associates. He could feel the weight of their dead relationship dropping from him day by day, no matter the pain that came up as a reminder of loss.

With Masako taking a brief siesta before they went out sightseeing, he busied himself reading through his recent notes on Heliogabalus' involvement in the mystery religions. Masako had turned over and was sleeping face down, and his eye was drawn to the little red heart tattooed above the crack of her bottom, an image so discreet, and at the same time loaded with sexual connotations, that he triggered erect with hard impromptu lust. Redirecting his attention back to his work, he savoured the sweet expectation that comes of denial and promised himself that if ever the time was right he would follow the tattoo as the directive to entering her body.

In recent weeks Jim had been preoccupied by the events leading up to Heliogabalus' decision to arrange a marriage for his god, an event that followed close on the heels of his own improvident marriage to Annia Faustina. Research had told him that for the union of deities the emperor had chosen the Carthaginian divinity Caelestis as bride for Elagabal. Recognized in Rome as the queen of the heavens, Caelestis was a variant form of the Phoenician Astarte. Her image had been brought to Rome and transported to the Elagaballium with immense ceremony, and the ritual marriage of the two deities had taken place in the temple. Jim's knowledge of the subject told him that Heliogabalus had chosen well, as the goddess was not only the chief divinity of Carthage but was widely known in North Africa and elsewhere around the Mediterranean basin. She also had a cult following in Rome, her worship having been established by Septimius Severus. Her popularity apart, Jim guessed that the emperor may also have been motivated in his decision by the enormous wealth attracted to Caelestis' temple. Commentaries differed as to the emperor's motives in arranging this marriage, and Jim liked best the report that Heliogabalus would accept nothing but two golden lions to mark the occasion, the spiritual significance of the event proving sufficient for his ends. He imagined the emperor being handed the lions on a jewelled leash and his sense of exaggerated style leading to them being fitted with tiaras and dressed in purple coats to match his toga.

Masako continued to drowse and tentatively put out a hand to reassure herself that he was still beside her on the bed. His eye again returned to the heart-shaped tattoo, the symbol growing to be an obsession that irritated his sex. She had shifted position slightly, in a way that distributed prominence to her right buttock, a gluteal fold of which was in contact with his thigh.

Distracting himself with work, he reflected on the dual nature of Caelestis as a fertility goddess as well as one who presided over the stars. In the role of earth-mother she was identified with Cybele in Africa and with the cult of Bona Dea in Italy. His reading on the subject of Bona Dea had told him that she co-opted into her rites an amalgam of other goddesses, such as Magna Mater and Juno Caelestis. In the largely syncretistic tendencies of Heliogabalus' age, the identification of Caelestis not only with Magna Mater but also with the worship of Mithras was commonly recognized. Jim doubted that Heliogabalus would have approved of this rival god but thought it likely that he would have endorsed Mithraism in the interests of gaining favour with the Army. It would follow, then, that his decision in choosing Caelestis as the complementary divinity to his own was probably a diplomatic one, aimed at securing the much needed, if temporary, support of the military.

He made notes and thrilled at the excitement of having Rome socketed to his nerves. He could feel the city turning over, its digital screens, office towers, e-commerce, manic traffic, sexual hunger, airports and cemeteries all compressed into the megabytes activating his sensory cortex. He was impatient to get out there and interact with the city's seething tempo but also happy to live in the charged moment of suspense.

Waiting his time, he continued to point up his notes on the mysteries pertaining to Mithraism and its largely esoteric rites. The bull, as its chief symbol of ritual sacrifice, was an animal associated not only with Mithras but with the goddess Cybele, too. It was while researching the emperor's attempts to win the confidence of Cybele's priests by personally sacrificing bulls on the goddess's altar that Jim had encountered the reference to castration which played directly into his study of Heliogabalus' gender. To be admitted to these rites the initiate had to undergo castration or a form of false castration. Given Heliogabalus' request to undergo a sex change, Jim entertained the suspicion that the emperor may have undergone the operation for real. The historians were at best ambiguous. Lampridius, for instance, alluded to the rite by using the words *genitalia devinxit*, which implied that the emperor's genitals were tied up for the duration of the ceremony, rather than removed. Aurelius Victor, however, was emphatic that the emperor was *abscissis genitalibus* and had undergone literal castration. Support for this theory was substantiated by a passage Jim had discovered in an unknown author referring to the fact that Heliogabalus had been ritualistically castrated and cared for by priests during his recovery. The same author reported that after the emperor had adjusted to the physiological change he claimed that his god had also changed sex and that necessary revisions should be made to the religious ceremonies conducted in his temple.

Jim pondered his findings, certain that his sources would be dismissed as apocryphal but determined to persist in his line of investigation. The subject of Heliogabalus' gender was to be central to his thesis, and while in Rome he intended to peel the issue of its sensitive skin. Masako shifted again as he watched, the alignment of her buttocks tempting his eye to probe the tiny chocolate punctum of a beauty spot existing like a detail in the fold joining the leg and buttock. It was a mark he had neglected and one that brought renewed excitement to his slow-burning anticipation.

He continued to keep his thoughts suspended in a gravity-free zone, like markers orbiting in space. Masako had moulded herself to his erection, not intrusively but lightly, in the manner of sand forming a contour on a beach. There was no urgency in the movement; it was tentative, like a drum brushed into sound, and almost without objective. Still determined not to respond, he continued with his notes on Heliogabalus. Whether it was because he was in Rome and the associations were charged or simply that his nerves were overstimulated, he kept having the mental image of a youth with bleached hair and a made-up face flash into his mind. It was the recurrence of the image, always the same and always precise in detail that made him feel unnerved. The thought crossed his mind that Heliogabalus as a psychic entity had taken it on himself to be his guide in the city. He put the idea out of his head instantly, refusing to believe that the living and the dead could occupy the same space. He assured himself it would go away and that the phenomenon was linked to the series of recent events that had jinxed his nerves.

He returned briefly to reflecting on another of Lampridius' character assassinations of the youthful emperor. According to the vituperative historian Heliogabalus 'had conceived the plan of establishing in each town, with the title of prefects, persons who make a career of corrupting youth. Rome was to have had fourteen; and he would have done this had he lived, determined as he was to elevate to the highest position everything that is most corrupt, and men of the lowest profession.'

He laughed out loud to himself at the thought of a youth going to these extremes to infect the capital with vice. He wondered all along if there hadn't been some fundamental misconception as to Heliogabalus' age and if the dates of his birth and death hadn't been falsified in the interests of distorting history. Was someone so young capable of the monstrosities ascribed to him by his biographers? The question was a flexible one and dug right at the roots of historic subversion. For a moment he had a terrifying vision of Heliogabalus having outlived himself, diseased and no longer recognizable, living to corrupt the system like random error occurring in the separation of two DNA helices.

It was a thought he quickly dismissed, only to find it almost instantly replaced by the return of the image that had been troubling him for days, but this time the eyes seemed to be staring directly at him, demanding his attention. He couldn't shut it out by thinking of something else and, as he watched, so the face broke into a twisted smile. It was the look of someone so disillusioned by life that death was the only possible option. It shook him, and he felt decidedly uneasy as he refocused the world back into his immediate surroundings.

Masako awoke at that moment, still fuzzy from her siesta sleep, and sat up and pulled her T-shirt down over a porcelain-coloured waist. She, too, seemed to have difficulty in reconnecting with her surroundings and came to only after struggling with visible disorientation. She gave no hint of the erotic pleasure she had received but instead reached for the bottle of Evian beside the bed and uncapped it to drink. She fluffed her hair back into shape, smiled at Jim and took herself into the green-tiled bathroom to shower.

Jim lay back listening to the torrential hiss of water coming from the shower, and checked his guide book prior to their going out. He wanted to avoid the scene, the cruisy bars, the pick-up places in parks and to access the city from the viewpoint of the *flâneur*, spending leisurely hours discovering the significant by accident.

But the subject of Heliogabalus's notoriety continued to frustrate him in his attempts to recreate his subject free of the prejudice of moral historians such as Gibbons, who had referred to the young emperor as 'a monster who abandoned himself to the grossest pleasures with ungoverned fury, and soon found disgust and satiety in the midst of his enjoyments'. Jim was increasingly aware that aberrant scholarship was only one of the obstacles to be dissolved in his quest to resuscitate the emperor from a long cryogenic sleep.

On the other hand, his reading of Antonin Artaud's deeply personal account of the emperor's life had put him on to valuable tangents of study. According to Artaud, much of the emperor's belief in the miraculous was triggered by his diligent reading of Philostratus' life of the miracle worker Apollonius of Tyana. Apollonius was still another fascinating subject for Jim to explore, a further lead in his attempt to junk-strip the DNA in the emperor's posthumous cells. Apollonius was supposed to have raised the dead, cured the sick, travelled to India and ascended bodily to heaven.

His thoughts on the subject were broken by Masako coming back into the room tented in a cerise towel. Removing the towel and wrapping it around her hair, she stood naked with her back to him. She fished a black Dolce & Gabbana T-shirt out of her travel-bag and matched it with washed-out Lee jeans. The red lipstick gash she applied was the livid matt of a carnation, her small mouth made up like a geisha's. Her simple definition complete, she turned around from the mirror and pouted complicitously at Jim, by way of acknowledging the unusual sex that had taken place between them. Jim, who had never before been aroused by a woman, felt beneath his confusion a dull expectant longing. He was determined to take his time and to follow the plot to its experiential end.

He suggested they head for the Trastevere district, so that they could eat at one of the trattorias for which the place was noted. They would walk wherever possible, as had been their practice for the past days, being the best method of getting to know the place. To his surprise Masako suggested they should visit the gay quarter and had read up on some of the high-profile clubs and bars, such as Alpheus, famous for its drag shows, or the delightfully named Garbo on the Vicolo di Santa Margherita or the oldest of Rome's gay spots, L'Hangar just off Via Cavour.

'I've never told you before,' Masako said, lowering her eyes, 'but I like girls, too. At least I'd like to experiment.'

Jim smiled, a little chord of jealousy sending out search notes as his heart missed a beat. He wondered if the measure of his response was simply infatuation and nothing more or if there was a deeper bonding of emotion at play in his feelings for Masako. Either way, a possessive ripple chased through him in series of needling jabs. While Masako busied herself with a mascara brush, he tried unsuccessfully to push her out of his thoughts. He told himself that, given his bias, he had no right to become attached to her on any other level than that of a friend, an idea that collapsed in the thinking. Hadn't they already exceeded the boundaries of friendship, he asked himself, and become intimate through sex, and hadn't he, in finding out Masako's foot fetish, made an inroad into the world of sharing? He wanted to ask her more about this particular sensitivity and decided he would at a later date. Right now, looking at her from behind in tight, worn jeans, the desire he felt overshadowed every other emotion. He looked away, ran his eyes up the blinds and stared out at a densely composed city sky. It was hot, oppressive, and a petro-carbon smudge hung over the late afternoon. He could see a couple moving about in the flat oppo-site, the woman watering geraniums in window-boxes and the man testing the flash on a camera. Although Jim didn't know Roman weather in the way he could assess a London sky, he could read storm signs in the air.

When Masako was ready, she came over and without saying a word kissed Jim on the lips. It was as though she had instinctively sensed his need for reassurance and acted on his uncertainty. Her kiss was like all her gestures, intimate but constrained, personalized but discreet. If he expected more it was because he had let his imagination outrun the reality of the situation. He had speeded up the development of their tentative relationship and was already viewing it as something based on deep foundations. In his mind, everything had taken place before it had even begun.

They went out into the pushy, crowded streets and decided to head for the city centre and cross over the Ponte Sisto to the Trastevere district. Although as a student she lacked the money to shop on impulse, Masako wanted to view the emporia of stores owned by the likes of Armani, Versace, Dolce & Gabbana, Gucci and Valentino. Design was the world with which she identified, and the women they passed were dressed with a simplicity that buried the outstanding detail in the rightness of the cut. Masako liked to spot the better labels and pointed out to Jim the ones she recognized, such as the grey Armani suit on a woman stepping out of a black Mercedes, the loud Versace jeans – backpockets sprayed with diamante – moulded to a blonde or a black dress that was obviously Galliano. Her eye took in everything by way of visual commentary and stored the contents for future reference.

Jim bought a chilled beer at a street stall and inadvertently made sustained eye contact with the assistant, who was undoubtedly a gay boy wearing a chunky gold chain around his neck. They batted eyes at each other in recognition of their secret, while Masako immersed herself in the guide book and manicured a pistachio ice with her compact red mouth.

They headed across town in the direction of Via Giulia, with Jim soaking himself in the atmospherics of a city in which Heliogabalus had briefly flourished. He told himself that, although the Rome Heliogabalus had known had been built over repeatedly in the course of history, somewhere beneath the macro-megatons of its modern counterpart particles of the emperor's world survived. He found himself against all reason hoping to encounter Heliogabalus in the crowd, half expecting that the image which had burned itself into his mind would become a reality. They browsed through streets glutted with tourists manipulating the obligatory hand-held camcorder or snapping at ruins. A fuming altercation was taking place between the woman driver of an open convertible and the male driver of a dark-blue Porsche. Both had got out of their cars and were conducting a mini gender-war in front of a vociferous crowd who resembled extras on a film set.

They walked in rhythm, sharing the attractions and feeding off the city's wired energies. They got lost repeatedly, rechannelled their footsteps, negotiated slabs of history on which they had no conceivable hold and finally ended up at the Ponte Sisto, tired but elated by their discourse with Rome's frenzied dialectic.

They stopped at a street café before crossing over to the right bank and sat outside in the nervy air. Jim looked up to see that the sky had come down like a flat roof on the city, its combination of violet, brown and crushed raspberry colours hinting at the prospect of storm to come. His mind was thrown back to the detonative rain that had accompanied the sex he had shared with Danny under Waterloo Bridge, an episode as apocalyptic as it had been emotionally lacerating.

'You look like you're seeing things,' Masako said, tilting the contents of a sugar sachet into her cappuccino. 'We're here to discover your emperor, Jim,' she added. 'We must look out for him.'

'We're also here to enjoy Rome,' he replied, his feet kicked away by shock at her insight. It seemed to him that she could access his mind and focus on his deepest inner preoccupations. 'It's good just being here with you,' he continued, attempting without success to sound casual. 'Maybe I'm imagining things, but time seems to slow down when we're together.'

'I'm finding the same. I feel I can be myself with you. Men usually crowd women out.'

'You're right,' Jim laughed. 'Men have a habit of allocating women a space they can control. I suppose it's like conditioning someone to fit a grid. The man does this, the woman that and there they stay.'

'It's because you know these things that you make me feel good,' Masako said, looking down and quite clearly engaged in the process of self-discovery.

Jim could smell the busy river as she spoke, its urban scent coming up with the flat tang of pollutants and an indigenous flavour that he associated with Rome itself.

'It's crazy, but I'm growing attached to you without trying,' he said, a wave of shyness causing him to look away at an indefinite point in the distance. He felt both frightened of committing and of not, as he listened to the confused mix of his emotions.

'Mmm, and me you,' Masako confided, with equal shyness, her

eyes fixed on the chocolate beauty spots in her cappuccino.

Jim was beginning to let go the emotional bruise that had lived in him as a dull persistent ache for weeks. He could feel with less pain, hope without an interposing negative and, most of all, begin to trust again.

'I'm enjoying each moment of our stay,' he said. 'There's so much to see and do, and, yes, I'm also keeping an eye out for the emperor.'

'You should,' Masako smiled. 'I bet he's somewhere in this crowd, reincarnated.'

'I hadn't thought of it quite like that,' Jim reflected, excited at the prospect of Heliogabalus starting out his life all over again in the place where he had been cut to the bone by his assassins. He suddenly had the vision of a blond boy biking through Rome wearing a rhinestone-sprayed jacket, a pink boa and flashily buckled biker's boots.

'Let's make a point of looking out for him,' Masako said. 'Let's find Heliogabalus. We can make that the point of our being here.'

'I'm excited. I keep getting these visions of a face I associate with the emperor. He's young, blond and persistent and incredibly made up. He wants something, I know that.'

'He's trying to communicate,' Masako said, bringing out a compact to check on her lipstick, the matt red doing a good job at holding its own.

Jim thought on it and was sure that she was right. During the time he had been researching Heliogabalus' life an extraordinary chain of events had occurred to alter the pattern of his own. He had broken with Danny, encountered Slut, been kidnapped and had, in part, changed his sexual orientation. Masako, as he saw it, was his redeemer, the person who stood between him and disintegration. That they were sitting together in a street café in Rome seemed in itself extraordinary. When he looked up at the sky he had the impression he was dreaming and that the clouds were neurons in his brain. He told himself that none of this was happening, then he refocused the world back into place, and Masako was still there tentatively retouching her lipstick with a completist's attention to detail.

'Let's go over the bridge,' he suggested, conscious as he spoke of the symbolism implied by making the journey to the opposite shore.

They crossed over the river's muddy tract, its olive spine branching away to black eddying pockets. Jim loved the sensation of straddling the city on a bridge and took Masako's arm as they walked across, stopping to watch a passenger ferry make roiling tracks downriver. High-rise slabs interfaced office towers and media emporia on both banks, but it was the river that held his eye, the same polluted one into which Heliogabalus had reputedly been thrown. Jim found himself wondering at what point along the shore the river would have deposited the remains of his body. A leg here, an arm there, an involuted scroll of organs on some lip of the shore? Heliogabalus' body had been dismembered like Osiris', and he felt it his duty to find the lost components and restructure them out of the city's burning grid.

Caught up in the frantic pace of the Trastevere, they made their way to various landmarks, including the Villa Farnesina, built by Baldassare Peruzzi for the Renaissance banker Agostino Chigi, and stayed a long time there taking in lunettes featuring scenes from Ovid's *Metamorphoses* by Sebastiano del Piombo and Chigi's horoscope constellations, frescoed by the building's architect.

From there they made their way under a glowering violet sky to the top of the Janiculum Hill and looked out from that high place over the city's stacked skyline. They found a small café in a piazza and sat outside under an umbrella that reminded Jim of a blue-and-white-striped petunia. They were both hungry and settled for generous portions of vegetable lasagne and a bottle of Chianti.

They talked and ate, and as Jim undid the stitches on his past so Masako followed, unpicking a seam fraction by fraction. He told her that his earliest memories were of the sea and of the rhythm of the tides that had punctuated his childhood days spent in Shoreham. His had been a lonely upbringing, and something of this had followed him into an equally estranged youth.

Masako had come from a large family and had three sisters and a brother. Her father, a wealthy Tokyo dentist, had left her mother for a leggy Californian blonde when Masako was ten. While she had continued to enjoy a privileged upbringing and education, the vulnerability she felt at the loss of her father had translated itself into an insecurity that required therapy. She described it as an acute undercurrent, the unsettling sensation of being vulnerable to a fear that was constantly there as a reminder of the grief she felt over her father's desertion. She called it a father-shaped hole, a drop through which she had dreaded to disappear.

They began to learn rudimentary things about each other, selecting with care the molecular building-blocks on which relationships are founded. The construction was by its nature tenuous, but Jim could sense a rightness in the process that made confession easy rather than unnerving.

'Let's go back,' Masako said after they had finished their meal, and they took a bus back to the Ponte Sisto and walked over the bridge with the lights on and the sky smelling of rain. The city was now a digital rainbow of imagery, a modem connecting the collective conscious of its inhabitants to their teeming informational highways. They watched an aircraft lowering on the city, its fins dipping in and out of cloud.

They bussed back from the other side, with the storm still building. A hollow rumble of thunder earlier had come to nothing, and when they got back Jim threw open the bedroom shutters on the oppressive heat. The city's roar came up to meet him as an electrifying soundscape, a medley of signatures dominated by the hot blast of traffic.

It was steamy indoors, and he noted how, on sitting down, Masako popped the top fastener on her button-fly jeans and lay back exhausted on the sofa. He took a bottle of wine out of the fridge and collected glasses and a corkscrew from the kitchen. As he did so, he had another flash of the image he had come to associate with Heliogabalus. It was so clear this time that he was left without any doubt as to its identity.

He poured out the chilled wine and heard Masako say, 'We'll find Heliogabalus tomorrow. I'm sure of that.'

'I believe you,' he said, as he looked out at the unshuttered sky-line with its film-set architecture, gantries and shape-shifting digital screens. 'I know it sounds crazy, but I have this hunch we're narrowing in on his trail. Do you think he's seen us in the crowd?'

'I'm sure he has. He's waiting for us to signal our presence. I'll tell you tomorrow where I think we can find him. I have a street in mind.'

'Are you serious?' Jim asked, thinking for a moment that Masako was losing it.

'Mmm. Of course I am,' Masako stated, giving him the impression she was busy image-scanning her thoughts. 'I have an idea and I'm going to commit it to my dreams. When I looked at the streetmap earlier, I was sure I had found the place.'

'I believe you totally,' Jim said, feeling the wine come up assertively in its lift. 'I think I'd follow you anywhere.'

'I would see things even as a child. I used to think it was normal, but on the rare occasions when I spoke about it I was told I was being crazy. It's like a window I look into. I've seen a house and a street and I know we'll find Heliogabalus there.'

'The reincarnated Heliogabalus . . .' Jim mused, sucking on the prospect like a sweet. 'What will he remember, I wonder? Everything or nothing?'

'Fragments. It's all that any of us remember. The pieces and not the whole.'

'I had no idea that you had access to the psychic world,' Jim said, amazed at Masako's ability to insight her thoughts about death with such clarity.

'Mmm. It's not something I've learned, it's something I know,' Masako replied, sleep starting to film her eyes.

Jim sat looking at his glass, making it the only point of focus in the world and looked up as a half-unbuttoned Masako made for the bedroom. The desire in him remained as a powerful reminder of what had taken place during their siesta, but the urgency had been replaced by other preoccupations arising from their talk about Heliogabalus and the dead. He felt marginally dissociated and had the sensation that only a part of him was really there in Rome, while the other part was marooned back in London attempting to make sense of his disrupted life.

By the time he went into the bedroom and undressed Masako was already asleep. Her discarded jeans looked like two disconnected lengths of piping draped over a chair. She was lying face down beneath the duvet, an open streetmap placed beside her on the pillow. Still doubting the reality of things, Jim slipped into bed quietly and fell asleep to a freeze-framed image of Heliogabalus daring him to follow down a sunlit alley to the muddy, fast-paced river.

9

Even as he lay back waiting for Annia Faustina to arrive, he knew he had made a big mistake. While there had been no marriage contract, and he had, in addition, refused to accept a dowry, he had exchanged vows with Annia before returning home alone. His mother and several of his council had been witnesses to the occasion, and he had effectively breached protocol by not attending the festivities that would lead to Annia coming to him later that night.

His pet leopard, Vesuvius, lay beside him on the couch, the animal's streamlined musculature uncoiled and flexing in a stretch that placed its forepaws out like two studded fists. He had no fear of a creature that could kill him on impulse but, on the contrary, felt secure in its presence. Most people, excepting his inner circle, backed off at sight of Vesuvius pacing the floor like a contained holocaust of energies, and he had little doubt that Annia would bolt from the room on sight of a leopard pounding across the marble floor.

Her father, a descendant of Marcus Aurelius, had insisted on the marriage celebrations taking place at his villa, and Annia was to be conducted to the palace by a procession of musicians and torch-bearers.

Heliogabalus picked at the tondo of baked dormice arranged on a silver plate for his pet and fed the plumpest to Vesuvius, who responded by dispatching the canapé with a single incisive bite. He felt no desire at the prospect of Annia coming to him on what was their marriage night, only a sense of obligation in having to pretend to perform the functions of a husband. The situation was additionally strained by the fact that Annia's previous husband had been put to death under Heliogobalus' government, and he wondered if her motives for marrying him were in part inspired by a morbid attraction to himself as nominal executioner.

Not that he really cared. His mother had suggested he remarry in the interests of pleasing the Senate, and he had acted on her advice. Annia was not only a widow, but she was middle-aged, conventional by his standards and doubtless little prepared for his unusual lifestyle. That he was prepared to spend all day arranging flowers in his room, disputing with the chef about the exact qualities of porcini mushrooms or deciding with Antony on the merits of a particular blond hair-dye, would, he imagined, exasperate any woman expecting a show of masculinity from her new husband.

He was determined, before Annia arrived, to spend time with Valentino, one of the boys he had met recently down on the docks. Valentino wanted to be a hairdresser, had come to Rome from Tuscany and had lived with a number of older men in the course of working as a hotly desired rent boy. He felt in some way responsible for this youth, who also gave him advice about his hair, discussing styles and methods of going blonder than blond. He himself would like the world to have existed of nothing but tiny details, and Valentino, he felt, understood the significance of his obsession in which a colour, a scent, an item of dress or some culinary flourish were of major importance in the universal scheme of things. He doubted from the little he knew about Annia that she would have any leanings towards his world of unashamed camp. Her character, although deferential, struck him as conditioned by disciplinarian parents. She lacked the humour to hold good with his entourage and was without the flair to take colour from his outrageous coterie.

Vesuvius got off the bed abruptly and took a lazy, swaggish roll into the adjoining room, where a platter of pheasant and goose-liver was waiting to stop his appetite. Heliogabalus bit into a black fig, tasting the seeds like they were memory cells infiltrating his saliva. The sensory associations took him back to childhood, to his mismatched relationship with Julian and to remembering the smell of sunlight as it came to meet him in parcels of photons.

Vesuvius came back to the bed and repositioned himself in a way that was redoubtable as it was slack. All of the taut wiring that could cause a fuse to blow in an instant was visible in every charged nerve. The coat looked like a solar-storm had erupted over the fur. The eyes were the green of high grasses bleached by the sun. It was the animal's brain's compact slaughterhouse potential that interested Heliogobalus, the fact that it could be triggered into killing by a spontaneously coded impulse and that he himself was not exempt from being butchered if the wrong switch was thrown.

He had beside him his favourite cookery book – Apicius' *De Re Coquinaria*. Apicius remained his authority on good food, and he delighted, too, in the author's accounts of the dishes enjoyed by the emperors Otho and Vitellius, who also served as role-models for his exacting curiosity about cuisine. He himself liked nothing better than to inject camp repartee into the kitchen and to introduce an air of stagy irreverence into the proceedings. He was also fascinated by the eccentric practice of one of his predecessors, Antonius Geta, who ordered dinners according to single letters: goose, gammon, gadwall or pullet, partridge, peacock, pork, pig's trotters.

As he leafed through Apicius' compendium of recipes his desire to recreate the dish that Vitellius had called 'Shield of Minerva the Protectress' was renewed. He read again of its contents: pike livers, pheasant brains, peacock brains, flamingo tongues and lamprey milt. He was determined to meet the challenge and prepare it one day for his inner circle. Certainly tonight was not the time, as he intended to downplay the occasion and formalize it only with the preparation of a cold buffet underlined by artichokes, asparagus, salad and a variety of fish. He would rather have amused himself with his history books, his coterie of pretty boys and the inexhaustible prizes in his cellar than attend a buffet aimed to please his bride.

He was interrupted in his thoughts by Antony coming into the room to tell him that Valentino had arrived. He carried a jewelled leash to harness Vesuvius and led the lopingly acquiescent cat off into another room. Valentino was terrified of the leopards, panthers and lions he had encountered in Heliogabalus' rooms and had threatened never to return unless they were locked up for his visits. Heliogabalus watched his pet slope off in a rippling blaze of emeralds and sapphires, the claw-pads raining amplified blows on the tessellated floor.

When Valentino came in his hair was arranged in blond curls

and his eyebrows were two black horizontals. He looked tired, as though his work as a rent boy had forced him a long way down into himself. Heliogabalus had noticed over the months how Valentino's mood fluctuated according to the treatment he received from his clients. He could be elated one day if his earnings had unexpectedly peaked or totally despondent if the sex had involved abuse or the failure to be paid. Tonight he looked strained with worry lines etched above his nose in the form of a deep-set W, indicating the problem was centred there in that particular site.

Heliogabalus poured out wine himself rather than call for a servant and had Valentino sit down beside him on the couch. There had often been occasions when they had talked instead of having sex, for their ages were similar, no matter the difference in their stations in life. He sensed that tonight was to be such an occasion, and he gently lifted Valentino's hand and placed it in his own. He could see that the boy was nervy and strung out and in need of being comforted. He watched him drink hard and fast in the attempt to have the wine wipe out his anxiety.

Heliogabalus knew that he had roughly two hours to himself before his wife was due to arrive and felt the need to maximize on that time. It was, in his mind, an interval standing between him and the loss of his freedom. He wanted, suddenly, to remember every word that passed between himself and Valentino as a record of a particular moment in his life.

It was growing dark outside, and he could hear a wind frisking the avenue of ornamental trees leading to the palace. He still hadn't learned all their names, but he knew the plane, the cherry, the ash, the laurel, ilex and oak. Nature demanded nothing of him; it was just there as part of the regenerative and degenerative cycles of the earth. He could trust in it, as he could an elephant, a leopard or an ostrich.

Valentino let go and rested his head on his shoulder, and he could feel the boy's trouble crumple in the process. He, who so wanted to be loved, was the victim of a loveless profession. Heliogabalus felt for him and the indignities he suffered as a rent boy selling his arse for money and at the same time expecting to receive love in return.

'What is it?' he asked Valentino, the woman in him surfacing to meet the hurt. 'Is it something that's been done to you? If it is, then I can step in and make my power felt.'

Valentino still wouldn't come clean. His eyes had the blank stare of the mad, who withdraw so far into themselves that they are uncontactable.

'Something terrible has happened,' Valentino confessed, his eyelashes doing sonatas in time to his thoughts. 'I've betrayed you,' he said, biting on his lip sufficiently hard to draw blood. 'Hierocles came to me yesterday and forced me to have sex with him in a way that was brutal. He really fucked me up.'

Heliogabalus savoured the irony of the situation like tasting a sharp grape. Neither he nor Hierocles were faithful to each other, but Rome provided sufficiently wide a cast of boys to prevent this sort of situation happening. He knew instinctually that Hierocles had done it as a form of revenge. His impulse to laugh was cut short by the intended nature of the hurt and by the anger he felt at Valentino for finding it necessary to confess.

'Why do you tell me this?' he rounded on the boy. 'Aren't there some things that are better kept secret? Who you fuck is your own business.'

Valentino looked shocked at the anger he had spiked. Heliogabalus got up from the couch and hot-footed it once around the room, the conflict of his thoughts tingling like pins and needles. He despised them both for trashing his feelings for, try as he did to deny it, he still loved Hierocles and needed him in his life.

He thought of throwing Valentino out on the spot but softened when he realized the boy's vulnerability and his messed-up state. As the declared patron saint of rent boys, he could hardly turn on his own. Instead, he slowed his walk, toned down the drama and went over and took the boy's hand.

'I'm not a Caligula or Nero,' he said. 'Doubtless they would have devised a punishment so disproportionate to the crime as to make themselves butchers. Instead, I forgive you. Your wrong was simply in telling me something better left unsaid. If you can learn from this, some good has been achieved.'

He watched Valentino's body unwind from its tautness, the W knotted above his nasal bridge starting to slacken and then collapse. Relief flooded his features, tempered by suspicion that he had been let off so lightly. He looked like he still couldn't believe what he had heard and that there was a catch in it aimed at tricking him into a false sense of security. Heliogabalus watched him look up like an animal that had been dropped by its captor.

'You mean you're not going to punish me?' he said, testing each word for its staying power.

'No. What you lack, Valentino, is discretion, and the absence of it can wound others. I was luckier than you. I learned my lessons from studying Seneca. I know what you suffer and the need you feel to blame it on the injustices done to you.'

He watched the youth bunch up defensively like a hedgehog, its ball of needles primed. He realized he had made a mistake by hitting direct at the truth. He had got Valentino on a raw nerve, and it stung. He poured more wine and quickly switched the subject. 'You may have heard I got married today to Annia Faustina,' he said. 'My mother insisted I do it to strengthen my position. That's why I needed to see you tonight, to touch base and be reminded of my true identity.'

Valentino smiled. 'You've been through all this before, haven't you?' he said. 'You'll never know what you want. Nobody does. My mother thinks I should marry. If she knew what I did for money, she would have my father kill me.'

'Most of Rome seems to know what I am,' Heliogabalus laughed, reflecting on the downside of public image. 'Not that it makes it any easier. I still get hurt by comments. Hierocles says they'll do us one day, and I'm sure he's right.'

He had deliberately risked bringing Hierocles' name into the conversational radar in the hope of normalizing affairs. He watched Valentino inwardly flinch, as though an acupuncture pin had turned on a nerve. He clearly resented being reminded of his indiscretion, but there was no other way. He wanted him to learn, and to do so the needle had to be punched home.

'I just live for the moment,' Valentino said, deliberately avoiding mention of Hierocles' name. 'I'm only concerned with sex, money and getting wasted. That way I don't have to think too much.'

'The mind is thinking all the time, even if it's not in use,' Heliogabalus said. 'What goes on in the unconscious is a pointer to another form of reality. I value my dreams more than I do my conscious thoughts. I once had a dream in which I saw myself hatched from an eagle's egg. I was high up on a mountain ledge, concealed in an eyrie, and the parent bird flew back to me with a purple toga in its claws. I'll never forget it. The bird was golden and its wingspan huge like the branches of a tree. When I relayed the dream to my tutor, he said it meant I would become caesar.'

He could see that Valentino was slowly starting to relax, despite remaining fractionally on his guard. It was something Heliogobalus had observed in all boys of his profession, an inability to trust. They would only meet you so far before a reaction set in. He had known it so often, the temptation to fall in love with a boy and forget that distinctions were necessary and that emotional involvement was out. It was the awareness of this tacit agreement that helped prevent him from imagining he was in love with Valentino or any other of the countless boys who hung out at the bath-houses and docks.

'The only dream I remember', Valentino said, 'was after my lover Paul died. I saw him standing in the crowd, and when I went over to kiss him he placed a hand over his mouth. I suppose you could call it a sign.'

'Undoubtedly. It was his way of saying he'd moved on. Not that anybody really dies. They just change address. The priests at Emesa taught me that, and I've reason to believe it.'

Heliogabalus watched Valentino settle, now that the conversation had made tracks from its stumbling point. He could see that Valentino was erect, but sex wasn't on the menu. There was something about this boy which fascinated him, largely, he suspected, because he was the personification of who he could have become under different circumstances. This, as he saw it, was the reason for his attraction to someone whom others viewed as a prescription for ruin. It was also why, in times of crisis, he had the boy over to companion the change. Valentino had, unknowingly, become the witness to psychological factors which in turn affected affairs of state.

As they spoke, a zigzag fork of lightning spiralled across the sky-line, its yellow voltage exploding above the city as an ionized fuse. The lightning was answered by a sizzling downpour rapping the spread fig trees beneath the terrace. He looked out, hoping the rain would cancel Annia's procession to the palace, but the storm was short-lived and, having announced itself, took off again. He could see the sky was coloured a dusty yellow, like Vesuvius, with here and there blotchy blue-black clouds fingerprinting the horizon.

He called for food to be brought, sensing that Valentino was hungry. A servant came in carrying a platter on which two cold lob-sters had been prepared. There were star-shaped seafood canapés spiked with flowers, a salad composed of primary colours and an almond cake for dessert. It was a light assemblage, for time was lim-ited, and he had no intention of having Annia discover Valentino in his rooms. That truth would come later, and she would have to accept it or go back to her father. He was determined to make no compromises other than for the sake of formality on his marriage night. Anyhow, he imagined his reputation had preceded him and that Annia, who was past child-bearing age, would expect little of him sexually.

Valentino stacked his plate with lobster brought from the blue coves of Capri and set to with appetite. Heliogabalus preferred to watch others eat and then to do so himself in private. Instead he drank to cushion himself from the pain he felt over Hierocles' betrayal. He knew from experience that if you drank enough the alcohol eventually reached the pain. It didn't stay there long, but it finger-tapped the chemistry sufficient to bring about a change. Of more importance to him was that the moment was starting to regis-ter as something significant in his life. He found himself reviewing it like someone looking into the complex nature of time and attempt-ing consciously to slow it down. He wondered if time had a shape like molecular configurations or sub-atomic particles and if the moment could be isolated in its particular form. He would like each distinct nanosecond of his time with Valentino to be transparent and teardrop-shaped like a diamond.

Valentino started to tell him about a client who was also a senator and who stayed in the closet to protect his reputation. This man liked to have him wear his wife's jewels and to act out her role in bed. He was mean and on the last occasion had refused to pay. Valentino wanted to get back at him and asked for assistance. He was determined that the man should be exposed, and Heliogabalus again found it necessary to remind him of the need for discretion even in the face of injustice. It was a lesson he was finding hard, unlike the easy way in which he demolished the lobster salad.

He liked nothing better than to be stimulated by tales of sexual excess. Valentino, like most of the boys in his profession, had pursued a life of such bizarre encounters that most of his stories sounded like fiction. He had little doubt that, properly written up, they would provide the material for a narrative documenting Rome's sexual underworld. It was something he hoped to see written in his lifetime to rival the more salacious works of Petronius and Juvenal. Only he wanted it hot, with garlic cooking in the writing.

Valentino had moved on to the almond cake and was worried as always about his figure. 'If you don't look like a girl you quickly go downmarket,' he said, his mouth dusted by crumbs. 'Waists are everything in my job, even if my clients are usually obese.'

Heliogabalus laughed. He, too, refrained from overeating to keep a figure admired in the baths for its defined wiriness. If he remembered age from a previous life, and with it the transformations his body had undergone, then it was as a reality, rather than something abstractly conceived in the way Valentino talked about it. Although he was still a youth, he recollected enough of age to know that it was a process with which you grew familiar, like most patterns in the body. It was something in the genes that you had to accept, like the flower entropy.

For all his self-conscious girlishness Valentino couldn't resist a second portion of cake, playfully smearing his mouth with the residue, so that it looked like he was wearing a dark lipstick. He leaned over Heliogabalus and smooched him with confectioned lips.

Heliogabalus lay back and luxuriated in the time granted him before Annia arrived. In the extended calm he drew Valentino to him and kissed his mouth into a scorched oval. He broke off, so as to keep the tempo down, took off a blue diamond, a clumpy hexagonal rock of a thing, and pressed the boy to keep it. The stone shone in his palm like a swimming-pool. Heliogabalus watched the confusion he had created. Valentino was too shocked to accept or refuse, his gobsmacked stare saying everything, as he continued to hold the stone up for inspection. The gift was worth more than he could earn in a decade, and he understandably handled it with suspicion, afraid it would suddenly dissolve or burn a hole in his skin.

He insisted that Valentino take it, not as a trifle but as a token of their friendship. 'Accept it,' he said. 'If I die before you, you'll have something to remember me by.'

He watched Valentino's fingers close over the ring, shutting it into his palm like a thief. Even if he declined to speak, it was some sort of acceptance.

Heliogabalus was determined to say nothing. He had no intention of forcing the gift on his friend or adding another word to what he had said. Instead, he decided to change the subject. 'Have you seen Marco at the baths lately? I've been asking about him, but unsuccessfully.'

'Marco with the wrist-thick cock?' Valentino exclaimed, momentarily put out by Heliogabalus' preference for size. 'I've heard he's ill. There's some sort of plague that's hit the baths. Boys are getting fevers, losing weight, dropping away. Nobody seems to know what it is.'

'So I've been told,' Heliogabalus said. 'I've heard reports that it comes from Africa and that it was brought here by slaves. It's within my powers to order an enquiry, but I haven't. Where does Marco live?'

'Don't know. He's got a sugardaddy who looks after him, so he never tells.'

'I'd like to offer some help,' Heliogabalus said. 'Marco's always been dear to me, and even I have never met his match when it comes to size.'

He could see that Valentino felt slighted, despite having just received an extravagant present. Like most of his kind he had a woman's jealousy and a tendency to identify with being perfect. He was likely always to construe allusions to others as an attack on himself. Heliogabalus knew him well enough to know that this couldn't be avoided. The boy's expression looked dented, showing the kink in his mood. His petulance expressed itself through the rapid flickering of his eyelashes.

'Marco deserves whatever he's got,' he said spitefully, the force of his indignation causing his lip to curl.

'That's taking things a bit far,' Heliogabalus responded philosophically. 'Do any of us really deserve to suffer, and when we do is it of our own making or is it due to circumstances outside our control?' He realized at the same time that Valentino had little or no aptitude for philosophic enquiry and instead offered him the choice of a plate of ripe figs. He still had Annia on his mind. The whole ceremony had smacked of hypocrisy on his part and insincerity on hers. He doubted, too, that the people would celebrate his marriage with any conviction. It was too obviously a marriage of convenience to merit the explosives of orgy. Annia was doubtless, to their minds, menopausal, stretchmarked and disfigured by cellulite – not a woman to colour the erotic imagination. His mother had taught him that there was no reason for embarrassment in these affairs and that they simply served as a means to an end.

But Marco, he had expectations for the boy, and felt a pit open inside him at the prospects of youth decimated by plague. He knew without having it analysed that the virus didn't come from the bathhouses or the river or the refugees on whom inevitably it would be blamed. There were no records as yet of a single woman in Rome having gone down with the disease; it seemed almost exclusively confined to the gay community. It simply hadn't shown up in any other sector, and he had cause to worry. If Marco had gone down – and how many more of his friends? – then he, too, could be a carrier. The virus even now could be circulating in his cells like an undercover agent.

He had a longing to be out of the palace and to sniff out the night. Always, when it got dark, he had this desire to dress up and become somebody else. A rent boy, a clown, a man openly wearing drag, a singer, a graffito or simply an anonymous person out walking the city. Even though it would cause offence if he was to go out now he saw no reason why he should remain at home to receive Annia. Antony would be able to handle the formalities of showing Heliogobalus' bride to the room especially prepared for her, the luxury of which he hoped would more than compensate for his absence.

'Let's go out,' he sprung on Valentino. 'I can't face the prospect of being here when she arrives. You doubtless know that the people call me obscene names like Tibernius, Tractatilius and Impurus, and so what have I to lose by creating an additional scandal?'

'People despise whatever they can't understand,' Valentino said. 'And in my job I'm hated even by my clients.'

'That's because you remind them of themselves. Self-hatred invariably leads to a person turning on their own kind. It's like smashing a mirror because you can't stand your own reflection. Let's go . . .'

Heliogabalus got up from the couch and put on an outrageous ankle-length leopardskin coat. It took Valentino's breath away, and Heliogobalus pointed the collar up so that it came level with his ears. 'The coat is probably made from three cats the size of Vesuvius,' he said, fitting it to his shoulders and moulding the line to his body. He stuffed the pockets with the money he intended to give away, the gold coins spilling as he kneaded them with his fists. 'Whatever comes to me goes. It's my way of being everywhere at the same time. Giving means being in circulation.'

He called for Antony and told him of his plans. That it was dangerous for him to go out without minders was all part of the thrill, and tonight he intended to end up in a riverside bar called the Pink Sailor. On the way across town he planned on distributing money at random to the poor. It was his way of playing games with the people, and occasionally he would make his identity known to the incredulous recipient by whispering, 'Antoninus gave you this.'

They were driven into the city by a chauffeur who never spoke. Heliogabalus liked the man's inscrutable discretion. He was off-beat, had only one arm, never asked questions and rarely if ever volunteered a word. His job was to park up out of sight and wait, something he did to perfection.

'Rome's too fat,' Heliogobalus said, as they walked out under trees to the car. 'Everything's here. The wines and fruits of Italy, corn from Egypt and Africa, oil from Spain, cured meats from Baetica. Shall I go on? Marble from Tuscany and Greece, ivory from Syrtes, gold from Dalmatia, glass from Phoenicia, spices from the Orient, stones from India, silks from Asia . . . This is the data that feeds the Senate. Men who are unable to identify with their opposite find it difficult to die. Remember that, Valentino. The richer you grow the harder it is to accept you're made of dust. It's easy to let go nothing, but what do you do with an empire?'

He knew that Valentino had taken in his outburst, even if he only understood it in part. People were like that, he reminded himself. They blocked everything they didn't want to hear and saw only what was like themselves.

Mohammed was his usual taciturn self as they burned across the city. There were people out in the streets celebrating his marriage, and a spermatozoa trail from a blue firework fanned out like a peacock's tail over one of the squares. He appreciated the irony of the situation in which he, as the groom, was busy on his marriage night escaping the bride. He shouldn't have been headed for the Pink Sailor near the Aventine, but there was no choice in the matter. Impulse was stronger than reason, and he had to obey.

There were more firework explosions in the form of scarlet and pink frothy detonations as they headed towards the port. The night had come on violently, and the city throbbed with nightlife. According to Antony, crowds had converged on the three ports of Ostia, Porus and the Aventine, and a number of ships had been set on fire as part of the celebrations. There had been trouble around the central halls of Trajan's Market, the banking and stock exchange district of the city, and troops had been called in to subdue a potential riot. He knew he was risking his life by going out tonight and that a soldier not recognizing him in drag could well cut him down as an undesirable. But he didn't care. He knew that his death, when

it came, would be a violent one and that like so many of his predecessors he would be butchered. His heroes had all gone that way
or had been forced into taking their own lives, like Nero and Otho
and, more recently, Caracalla and Geta. He came from bad blood
and he knew it, and while he smiled at being both the most powerful and despised of men he flinched from the idea of being carved
up alive.

They drove by the Horrea Agrippiana between the Clivus Vic-
toriae and the Vicus Tuscus on the fringe of the Forum and headed
in the direction of the Aventine. People were out carrying torches
and candles, and he wondered if there wasn't a very real chance of
the city being set on fire. A group of clowns caked in theatre makeup
were carrying candles shaped like giant phalli down an avenue to the
side of the Forum. The scatological black candles, complete with
heavy balls, were, he knew, not only a reference to an imperial
marriage taking place but also a deliberate pointer to his renowned
preference for size. There was no way of hiding secrets from the
media, and his sexual tastes had become common knowledge.

People were on their way to opera and to the theatre, and he
himself had agreed to sing in a production that was coming up in
the next weeks. He was to be the soloist who incarnated the show's
entire action and, unlike Nero, who would sing for hours, he
intended to keep his appearance short. He was fascinated by singers
and their obsession like all stage artists with maintaining a youthful
appearance. They kept away from acid foods and hydrogenated fats
and did breathing exercises to extend their note range. It was their
ethos of makeup and stage glamour that appealed to him and the
way, too, in which their occupation dissolved all notions of gender.
They were people like himself who devoted their lives to their looks
and agonized over a facial spot or being seen out of context.

The area of the port in which they parked was relatively quiet. It
was in a slum complex, and most of the disused warehouses were
deserted and the empty tenements taken over by rats, alcoholics
and the mad. He remembered encountering a sailor here in the past
who professed to be emperor. The man had painted his face and
arms blue and was looking for a prophetic snake he claimed to have

brought back with him from Africa. According to the man, the python knew the whereabouts of all the treasure buried in the empire . . . He remembered the incident like a hallucinatory flash-back, as he stepped out of the car leaving Mohammed in his usual catatonic state at the wheel.

When they walked into the lowlit bar there was a castrato singing on a small stage in the middle of the room decorated with ostrich feathers. He recognized the singer as the Queen of Sheba, a young man who worked the bars and whom he intended to invite to perform at the palace. He, too, hung out at the baths, a fugitive who slept by day and came out at night. It was a pattern adopted by most of his friends with their unconventional lifestyles and avoidance of normal society.

Heliogabalus' coat drew everyone's eyes away from the singer. In his own mind he was covered in hundreds of black eyes all star-ing out at the attention they attracted. While the entire bar was aware of his identity, people let him be and never imposed on him for favours.

He and Valentino sat down at a corner table to watch the per-formance. The singer paid no attention to the fact that the emperor was in the audience and continued to dramatize his coloratura.

As Heliogabalus listened, so he felt his own involvement with the song grow. He planned on rewarding the singer with the fist full of gold concealed in his pockets. There were men openly kissing and exploring each other. He felt excited and open to adventure. The sexual tempo of the bar lit into his nerves. There was news of a new substance being used, different from a psychoactive such as hashish and more powerful in the visions it generated. It was called soma, an extract from the fly agaric mushroom or perhaps, more rightly, as he believed, a compound extracted from harmel, or Syrian rue, a plant native to his own country. The priests at Emesa had called the drug hoama, a plant mentioned in the Zoroastrian teachings, and also mang.

He had an insider's knowledge of the drug's visionary properties but had never considered using it purely for kicks. When he looked around the bar he could see that the greater number of its occupants were somewhere else, out to lunch and smashed on something other than alcohol. The Queen of Sheba was singing a song about unrequited love, in which he had changed the woman's role in the song into a man's, so that the relationship was a same-sex one.

Encouraged by the song's gay bias, a number of men close to the stage were engaging in group sex. Over it all, the voice built a tragic scaffolding, an ethereal falsetto spiralling into the reaches of pain that only the genderless knew. He signalled to one of the bar staff, and the man returned carrying wine and drugs on a silver tray. He could see people's inhibitions breaking down as the drug came up, and he, too, wanted to dip into the hallucinatory stream and see where the current took him.

While he and Valentino waited for the substance to kick in, he singled out another pretty boy who was sitting at the bar. He was about his age and had the look of a cowed teenager who had run away to the big city. He almost knew the story without asking: he had come to Rome from the provinces, been disowned by his family, lacked a permanent address, had no stable job, found it difficult to adjust, worked the baths and docks, hated himself for doing it but had no choice.

He decided to take a risk and went up to the boy, who was called Zozi and who wouldn't look him direct in the eyes having heard that he was caesar. He was clearly on the drug, and as it took effect in himself he could see the boy's skin glow and turn radiant, each pore distinct and alive with molecular energies. He felt for a moment that he had conceived Zozi as a brain thing, a simulacrum cloned by the drug. When he embraced the youth he had the feeling his fingers had bypassed skin and were tuned right into being itself. He was somewhere in Zozi's nervous mains searching for the DNA signature to his identity. It was a place he hadn't accessed before, and configurative shapes were coming up opening gateways into the billions of cells contained by the body, each windowed as a complex microcosm and taking on colours such as purple, blue and red. It was the first time he had ever been inside someone's psychic space, and the experience was awesome. He saw helices the shape of pasta twirls, and both he and the body he was exploring appeared light enough to float. He had the impression that both he and Zozi were free falling through space, and once he let go the initial fear the feeling was pleasurable like flying.

He wanted nothing more than to touch and explore the taut map of Zozi's skin. Each pigmented inch was like the cratered surface of a planet, the contours and indentations gridded like a road-map on the epidermis. At the same time he felt connected to everyone; his touch extended to the room and all its occupants. Every sensation was heightened, so that through Zozi he found himself caressing the fifty or sixty men gathered there with an intensity that was dangerous. The plurality of touch was what thrilled him, and when he drew back for an instant he missed the contact and felt suddenly disconnected.

Whorls of colour exploded in his mind like a neuronal blow-out. They were like sequences or building blocks, and he realized in a blinding flash that inner and outer were seamlessly joined in a continuous pattern and that under the influence of altered states the split between subject and object disappeared.

He had kept his coat on, and it struck him that he was like his pet Vesuvius, a leopard playing amongst men. He was still too cautious of the drug to fully let go, but he could sense layer after layer of resistance dissolving. He wasn't aware now of who was touching him or why or of his own part in reciprocating trust. He was being drawn centrifugally into a vortex of bodies, which in turn were objects lacking all boundaries. This time he gave in and connected to the central design. He was everyone and no one as he abandoned himself to contact and sped neatly and unhesitatingly into the eye of the whirlpool.

10

When Jim awoke to the loud Roman morning outside Masako was sitting up in bed reading. He flickered in and out of consciousness for a while before coming to. It always seemed unreal to wake up in Rome next to Masako and even more improbable to be on Heliogabalus' trail. None of it added up, but by now he had come to accept that unconscious dictates were as powerful as those governed by reason in determining the major issues in life.

He sat up and shook himself fully awake, feeling the strength of his erection rooted in the erotics of sleep. He noticed Masako's streetmap still open beside the bed, only the grid was different from the one he remembered last night and the page had clearly been turned.

'How was your night?' Masako asked, without taking her eyes off her book.

'I had strange dreams,' he replied, finding her gentle manner the ideal accompaniment to dispersing foggy morning blues. 'I'll tell you about them later,' he said, a flashback as he spoke reminding him of one in which he had been sorting through rubbery squid on a fishmonger's stall to discover Masako's handbag buried beneath a spaghetti cradle of knobby tentacles. He recalled trying to pull it free of the attached suction pads and in the attempt having the tentacles snake up his arms.

'Mmm. Wait until I tell you my dream,' Masako said, still not looking up from the Kundera novel she was reading. 'I dreamed of the exact place where we'll find Heliogabalus. It's in an alley off the Via Cavour, near the Forum. He's up on the third floor.'

'How can you be so sure?' Jim asked, astonished by her certainty that she had discovered the place.

'Because when I ask a big question, the dream answers. I only do it sometimes. I told you how I discovered it for myself as a child. I'd wake up knowing what I'd learned was for real.'

Jim still felt marginally stunned by Masako's access to the specifics of dream, as well as disconcerted to be in the presence of somebody able to commit data to the unconscious and have it processed to resolution. It was uncanny, but he knew enough about the psychic to be convinced of its authenticity, together with the whole contingent science of synchronicity. His recent experiences had taught him that one reality interfaced another and that the two were separated by no more than a window.

'I suppose I find it frightening,' Jim said, his voice signposting a hint of uncertainty. 'I never thought when I started this whole Heliogabalus thing that I'd wind up in such a mess.'

'Mmm. But you have me as your guide,' Masako said reassuringly, surveying a fingernail that smouldered with a sheened burgundy.

Jim sat up, aware that he was dressed only in his tiny black briefs. He was still confused about his feelings for Masako and reluctant to make sexual advances, no matter his desire. At the same time he was aware from past experience that if avoidance became the norm then it grew increasingly difficult to sexualize a friendship. Masako, with her boy's torso and girl's bottom, was how he imagined Heliogabalus to have been, the androgynous ideal playing into one of his recurrent fantasies.

He watched her pull on a white T-shirt with a glitzy pink, heart-shaped logo before manipulating herself into skin-tight hipsters. He could feel the hair-fine balance between desire and action dissolve as she fastened the top button of her jeans, aware he had missed an opportunity that may have left her disappointed. The issue was so delicate that he feared the least wrong move. Both of them, he sensed, were so alive to the possibility of rejection that neither was able to act. They were freezing themselves into corners from which it was impossible to manœuvre. It would require something spontaneous to happen for the pattern to be broken, and he was anxious to avoid the sort of preconceptions that would prevent this coming into play.

He still felt up-ended by the inchoate fragmentation of his dreams, the jump-shots remembered, the transitory flashbacks that even now he was experiencing. It was as if a parallel landscape had been superimposed on consciousness, leaving him, on waking, with sketchily hinted clues as to its reality.

He dressed quickly, after briefly observing the sky outside. He could never get away from skies, and wherever he was his eyes telescoped straight up there on a vertical axis. Today the skyline was choked with ivory-coloured clouds. The overall effect was a luminously oppressive heat-trap. Jim half expected to see vaporous statues up there amongst the clouds and low-flying aircraft.

'It'll rain tonight,' he told Masako with a seriousness that made her laugh. His predictions of weather change had become a private joke between them, causing Masako to pout as she applied the finishing touches to a scarlet lipstick bow. He liked the way her eyes contained her laughter and kept it visual rather than vocally demonstrative. It was her quiet way and one of her characteristics that pulled at a lead to his heart.

Despite the heat he put on a black cashmere V-neck, something he felt created a mood suitable to the occasion, and as he did so the face appeared again. But this time the image was more disconcerting, as a rusty trickle of blood escaped from the youth's mouth and the impact of what could have been a blade ripping into his intestines registered in the shocked eyes.

'What's wrong, Jim?' he heard Masako say, as he sat down, afraid he was about to faint.

'I saw him again. Just as I was looking out of the window, only this time his mouth was full of blood. I'm frightened I'm going mad.'

Masako brought him a glass of chilled water and took his hand. 'Are you sure you want to go? We don't have to meet him, you know. We can just relax and enjoy ourselves for the day. There's no pressure, Jim.'

He hesitated for a moment, but there was no doubt in his mind as to what he should do. He knew he had to go through with it and meet the person whom Masako claimed was Heliogabalus. Only by doing so, he told himself, would he be able to find out if this person was in any way identifiable with the face he kept on seeing.

After collecting their things they went out to a local café and had rolls and black coffee that tasted dark and bitter as the blues. The caffeine hit him alive, as though he was at the wheel of a Jag. Whatever reservations he may have felt at the prospect of going in search of Heliogabalus were starting to disappear. He knew instinctually that he had to go through with it, no matter the consequences. The whole thing was so intricately tied up with his relationship with Masako that the two seemed to exist coextensive of each other.

They took a brief walk through the neighbourhood and bussed over to Via dei Fori Imperiali and from there walked in the direction of Via Cavour, the air fried with toxins from the persistent grind of traffic.

Masako took his arm as they negotiated the crowds and the culture-hungry tourists busy with their Nikons and camcorders. The sky was still cornea-white with a dark-grey pupil opening ominously in the east. He could smell the rain up there above the politicized ruins and feel its heaviness fitted over the city.

Masako insisted on stopping at a florist's to buy six dark-red roses to take to Heliogabalus. She selected each individually and instructed the florist as to the flowers of her choice. She looked at each one fastidiously, like it was her own lipsticked mouth she was admiring.

'You know who these are for?' she said, throwing Jim a curtained look.

They moved on, constricted by the crowds and working to find gaps in the wedge. Masako protected the roses by holding them upright against her, like six pouting mouths competing for her attention.

Jim could feel the sweat breaking out on his palms. He was nervous, and the crowd didn't help. Masako was all bumped-up eyes for the window displays that swam out at them with tropical intensity. Blues, reds, pinks, violets and blacks brought her up against shop windows as she scrutinized new collections from any number of Italian and French designers.

He bit his lip and said, 'Are you sure we're doing the right thing? Wouldn't you prefer to go to the shops?'

'Trust me,' Masako replied. 'Everything's going to be fine.'

He wondered again if he wasn't on the edge of a breakdown. The sky appeared to be moving in ways he hadn't seen before, and he had the feeling that somebody was watching him in the crowd. He put it down to panic and increased his hold on Masako's arm. He found himself resenting being looked at by strangers and interpreted their natural curiosity as some sort of invasion of his rights.

With the aid of her ubiquitous streetmap Masako guided them off the main avenue into a quiet sidestreet which branched out into innumerable alleys. The tempo was slower there, and Jim felt able to breathe again. There was a young man, hair blown back into a gelled quiff like Elvis Presley, standing uncertainly against a lamp post and holding a beer bottle. His girlfriend was sitting astride a scooter, haranguing him for his wasted state.

Leaving him behind as an unsteady landmark Jim and Masako made their way along the narrow streets, Masako leading the way with a certainty that astonished him. She seemed totally sure of her direction and to be stopping simply to reacquaint herself with familiar surroundings. They skewed into an alley that smelled pungently urinous, a downpipe overflowing and somebody's A-grade argument issuing from an open window. They went right down to the end and turned left into an impasse.

'It's the third one along,' Masako said. 'This is the place I visited last night in my dream. It's exactly as I saw it. He's on the top floor. Just wait and see.'

Jim followed reluctantly, wishing he could dematerialize on the spot. He couldn't quite believe what he was hearing and looked up at a balcony full of washing like coloured flags as a means of distraction.

'See the name on the third-floor flat,' Masako said excitedly, as they stood outside the last house in a row of four that had been converted into modern apartments, each with its spill of geraniums and petunias tumbling from window-boxes on balconies. 'Antonio Tiberinus. Didn't you tell me that this was one of the derogatory names given to Heliogabalus during his lifetime?'

Jim swallowed hard and tried to think of something else. The evidence was there in front of his eyes, but he didn't want to know. He still clung to the idea of it being a coincidence, the mischievous factoring of someone who had decided to adopt the name as an alias.

'Don't worry,' Masako reassured him. 'He'll know exactly why we're here. Why else would he be communicating with us?'

'I wish I could be as sure. I still think we're embarking on something crazy. This person might throw us out.'

Masako held the roses up for him as a confirmation of trust, their compact turbans just starting to open and fleshy with the palpable illusion of tissue. 'Let's try,' she said. 'We've nothing to lose. I'm sure from my dream that the two of you will recognize each other on sight.'

Jim watched her depress the buzzer with a sleek burgundy fingernail that almost matched the roses for colour. There was a pause before the voice answered, the tone full of high-pitched curiosity, before quickly switching to English in response to Masako's enquiry.

'Yes, you have the right name,' the voice said with exaggerated politeness. 'But who are you?'

'We're from London,' Masako explained. 'I'm Jim's friend Masako. He's been seeing you for days, and he's here with me. It's important that we speak to you.'

'All right, you'd better come up,' the voice said, clearly fazed by the bizarre introduction.

Jim followed Masako into a dark hall with a tiled floor. There was no lift, and the staircase went straight up before spiralling out of view. He found a light switch to the left of the front door and threw it on, before leading the way up a narrow flight of wooden stairs. Somebody was playing pop in the first-floor flat, a surfy REM song that he recognized as coming from *Reveal*. They continued up to the top floor and found the front door to Tiberinus' flat painted purple, with the number three standing out in gold. Jim felt his heart do a Le Mans, as a voice anticipating their arrival called out, 'It's open. Come on in.'

He followed Masako into a small entrance hall done out in the same purple and gold, with a rococo mirror creating the illusion of space. They walked through to a large sitting-room with scarlet-painted walls and found a slim youth of indeterminate age leaning with his back to a window that gave on to the city. There was something about the place that stopped Jim in his tracks. He knew he had been here before and was experiencing an acute crisis of *déjà vu*. When he caught the young man's eyes he felt zapped by the exchange. The face was exactly the same as the one that he had seen in his visions ever since his arrival in Rome. Thick blond curls framed eyes that appeared more green than blue, the prominent high cheekbones formed a triangle, taking the chin for its base, the nose was pointed at the tip and the mouth surprisingly small and feminine. Jim couldn't help but feel that this particular face would have excited curiosity in any age. It wasn't so much that the youth was attractive as compellingly sexless. His shoulders were narrow and his hands small with elongated fingers. His appearance apart, what impressed Jim immediately was the sense of conviction that the young man carried. For all his apparent vulnerability he appeared absolutely sure of himself. It was clear he could hold his own on the street, and did, for he had the air of somebody who was streetwise rather than a fugitive.

Jim sat down next to Masako on a blue sofa, while Antonio, as he had introduced himself, went into the kitchen to make coffee. He could hear a kettle being filled and the clatter of cups and saucers being given a quick rinse.

He took the opportunity to look around a room that was individual rather than ostentatious. While the colours were bold, the furnishings were tasteful, the design nearly always avoiding drawing attention to itself. There was a rack of CDs on one wall and floor-to-ceiling bookshelves. Jim's inquisitive eye picked out a line of Roman and Greek classics in the green-jacketed Loeb edition, the names Pliny, Tacitus, Juvenal, Herodotus and Livy catching his scattershot visual enquiry. There was a handsome writing-desk placed beneath the wall of books, while central to the room was a leather-topped, circular library table filled with an ordered miscellany of papers and books.

Antonio came back into the room carrying Masako's red roses in a black vase and placed them on the table. Jim watched him stand back from the arrangement, choreographing it with his eyes, before he disappeared back into the kitchen.

They sat and waited for him to return. Jim noticed with relief that the double glazing kept out the persistent dynamic of the city's scooter-crazed traffic. He had the impression that the cul-de-sac in which Antonio lived had become time-warped, almost as if protecting its occupant, who continued to sound busy with coffee things in the kitchen.

Antonio reappeared carrying a tray with a coffee-pot and cups and a plate of florentines. Jim couldn't help but pick up a signal from the purple shirt Antonio was wearing as yet another clue to his hidden identity. There was a breeziness to his walk as he came in, and he seemed, for all his remoteness, glad of the company. He poured the coffee into a blue set and offered round the dark-chocolate florentines. 'The coffee's from the local deli,' he said, 'but it tastes Turkish. It's like a swamp brew.'

Jim took in the camp inflections colouring the voice, aware that Antonio's conflict of gender surfaced through this instrument. The man and the woman in him both manœuvred for space in his words, with neither assuming precedence. He found it oddly winning, this listening to the core of a person in which masculine and feminine played for options.

'I hope you don't mind us calling out of the blue like this,' Masako said. 'I know it must seem rude to just drop by.'

'Apologies aren't needed,' Antonio said. 'It was necessary that we meet.'

Jim continued to sit on the sideline as a silent spectator to events, disconcerted and uncertain where this was leading or how it would end. He kept asking himself how he could be so incredulous as to take a stranger he had never met for the reincarnation of Heliogabalus. Nothing added up, but by now he didn't expect it to. He suddenly found himself facing Antonio's level but benign stare, the eyes sizing him up for identity. In return he found the courage to meet this uncompromising scrutiny and stay with it until a bond was formed. There was kindness in the expression, as well as a tacit understanding of the contact they had already shared. It was doubly strange for Jim to encounter in the flesh somebody he had taken for a trick of his mind.

'I think I know who you are, crazy as it may sound. I'm in Rome to get some background to a dissertation I'm writing on the emperor Heliogabalus, and for some reason I can't get the picture of you out of my mind.'

'Of that I'm perfectly aware,' Antonio smiled, deepening a plot that Jim was desperate to believe for fear of going mad otherwise.

'Jim's had freaky things happen ever since he started his dissertation,' Masako added. 'He'll tell you himself about what happened in London and also of how he's been seeing you ever since we arrived.'

'Seeing me?' Antonio questioned, arching his eyebrows. 'Whatever's going on has been happening quite independent of me. It's been as involuntary for me as it has been for him.'

'Just hearing you talk about it makes me feel better,' Jim said. 'I thought I was starting to lose it.'

'Me, too,' Antonio said. 'The last few days have been impossible. I've never felt under such strain. My problem is that I have total recall of a past that happened thousands of years ago. I know at the time I was the emperor Heliogabalus and that you have chosen me to be the subject of your dissertation.'

'But why should that bring us together?' Jim asked, still baffled by the sequence of events.

'I have no idea,' Antonio laughed, attempting to make light of something too serious to be patched with humour. 'I suppose we can see if my reconstituted life fits with your thesis.'

'I'm afraid I've interpreted history quite freely,' Jim said. 'I've relied more on recreating my subject – or should I say you?'

'Absolutely right,' Antonio replied with incisive clarity. 'The individual is always too close to his age to know what is really happening. To live in time is to experience only its events and never their meaning.'

Jim reflected on the profound truth in Antonio's words, as well as the dynamic needed to compress thought into such telescoped expression. He realized at once the psychological depth attached to Antonio's character, and the intellect that backed it up. The two together were a formidable tool, and he found himself weighing up their potential, as an analyst might make a preliminary reading of a patient.

'Writing about you has got me into deep trouble,' he said, 'or at least I attribute some of my recent problems to my choice of subject matter.'

'What sort of trouble?' Antonio asked, curiosity adding brilliance to his eyes.

'It's a long story,' Jim said. 'The person I was having a relationship with, Danny, not only betrayed me but did so by becoming involved with a sex cult that meets on Hampstead Heath. They have their saint, a man called Slut, who presides over the group and elects to be crucified by his cult.'

'Go on,' Antonio said, clearly fascinated by the subject.

'Well, Danny managed to inveigle me into attending a meeting of the group in Soho. Naturally I wasn't prepared for what I was to encounter, and finding Slut repulsive I walked out. I then received a threatening message from Danny telling me that Slut was looking for me and meant trouble.'

'That's where I come in,' Masako said. 'Jim decided to come and stay with me for a few days to lie low.'

'But unfortunately they found me. I went out one evening to buy a bottle of wine, was abducted in a busy area of Soho, bundled into a car and handcuffed. To cut a long story short, I was driven to Hampstead Heath, forcibly initiated into the circle and made to witness a ritual culminating in Slut's crucifixion on the orgy-tree.'

'Did they force you to have sex?' Antonio enquired.

'I'm sure they would have, but the police arrived in a van and there were men running through the trees blowing whistles and carrying torches. I took advantage of the confusion to make a break for it and ran off into the woods. It was pouring with rain and I was convinced I was being followed. Eventually, after what seemed hours, I got back to the road and was lucky enough to stop a passing taxi.'

'What you describe is very close to an experience I recall from my life as emperor in AD 218,' Antonio said, his eyes appearing to look backwards in his head to meet with the recollection. 'You will know from my history that I incurred the Army's hatred by being openly gay. Well, a group of us used to meet in the gardens at night, and we called ourselves the *onobeli*, which, loosely, means well endowed. One of our group, a youth called Zoticus, had a Christ fixation, which was unusual, given that Mithraism was the popular religion at the time. Anyhow, he came to identify with the image of the suffering god, and I remember the night on which he insisted we haul him on to a tree and tie him there in the crucifixional pose –'

'I find this incredible,' Jim interrupted, as his mind meshed with Antonio's narrative.

'But I haven't finished yet,' Antonio said intently. 'We were all drunk and out of our minds and most of us naked. Suddenly our sanctuary was invaded by the soldiers who policed the parks. They ran in on us making superficial cuts with their weapons and shouting out abuse and ridicule. In the confusion I was pinned up against a tree by a soldier who spat at me. He was about to run me through when I made clear my identity. I can still see the man's face now. The terror in his eyes at having spat in the emperor's face and the realization he was only seconds away from murdering Caesar showed in his shocked expression as he recognized me. He dropped to his knees immediately, shouting out to the soldiers to desist. I took no action against him or the others. I simply ordered them to go and told them that learning tolerance would make them better soldiers.'

'But that's extraordinary,' Jim said. 'It's a perfect instance of synchronicity, or the fusing of two separate incidents into a shared time. In our case it's a way of having past and present unite through a singular theme. I'm sure you don't know any more than I do why this is happening.'

'Sometimes the truth needs to be heard, and perhaps we've been

175

drawn together on account of that. To make good something about my past? Does that sound incredibly naïve?'

'No, it doesn't,' Jim said pensively. 'After all, history invents lies. Most of the accounts I've read of Heliogabalus' life have been cobbled together by hostile biographers like Lampridius and read totally over the top.'

'I have to be in London in three weeks on business. I would welcome the opportunity to look at your thesis, if you would allow me to read it. Nobody's memory is infallible, but I seem to have inherited partial if not total recall of my life as emperor.'

'I, too, find the whole thing amazing,' Masako said, as she toyed fastidiously with segmenting her florentine. 'We found out where you lived only because I asked my dream to locate it for us.'

'I believe you,' Antonio said. 'We sound like we're creating a fiction, but it's for real. That's probably why we've all met. We share in common a particular psychic faculty, one that belongs to the brain's right hemisphere. It allows us to convert dreams into reality.'

'That's well put,' Jim said, feeling his wired tension come down a notch at the recognition of shared experience. He could sense a current in the room working as an interactive lead. They were all connected to its source while retaining their separate identities. It was a good feeling, being up after having been so down.

'What I've learned,' Antonio said, 'and I suspect I knew it also as Heliogabalus, is that magic is a far more potent instrument than reason. The latter has to cut through too many layers to find a solution, whereas magic goes directly there.'

'Again, it couldn't be put better,' Jim said. 'Life is, after all, a process of relearning what we have forgotten. Imagination and magic allow us to access the molecule inside the junk.'

He watched Antonio sight him with approval. He could see from the complete absence of shadow on the young man's face that he had never found it necessary to shave. There were no blue runways structured by a razor and no rusty craters indicating nicks. The face was androgynous, in that the hormonal baseline was a selective pairing of male and female. There was strength in his vulnerability, suggesting the feminine was compensated by a masculinity adept at managing to hold its own in life.

'Still, it's a sort of miracle that has brought us together,' Antonio observed. How else to explain it?'

'Mmm. It's a long time since I last asked a dream for a solution,' Masako said.

'But tell me more about how you managed to find my address?' Antonio asked, all curiosity.

'Well, I'm certain we saw you in the crowd a few days ago,' Masako replied. 'I had a hunch then that you were the person we needed to meet, as Jim was experiencing these visions. Yesterday, before going to sleep, I concentrated on looking at the exact grid on the streetmap that I visualized as your neighbourhood. I then asked the dream to come up with the answer. And it did. When I woke up I knew the name of your street, the house number and the floor on which you lived.'

'I chose this place because it's so well hidden,' Antonio said. 'I've always felt the need to shelter my true identity – and anyhow I'm something of a recluse. I don't have to work. I come from a wealthy family who provide me with an income. I can pretty much do as I like.'

'It's a weird case of subject and author meeting, on my part,' Jim said. 'It's not what you anticipate when you start writing about someone who was supposed to have died in AD 221.'

Jim's remark had him telescope into imagining a world in which people endlessly exchanged identities and in which nobody ever died. He wondered if friends who had died young from the ravages of AIDS were already back in circulation as young children and if their former identities were now reincarnated in still other lives, in the endless cycle of existence. He found the prospect a scary one. Was his dead friend Robert now a seven-year-old child whom he might inadvertently encounter somewhere, and would it dawn on that child one day that he was Robert, a serious young film director who had run out on life too early?

He was rescued from his train of thought by Antonio announcing that he was going to fetch a bottle of wine from the fridge and by

Masako playfully brushing her foot against his shin with character- istic discretion. He took the gesture for what it was, a reassuring sign that they were in this together.

'I think it's sufficiently chilled,' Antonio said, producing a frosty bottle of Chablis and holding it up for inspection, the condensation clinging to the bottle like a blue négligé.

'Let's drink to the unravelling of our plot,' Antonio said, releas- ing promise of a grassy bouquet as he uncorked. 'When I said I first started having contact with you a few days ago, I wasn't being entirely truthful. I became aware of your existence some time earlier, largely through dreams and the sort of flashes that you've been experiencing and also through hints, like seeing a face in the crowd. It was unsettling, so much so that at one time I consulted an analyst. I had the feeling that someone out there was looking for me.'

Jim sipped at a wine that tasted like sunlight lying down in deep meadow grass. Its blond chill opened out on his palate, like an act of disclosure. He watched Antonio take his glass over to the win- dow and stand looking out over the neighbouring rooftops. The knowledge that they were, all three of them, linked by some form of psychic network was still something to which Jim needed to adjust. He had always believed in the existence of subtle energies at play in the body, but not as a force that made its presence directly felt in the external world. He struggled with its possible meaning, knowing at the same time that it was necessary to make radical shifts in his thinking. 'And I suppose, if I'm truthful,' he said, 'then I half expected something like this to happen, although not quite like this. You know the feeling you get when you're expecting the perfect stranger to walk through the door, and at that very moment they do. I'd had a presentiment like that ever since I started my thesis.'

'That's the moment we're all waiting for,' Antonio said, turning around from the window. 'I had it once with Hierocles. I haven't found it this time, at least not yet.'

Jim, with his obsession with clouds, could see stringy, low-flying formations churning outside the window, white textured with grey, like a snowfall turned dirty. Further off, a shoal of whale-shaped cumuli were inertly suspended over an office tower.

'As you will see, I've collected as much evidence of my past as I can,' Antonio said, pointing to the bookshelves. 'You have every right to consider me delusional, but I have absolute belief in my identity.'

'Everything makes sense to me,' Masako said, turning her wine glass around like somebody coaxing a thought to conclusion.

'The way I see it', Antonio said, 'is that sometimes a person is born with the memory of a previous incarnation, and this mind-set attracts others to it like a wavelength. I imagine there's a lot of people out there who have recall; it's just that they're too frightened to speak.'

'It sounds like a whole parallel universe,' Jim said, feeling the wine give him a lift. 'I suppose if you couldn't handle it you'd run the risk of cracking up.'

'I don't know if either of you are hungry,' Antonio said, changing the subject, 'but I'd like to take you to my favourite local restaurant. It's sometimes good to step thoughts outside.'

Jim, who had been looking out at a blue-to-grey sky-change, welcomed the idea. Most of what they had discussed was so remote from his viewpoint that he needed time in which to let his thoughts settle. If he was to believe Antonio's claim to be the reincarnated Heliogabalus, then he had to abandon his idea of history being in large a study of the dead. He was faced now with the prospect that some of its characters were alive, and for all he knew out shopping at this moment in cities radically altered by the constant revisions of time. He sat thinking of a nightmare scenario in which Adolf Hitler was coming alive to a schoolboy out walking with his mother in a Berlin park. He was telling the boy that he had once been the Führer and that he was to own to this as his true identity . . .

'You're miles away,' Masako said, recalling him to the present and the decision they had made to go out.

Antonio had slipped on a linen jacket and was busy checking his pockets for keys. The light had gone out in the sky, and a dense slab of grey cloud obscured the sun. Jim noticed that the room was suddenly dark. He had the impression that he had gone missing for a while or that something had significantly changed since he last spoke. He felt displaced, like someone woken from a siesta without remembering having fallen asleep.

He panned in and out of consciousness, as Masako stood up and ran her hands in a flattening motion over her denimed buttocks. He was struck again by how lucky he was to have her with him in Rome. Her fine-tuning to his needs was something he hadn't experienced before with anyone. Her sensitivity was rare, and it shone translucently in her features.

Jim got up, and together he and Masako followed Antonio down the stairs and out into the alley. Rome was under clouds and the streets seemed altered. The whole city had shifted mood in response to the change.

'I've decided, on second thoughts, that we'll go somewhere more special than my local,' Antonio said. 'What about my taking you to Il Guru on the Via Cimarra? We can catch a bus there if you look out for a number 75.'

Antonio led the way through a complex of alleys towards the avenue. Jim still felt he was daydreaming, as the late afternoon graduated on a soft pink curve towards evening. A young man met him eye to eye with busy sexual signals, his slim figure tubed into white jeans. He smelled of Acqua di Parma, sex and something else that Jim preferred to call mystery. All of his same-sex longings hit into his cells as his over-the-shoulder look was fielded by the stranger's simultaneously thrown head.

When a bus came into view they ran for it. Jim stood on the packed aisle between Antonio and Masako. He knew he could have gone off with either. His life was like that, it pointed east and west, north and south. He held on to the overhead strap as the street got eaten up. There was a girl outside the station running to meet her lover. He watched her place a restraining hand on her floating hair as the bus came level with her before accelerating away.

II

He knew he had made an error of judgement, but he couldn't help himself. He had ordered the defacement of all the statues raised to Alexander in public places. They were to be smeared in mud and excrement and slashed with graffiti.

Alexander Severus, his cousin and heir, was straight and dangerous, and Heliogabalus had reason to fear an uprising. There had been previous insurrections, he reminded himself, the first as early as 218, when the Third Legion, 'Gallica', stationed in Syria, had defected in the interests of making Verus, their commander, emperor. Subsequent to that there had been attempts by the Fourth Legion, the fleet and a pretender called Seleucus, all of which had been suppressed by Heliogabalus' guard. In a self-critical mood he thought back to the beginnings of his antagonistic policy towards the Army and how much of it stemmed from his appointment of a gay lover, Publius Valerius Comazon, to the position of commander of the Praetorian Guard. This ill-considered move in his first year as emperor had lost him the support of the military for good.

But in Alexander, even though the boy was only thirteen years old, and in his inveterately dominating mother, Julia Mamea, he had made powerful enemies. He had grown to hold both in contempt, more for the undercurrent of their ambition than for any direct plot to remove him from office. There was something about Alexander and his refusal to drop a predominantly passive guard that Heliogabalus not only disliked but mistrusted. The boy was too anxious to please, and the lack of conviction apparent in his ideas suggested he could be easily manipulated. Alexander reminded him of still water: no impulsive ripple entered his behaviour; no oscillating current rocked his mood. He was to be found reading politics, law and equity or discussing with the Senate ways of keeping the empire stable by using Rome as the baseline for a civilized community.

It was winter. Heliogabalus was finding it hard to cope with Annia Faustina's demands as a woman. Contrary to his expectations, she expected him to perform in bed and on his refusal had stonewalled him with an angry silence whenever they found themselves together in private. The relationship was becoming a mess, like so much of his personal life, and part of him wished he could take off with Hierocles to one of the islands, maybe to Capri. He had begun to dream of blue spaces and of setting up an exclusive gay community on one of the outposts. He had talked about it with his closest friends, most of whom had encouraged him to pursue his aims. He was tired of the admin expected of him, and he longed to be free of the Senate's conniving spin.

He sat eating a light meal of olives, goat's cheese and a variety of vegetables and was glad of having Antony there to prepare his clothes for the day. He felt on edge, knowing there would be reprisals for the ugly method he had chosen to assassinate Alexander's character. His message was clear: if there wasn't a turnaround in public feeling then he would abandon Rome and set up his island community. And if they came after him and burned the island, then he couldn't care. He would at least die amongst his own.

He had arranged today to take beauty tips from Laura, the exceedingly beautiful prostitute he had bought outright for a hundred thousand and kept untouched in his own wing of the palace. She was his platonic distraction, and her presence at dinner annoyed Annia in the same way as she was unable to accept the importance of Vesuvius in his life. The more he thought of it the more he recognized the need for a separation. He hadn't the time to cope with domestic conflict, particularly with Hierocles demanding constant support as he slammed from one drunken state to another on a self-debasing trail of excess.

Laura came into the room, wearing a black piled-up Indian wig, and took a place beside him on the couch. The heating in the palace was never sufficient for him, and he shivered. He envied Laura her body. No matter how much he imagined what it was like to be a woman, he was acutely aware of his separation from the actuality. Laura was his compensation, the woman he would like to have been if things had been different. As it was, he remained fascinated by her looks, his only demand on her being that she saved herself for him while at the same time accepting that the nature of the relationship ruled out any possibility of sex. She had put on her day-face and wore a purple silk dress, an item likely to offend Annia with its imperial connotations. He liked to give her presents as a consolation for the tedium of her life. She was his doll, and it was her job to blink her big green eyes at him from behind a defensive screen of mascara. Laura had come from a good family but had been disowned by them after an early sexual scandal. She had never confided the details, but he knew enough of her sketchy background to guess that her social defiance was aimed at her family. Penalized for sex, she had come to identify totally with it, compelled to make this aspect the cause of her ruin. He had given her books, including Ovid's racy celebration of love, but he suspected she never read them. She shared a flat in the palace with his personal beautician, an Egyptian called Leila, and appeared to have settled into a life of uneventful luxury. It wasn't something he had the intention of indefinitely extending, but for the time it gave him a perverse satisfaction to know that he was denying other men access to her body. She was the feminine ideal he could look at but never touch.

He performed his usual little acts of homage, giving her rings that sparkled like frozen waterfalls or blocked facets of ice windowed on a high peak. What he liked was her genuine fascination with the beauty of stones, irrespective of their worth. He watched her eyes bump up at sight of a brimming emerald, as she turned the ring over in her palm before giving it the attention of her finger.

Together they looked at the jewels he had chosen on impulse from the thousands he hoarded in chests in his room. Stones that had been fetched from all parts of the empire and cut and set by Rome's best jewellers. They were the cold currency rainbow that he turned over in his hands whenever he felt insecure. He liked the way Laura would study a ring by widening her left eye, while correspondingly narrowing the focus of her right.

Laura's surprise on closing her eyes and reopening them to a colour-impacted hexagonal stone was decommissioned by Antony hurrying into the room to ask for his urgent attention. He could see from the anxiety in his face that it was an emergency. He knew intuitively and without having to be told that his plot against Alexander had misfired. He had felt uneasy all night, hoping against hope that his method of vilification would be endorsed by the people but at the same time knowing he had made a big error of judgement.

According to Antony, there was no time to lose. A contingent of soldiers was on its way to the palace, demanding either his resignation or his life. A splinter-group in the Army were adamant that Alexander should be appointed emperor in his place.

Unwilling to desert his side for a moment, Antony suggested they go into hiding in the Spes Vetus Gardens until the soldiers had come and gone. They would have to count on the fact that the rebellious faction were still under an oath of allegiance and that the majority of the Army had chosen to remain at their barracks under the leadership of the tribune Aristomachus.

Heliogabalus left Laura with brief instructions to take the rings and return to her rooms. He said he was needed elsewhere and that there wasn't a moment to waste. He followed Antony and a group of his close supporters through a series of underground corridors beneath the palace and out into the wooded parkland. The air was foggy-blue November. A mob of crows were policing the area like mafia. He felt suddenly exposed, believing that by running away he had forfeited his office. The short distance he had placed between himself and the palace was like the separation between the living and the dead. He was starting to panic and feared that if the soldiers were denied killing him then they would turn their vengeance on his mother and Hierocles.

He felt helpless as he stood there in the cold fog, before being hurried on by Antony and a group of armed guards towards a pavilion that overlooked the mashed circuit used for chariot races. He had put out a contract on his cousin's life, and now he feared the plot had been uncovered. He regretted having acted without consultation. He should have had him poisoned or drowned in the baths or hit by falling masonry on some public occasion.

He scrambled through woods in the direction of the royal pavilion. He was just coming in sight of the building when a bodyguard in front brought him to an abrupt halt by stopping him with a powerfully opposing arm. Directly in front of them a body bound by ropes had been pinned to the tree by a knife going clean through the heart and out the other side. When the guard held the head up he recognized it as Marco. The chunky diamond he was wearing at the time had been left on his finger as a warning. He knew the sign was intended for him, and he froze in his tracks, his throat furred, his heart pounding. He stood there paralysed, hardly able to believe what he was seeing, before his group forced him on. They hurried across the clearing and, after his minders had searched the place, he went on in. The pavilion, although it was stamped with his inimitable style, had been left unused because of his lack of interest in chariot racing. It had the musty air of a place thrown in on itself and shocked by their arrival.

He sat down and watched a gold chink of light make it through the closed shutters and tried to distract himself from thinking about Marco's mutilated body and the suffering he would have undergone before the blade was punched home. He sat there dejected, knowing he would never have it easy again as long as Alexander lived. Part of him looked for a political loophole and to making some sort of compromise with the Army, while the other part wanted out and conditions of peaceful exile.

He sat there stalling for time. The seconds seemed to slow to manageable chunks of time, identifiable components in which he evaluated the major events of his life. Each moment he reviewed presented a time frame and accompanying visual. He stared at the irreversible contents of a film played in slow motion, each of the experiences coded with his individual signature.

Whatever interlude he had been granted was dramatically shattered by one of the guards running into the room to announce that a group of soldiers under the leadership of Antiochianus were drawn up outside and were threatening entry. Antiochianus was apparently the mediator, intent on negotiating terms, while the soldiers were for liquidating the entire company. The guard remained armed, ready to die defending Caesar, his whole body wired for efficiency of purpose.

Before anyone could act, it was Antony who tore out of the room insisting he would negotiate terms. Three or four of his guards hurried in pursuit to offer protection to a man who was unarmed.

Heliogabalus couldn't find it in himself to respond. He hated confrontation and tried desperately to convince himself that none of this was happening. He was terrified and tried to take refuge by dreaming of the imaginary island he would colonize with gay youth, its white beaches overrun with their naked bodies. The waiting seemed interminable, and he expected at every moment to be confronted by his assassins. He listened for angry shouts or gestures, but there were no sounds of an offensive, only the querulous holler of a rook signalling from the wood. After what seemed hours, Antony came back into the room and told him in a faltering voice of the conditions. The demands were that he expelled his gay entourage from the palace and, in particular, that he removed Hierocles, Gordius and Myrismus from office and from his personal company. He was also required to designate Alexander a joint consul and to respect his voice in government. If he agreed to the conditions stipulated by the Army, he would be allowed to return to the palace and continue in office. If he failed to compromise, then he could expect a military *coup*. The terms dictated were nothing less than a charged threat: change or die.

He listened with horror to the Army's attempts to strip him of all that was meaningful in his life. Their demands shaved him to basics, but he knew he had to accept for his mother's sake and for the nagging sense that he would otherwise be deserting his destiny. He agreed to the terms outright. He had no idea until then how much he feared death on any other terms than his own. He was too shocked to speak but managed to signal his agreement by the violent nodding of his head.

He sat and stared at the gold chinks of November sunlight atomized across the floor as Antony went back outside to accept terms. Again the wait seemed interminable as he paced the room in the attempt to keep track with his thoughts. He had no means of redressing Marco's death, and the image of the boy with his chest slashed open cut him up deep. The atrocity reminded him of his own precarious mortality and, when Antony came back in to tell him that the soldiers had gone, he felt an overwhelming sense of dejection. All the way back through the parkland he couldn't free himself of his preoccupation with Marco and the way his friend had died. Rooks mobbed their progress, spilling a black calligraphy on the autumn sky.

When they got back Heliogabalus was met by a drunk Hierocles, his eyes black from the makeup he had slept in and his body draped in a woman's négligé. He came towards him on an oscillating pivot before collapsing back on to a sofa. The man he loved and whose emotional support he needed was little more than a wreck.

Heliogabalus went over, shook him to no effect and stormed out. Inwardly he blamed Hierocles for his trouble with the military and his loss of political clout. By devoting all of his time to his lover he had lost sight of the main issues and allowed himself to become sidelined. He had somehow to pull things around if he was to continue as emperor, and this also meant cleaning up his life in accordance with the Army's wishes. But it was a resolve he knew he would never keep. The rot in his relations with the state had gone too far. It was like a pernicious virus that had come to affect the entire organism.

He went in search of his mother, knowing that only she could calm his nerves. He found her in bed with a boy half her age, her stripped-off gown shredded like Vesuvius had slashed the transparent silk. She was sitting up in bed, her full, conical breasts on view, picking at a fruit bowl. She caught his eye simultaneous with shredding a grape and patted the bed beside her as a signal for him to sit down.

He hung back, conflicting emotions of anger and jealousy tuning his temper. The boy asleep in the bed was younger than himself, and he took it as a personal affront that his mother should turn to a toy-boy rather than himself for pleasure. But, looking at her now, a sensual ribbon of juice escaping down her chin and her eyes puffy from drink, he felt nothing but contempt for her ways. His thoughts were still aimed at the reform necessary to change his skin. His mother, like Hierocles, was a liability. Her unpopularity with the people made it impossible for him to delegate power and take a brief period away from Rome. He knew the payback would be disastrous and that such a move would play directly into Antony's cause.

He pushed his mother's hand aside, as she tried to direct it to her breasts, and stripped the sheet off the bed. His anger blown, he calmed down, recognizing in her a bond that stitched them together along a crooked seam.

'Things are bad,' he said, sitting down beside her with his head in his hands. 'The Army have given me an ultimatum. I either acknowledge Antony as a joint ruler or I'm as good as dead. I've also been told to clean up my household and get rid of the people closest to me, like Hierocles. I've been given no options. It's do or die, that simple. They've threatened to kill us all.'

He watched his mother sober up instantly. Her mind came on with all the instincts of survival. She stood up naked, shocked into awareness, and he could see the plum-coloured love-bites blotched in clusters on her body. Her life without power and the wealth it brought would be nothing, and he dreaded proposing to her his scheme of exile and their ruling jointly over the island community he intended to establish. She had, for all her faults, been the first woman to impose laws in the Senate and, no matter how controversial her platform, her influence had carried.

'What are we going to do?' she asked him, turning on him with panic in her eyes. She held on unsteadily to a marble bust of herself that faced a luxuriously decorated room. He had never seen her this scared or, in a dissolute way, this beautiful. Her hennaed hair was brushed out straight, the curve of her buttocks heart-shaped and full. She stood with her back to him like an artist's model, hands slung indignantly on her hips, her thoughts fixed in some obsessive frame.

'We have to accept', he said, 'if we let go now we concede to Alexander. He has the Army's support.'

Symiamira turned around to face him, eyes full on and powered up. She walked straight at him and continued to shunt him all the way to the bed, where he collapsed under her weight. Her mouth sealed his like a cork in a bottle. He gave himself up to her rooting tongue as it choreographed a circular groove around his mouth. He forced her hair back from his face and tried to struggle free. The boy she had taken to bed last night continued in his drunken sleep, oblivious to everything. Glancing at him Heliogabalus thought he looked dead, except for the lift of his chest in breathing.

He managed to stall Symiamira's passion and push her face away by placing a hand on each cheek and looking directly into her eyes. He sat up in order to gain space and positioned his hands on her shoulders. 'I'm ordered to appear with Alexander at the calends,' he said, 'as a sign that we're joint rulers. If I don't comply with this request then they'll come for us.' He watched Symiamira look away, as though by refusing to believe him she would succeed in erasing the danger. She sat back from him, still disappointed at his unwillingness to have sex but aware now of the reality of the situation.

He shook her to get her attention before telling her of his newly formulated plan to set up a community on Capri. 'We'd be safe there,' he said. 'As well as becoming the leaders of a new race, we'd attract to the island the world's most beautiful youth, and all of them gay. Why shouldn't we strike out in this direction and create an alternative society?'

Symiamira looked at him suspiciously, until the idea clicked. 'Do you mean that buying us out would be the condition? That we'd settle and let Antony take over?'

'Sort of. I would agree to take a less active role in government and live in exile like Tiberius. I had in mind his old hiding place.'

Symiamira played with the thought, committing it to her system like a substance of which she was unsure. He half expected her to come back at him with suicide as the only resolution to their dilemma. He didn't tell her that his sexuality was the root cause of military hostility. He had read his own graffiti epitaphs too often to doubt the reasons for his unpopularity. Heliogabalus the bitch. The faggot pretender. The bath-house slut. He had memorized each ugly inscription and had retaliated by a smear campaign against his cousin. He had been warned by Syrian astrologers that he would meet a violent end, and their prophecy came back to him now, as his mother answered him simply by curling up and taking refuge against his side.

He lay next to her, the day's incidents coming back at him like a traffic accident to which he had been a spectator. He had never felt so alone in his life. He was wanted by nobody, not even by himself. As he understood events, the Army had taken Alexander into their custody so as to ensure his safety. He knew for sure that his mother's sister Julia Mamea was a party to the plot, for she wanted to see her child Alexander as emperor, but he felt unwilling to pursue this line of investigation. He was too confused to think properly and kept hoping against the odds that the situation would reverse itself. It was the shock of it all that he couldn't shift. It was inside him like an air-pocket that kept buffeting his nerves. He knew he could never again be the person he was two or three hours ago, and that the cutting of his privileges was like halving his identity.

Eventually he got up and decided on a course of action. He had to do something to make amends, and he decided he would start by throwing Hierocles out of the palace. That whole scene had started to get on his nerves, and now was the time to end it. Determined to act on his resolve, he left his mother and went in search of Hierocles. He found him sashaying around the dining-room on high heels, a bottle in one hand and a blond wig in the other. He looked like someone trying to drink himself sober as the agenda for the day.

Heliogabalus came up behind him and steadied him by placing his hands on his shoulders. 'Hierocles, you've got to go,' he said, gently but with authority. 'Otherwise they'll kill us sooner than even you predicted. Get out and stay out until times are safe. And take all the trash with you. All the rent you have brought here from the baths. They've all got to go.'

When Hierocles said nothing he shook him. It was tragic seeing the man he loved in this condition. His face was bloated, his nose swollen and rashed with broken blood vessels, his eyes shot with scarlet fleck. Heliogabalus stood looking at him, fighting back the tears and holding his lover out on a long arm, appalled by what he was seeing.

Suddenly Hierocles broke free of his hold, positioned the blond wig for effect and looked him dead level in the eyes. 'I hate you,' he said vehemently, his voice shot through with malice. 'You'll die as you deserve. Like a dog.'

The force of his lover's hatred cut him deep. He felt the blow like somebody randomly slashing piano strings with a blade. He should have stayed calm, should have held back from confrontation, but instead he screamed, 'Get out of here at once. All of you. It's an ultimatum. If you don't go I'll have my guards remove you. Do you hear?'

He didn't wait for an answer. He stormed out, glad of what he had done. He knew there would be no going back on his word and that his marriage to Hierocles was over. He had torn up its gossamer threads like ripping apart a spider's web.

He went straight back to his mother and found her dressed and making up in front of a mirror. Her expression was serious, and she seemed to be busy making plans in her head. She was deep in thought as she filed a fingernail, his concentration having him believe it was the thought she was addressing, rather than the crescent of red gloss applied to her left thumb.

'You're right,' she said without turning around. 'We must stay at all costs. If we run at the first threat they'll know we're frightened. And that way we'll never negotiate terms.'

He noticed that the boy who had still been asleep in her bed ten minutes ago had disappeared without a trace. Clearly his mother had thought it wise not to exacerbate matters by drawing attention to her untiring sexual conquests.

'But it means a divided power,' he argued. 'The Senate support Alexander, and I'll be without any ruling voice. At least there is dignity in exile. Tiberius found it.'

'It's not something to consider now,' Symiamira said. 'Let's wait and see how events unfold. I'll speak to our advisers.'

'The astrologers have warned me I'll meet a violent end,' he said, hoping the awareness of it would have his mother reconsider.

'The calends are coming up and, as I told you, I have to make a gesture of goodwill and appear with Alexander on the occasion.'

He stood there, ashamed of the concessions he was making, his hatred of brute machismo urging him to show defiance. He wasn't going to be the wall against which the Army pissed. His tolerance, his generosity to the poor and the lotteries he had introduced, conferring huge prizes on the winners, had made him popular with the people. They liked him even for his extravagance, and he felt confident in their support. His enemies were largely the common soldiers, whose continuous demands for money he had of necessity silenced. Unable to get their own way they had taken to using his sexuality as a form of blackmail. He knew from experience the false sense of camaraderie that men derived from feeling part of the sexual norm. It was a bogus security to which they clung in the interests of identity. His own education by Syrian priests had placed an emphasis on the androgynous unity of male and female as the desired ideal. For them, gender was considered to be without boundaries, and he had been genuinely shocked to encounter prejudice in Rome and to find himself the victim of persistent homophobia. It wasn't how he had imagined life to be in the capital, and intolerance had forced him into the corner in which he now found himself.

He watched his mother pencil a blue horizontal eyebrow, meticulous to the last detail, ensuring that that the line was perfectly straight. He knew that if his mother's thoughts were on death, then they would equally be on how to present herself at her best, should the moment arise.

'You're right, of course,' he said. 'We'll stay. It would be crazy to leave, and anyhow there's nowhere to go. An enemy is someone who gets under the skin and knows everything right down to the details of your blood group. There's no chance of running away.'

He took the little box containing poison out of his pocket and toyed with it, knowing full well he had caught her eye. The gesture was an indication of how he felt rather than an attempt to initiate a suicide pact. If necessary, that would come later, as a final act of freedom, the ultimate push into the unknowable dark.

'That's our only certain death,' his mother commented, seeing the container in his hand. 'I'm prepared for it if you are.'

He wasn't, and he attributed his reluctance to fear. He had read in Seutonius of how Nero, finding it impossible to put the blade through himself, had to be assisted by aides.

He thought of all he had hoped for as emperor and of the temples he had raised to his god. Nothing withstood the ravages of time, least of all the human body. Everything material had a disposable audit. Love he considered the exception, as its qualities were subjective, and if anything of him lived on he hoped it would be because of this emotion.

He was lost in his thoughts when a servant came into the room carrying a written order for his attention. It was a demand that he should appear at the barracks at noon the next day, in the company of Alexander, to review the troops. They were clearly trying to force his hand, and he guessed the object of the exercise was to point up ridicule at his effeminacy. He had no purchase on his cousin's masculine bearing and his ability to acquit himself well in the eyes of the Army. The whole thing was a set-up to show him at a disadvantage, and he resented the politics behind such a scheme. While he couldn't be forced to attend, the failure to do so would play directly into his rival's hands.

For no reason at all, he suddenly let go the whole misery of his being and started to sing. He stood facing his mother and in his trained tenor's voice sang an aria extracted from one of Ovid's tales. When he sang, he visualized the notes, shading one part blue, another yellow, another red. Singing for him was like creating a sonic rainbow, one that bled words into sound in a controlled stream of molecular collisions. It was the chance to enter so deep into himself that he forgot his troubles. He watched his mother put down her eye-pencil and transfer her attention to his impromptu performance. He had done this in childhood, back home in Syria, sung to alleviate a situation when it looked impossible, and now he was doing it again. And, as he sang, so his resolve to remain emperor returned. He had no doubt in his mind that he was going to have his way even if it cost him his life.

His song finished, he sat down and wrote a reply on impulse. He ordered on command that the Senate should disband and all its members leave the city. He said that he no longer recognized them as the governing body but as supporters of a faction opposed to the emperor. They were to be gone by dawn, and the punishment for remaining behind was death. He repeated that he was not going to tolerate a conspiracy against Caesar, and singled out the names of Ulpian the jurist and Silvinus the rhetorician as foremost amongst the offenders. With his typically soft touch, he offered them exile rather than execution, preferring to keep his reign clean of blood to the end should signing the document prove, in effect, his suicide.

He briefly showed the letter to Symiamira and decided to have it delivered immediately. He wanted, for once, to assert his authority rather than reflect on the consequences of doing so. He didn't hold out much hope other than in the possibility of shocking the Senate and the Army into the realization that in supporting Alexander they were in fact undermining the emperor's sovereignty. He knew that by the time the people rose in his support it would be too late. The community were always the last to be consulted about events concerning them, so that a people's rebellion was invariably a reaction to something that had happened, rather than a determining force in its prevention.

He felt incredibly tired, almost as if his nerves had been broken up like a road. Symiamira, in contrast, looked surprisingly calm now that a decision had been made and busied herself arranging a number of gold vases on a bedside table. Looking at her attachment to things reinforced his belief that it would be wrong for them to go into exile. He didn't want her to have to change, and he knew her to be incapable of denying herself the least pleasure. He was more resolved than ever that, if they were to die, then it would be in the manner of how they had lived.

There was nothing to do now but wait. He had made the only real legislative demand of his reign. It amounted to a vindication of his rights to be sole emperor, and he hoped it would generate terror in the government. It gave him huge satisfaction to think he might, if things succeeded according to plan, force the Senate out of their corporate stranglehold, even if it was only for a short time. They and the interests they represented were what he hated most about the empire's burnt-out constitution.

He quickly changed into his *toga praetexta*, as a means of feeling more secure about his decision to take authority, and tried to distract himself by thinking of his achievements as emperor rather than allow his desperation to make a mental inventory of his defects. He talked himself through his various successes and reminded himself that he had been responsible for the completion of the Antonine baths as well as the Thermae Varianae on the Aventine and having built temples and a vast hall for the women's senate on the Quirinal. He had given generously to the people, preferring almost every walk of life to that of the autocratic ruling classes with whom he was supposed to mix. The latter had never forgiven him his origins, his religion or the towers he had built in the city according to the instructions of Syrian priests, one of which had a courtyard paved with gold as a symbol of his solar birth.

He didn't know how long he had sat there with his mother, only that a messenger returned at some point with news that the Senate were in flight from the city. They had taken him on his word and fled, and only the refractory Sabinus, a man of consular rank, had remained behind and resolutely refused to budge. He accepted the news gladly but remained suspicious, convinced that their exodus was mere show and that secretly they would be plotting a *coup*.

He hoped, too, that Hierocles and his entourage would be gone by now, although the pain of separation cried out in his heart like a small trapped animal. He went out of the room to look, part of him dreading to find the apartment empty, the familiar scent of his lover everywhere and his possessions gone. He knew there would be a comeback on his decision and that regret would force him to reconsider. Their history had been one of salvageable tantrums, glass splinters of jealousy, holocaustal tempers, but beneath it all they had known a love that at times had run deep like an underground river. They had faced hostility together, taken disapproval square on the jaw and somehow survived.

He knew from the quiet of the corridor as he approached it that

Hierocles had gone. The usual shrieks of camp hysteria igniting the place were absent and, for once, this particular wing of the palace was silent. He hadn't known it like this before, and he had the sudden fear that his entire staff had deserted him and left him to be butchered by the Army.

Of course the rooms had been looted. Hierocles and his circle had made off with all the valuables. He should have seen this coming and had Antony supervise their leave-taking, but at the time he had been too shocked. It wasn't his own losses he regretted, it was more his mother's anger he feared at his having mismanaged the whole affair. Most of the jewellery and the silver and gold objects they had stolen were her family heirlooms, and he dreaded having to tell her of the theft. He recognized it as still another instance of the payback he invited by mixing with lowlife. As he stood contemplating the stripped rooms, he couldn't decide whether it was his sexuality that compelled him to search out such people or if it wasn't that he himself shared their essentially underworld nature. Hierocles had clearly cut and run and decided to avenge himself by turning the apartment upside down. Expensive silks had been slashed, screens kicked over and books by Heliogabalus' favourites ripped up and kicked across the floor. The rooms had been devastated, and as he sorted through the debris, lifting with his foot a string of pearls that had belonged around the neck of a bust of Dionysus, he realized the tremendous force of a lover's hatred. Threatened with loss of material privileges, Hierocles had gone on a cyclonic thrash to compensate for being rejected. Glasses and mirrors had been smashed across the marble floors. Heliogabalus stood there, fascinated by the trail of maniacal destruction Hierocles had left in his wake. He cut his finger on a needle of glass as he picked up a gold frame he had once given Hierocles as a gift. The scrolled jeweller's work depicted ambiguously sexed Cupids and had been a present at the time of their audaciously staged marriage.

He felt totally alone in the biggest city in the world, at the hub of an empire over which he presided. He had everything and nothing, as he stomped through the litter, expecting at any moment to be surprised and run through by a member of his own guard. He couldn't believe he had really brought all this on himself. He was too young to account for the reckless extravagance by which he had lived. Being emperor had seemed as much a delusion as a reality. He had acted out the part without thought for the consequences. Everything had been at his disposal, and he had torn the building down to get at the contents. He had crossed the city once too often in carriages drawn by lions – or sometimes by naked boys. He had worn dresses and openly disparaged the Army. He had spent too much time perfecting sauces and too little on government. His extravagance had known no boundaries. He had driven to the Forum through streets sanded with gold dust and had funded the lives of the city's rent boys. He saw himself as he had addressed them in a dockside bath-house, promising them everything, including his patronage. His personal advisers had been encouraged to drag up outrageously and to adopt the appearance of women.

He picked up a gold candlestick that Hierocles' lot had left behind and debated leaving the palace in disguise and simply disappearing. He didn't know where he'd go, but in his confused state it didn't matter. He still believed that somehow he could turn events around and remain emperor. He thought of appealing to the people but knew that to do so would lose him their respect.

He hesitated as always, afraid of the immense silence that seemed to have fallen over the palace. Something told him that he had been abandoned and that his assassins were closing in. The building's nuclear activity appeared to have shut down. All the officious buzz of the place, its executive departments and the turbo of its activities seemed to have disappeared. His wing in particular had the silence of a mortuary, and clearly nobody from his guard had attempted to stop Hierocles when he went on the rampage. He called out for Antony, and his voice came back at him on delayed echo. It was impossible to imagine that the person closest to him had deserted. It didn't bear thinking about, and he raised his voice in the effort to attract Antony's attention. He expected at any minute to hear his familiar hurried step suddenly come into hearing. In the absence of it, he hallucinated the sound and finally, desperate, went running in search of him.

His assumptions were right. His quarter was deserted and, starting to panic, he hurried towards Antony's room. He repeatedly called out his name, hoping for a response that would explain his friend's silence and bring him running to his side. He was, as always, unarmed and totally vulnerable to attack. When he got to Antony's room he pulled back in alarm from the rash of blood-spots on the floor outside. He simply didn't want to believe what he was seeing. He was prepared to lose everything in the world but not Antony. He dreaded what he would encounter and stalled outside, his heart beating so fast it threatened to explode.

He edged his way in, tentative step by tentative step, his body wound taut in anticipation of shock. Antony had been stabbed clean through the thorax in a way reminiscent of Marco, with the blade left impaling the victim against a lacquered oriental screen. It was an exact repeat of the horror he had witnessed in encountering Marco in the park, and he sprung back in acute shock. It was intolerable that his gentle friend had died in agony at the hands of a butcher, and for the first time in his reign his whole being cried out for vengeance. The thought flashed through his head that Hierocles had stabbed both men in a fit of insane jealousy, but deep down he suspected the murders were the work of the Army. They were clearly systematically eliminating those closest to him as a way of cleansing his circle. He read it as a warning that he would be next on their hit-list.

He was terrified, and he started to run. He headed towards his mother's room, then abruptly switched direction. He felt as if he was being tracked by a spotlight, as he heard the brutal shouts of soldiers on the floor above. There was no time to waste. He ran down a long passage and through an empty hall, cleared a terrace and made it outside to the grounds. In his confusion he decided to take refuge in a latrine under cover of a group of ilexes. The place was little used, except sometimes by himself and staff working in the grounds. He had an attachment to its mildly fetid air, its discoloured marble urinal and the fact that it was like a cottage set apart for privacy. It had been there since the time of Severus, and little or nothing had been done to maintain it. Heliogabalus had gone there in the past when he needed absolute privacy and sat there listening to the rain knuckle the tiled roof.

This time he was desperate. He sloped in under the cover of oily green camellia bushes and flattened himself up against the cool marble wall for comfort. The unattended stench of the place cooked in his nostrils. Cloaca and urine gone to earth formed a cocktail of bad odours as his life went on fast-forward. All of its highlights panned from one brain hemisphere to the other. He could feel the speed of the retrospective zap his brain cells.

Suddenly he heard shouts in the nearby trees and the sound of men beating their way through the bushes. He was without any means of killing himself, for the poison would be too slow. He thought of his mother, his home, the priests chanting in the temple at Emesa and prayed he would be given another chance. At the same time his mind began to fill with an intense white light. It flooded in, despite his fear, permeating his entire being, as he visualized his early days in the temple at Emesa. The rest, he realized, was nothing. Fame, extravagance, being emperor, they were parts independent of his real self.

The light was in him as he heard men running towards his hiding place, their footsteps scrunching the gravel path, the staccato impact sounding like there was a group of them. When the first entered, sword in hand, it was hatred he saw in the man's eyes – that and the ugly group of pimples clustered each side of his nose. He turned his back on them so that he wouldn't see his murderer. When he fell under the ferocity of the first hit, he connected with the light. It was a pure luminous stream he entered. He knew he was going back home, and that home meant integrating with the universe. He simply wasn't there any longer when the soldiers carved him up. He had connected with the light, simple as the click of a mouse. He looked back at his absent body once and was gone.

'Most facts are errors,' Antonio said. He was seated on a purple cushion on the floor of Masako's Soho studio as Jim tentatively showed him extracts from his dissertation. He felt embarrassed about presenting his version of a life to someone who claimed to have been its subject.

After their holiday in Rome Jim had moved in with Masako, an arrangement consolidated by their having become lovers. While both of them retained a sexual ambiguity, they found a common meeting-point in precisely that area of confusion. Looking up from where he was squatting on the floor, Jim's eye was routed both to the jeaned curve of Masako's thigh where it joined the buttock and also the sensual meniscus that comprised Antonio's lower lip. He was attracted to both in equal degrees and, while his emotional bond was with Masako, he none the less felt the divided pull of interests that he had come to recognize as his own. It was reassuring to know that Masako was a journeyer across similarly conflicting territory, her orientation having been split since her early teens when she had entered into a series of same-sex relations. It was the boyishness in Masako that triggered his desire, while correspondingly she claimed it was his feminine side to which she was most attracted.

Jim felt shy of Antonio as he fed him selected pages of his dissertation with the promise that he could take a copy back with him to his hotel. Antonio had opted to stay at the Piccadilly and had twice invited them to dinner at the hotel's terraced third-floor restaurant, a level that allowed visual access to the whole Piccadilly sweep, with its decorative roof-top cupolas and gargoyles tucked into the architectural skyline. Jim liked the place for its fantastic displays of white arum lilies and for the fact that its glass roof provided a panoramic view of clouds building and rebuilding their state-of-the-art monuments over the West End. There they had spoken of Heliogabalus' obsession with preparing the ultimate fish sauce, with Antonio claiming he could still remember the ingredients of some of his more daring experiments and promising one day to give them an example of his cooking.

Jim, while still living in terror of Slut and his nocturnal coterie, was beginning to feel a distance had opened between him and the perverse saint of the Hampstead woods. Or perhaps it was the cushioning provided by his intimacy with Masako that allowed him to feel screened from the fear of being abducted again. Reacquainting himself with Soho and its topology of alleys had required a cognitive effort on his part, but he had succeeded, little by little, in refocusing the world as a place of trust. Accompanied at first by Masako, then later going out by himself, he had taken up with his familiar café circuit and with his exploratory walks across the city. The initial paranoia he had felt whenever someone appeared to be following him had gradually dispersed. At first he had stopped in his tracks if he felt himself pursued, then turned around and walked directly towards his imagined stalker. He had found it a successful means of disarming terror and after a few days had abandoned it altogether, secure again in the knowledge that he was just another stranger in the anonymous crowd.

Antonio laughed to himself over some observation he had made in Jim's thesis: the knowing sound of someone alerted to an incident from the past. Jim couldn't help observing his friend's sense of detachment in human relations, a sort of distancing of his thought processes, suggesting he came at things from a deeper, roomier locale in the unconscious. He was like someone permanently bi-located, split between a referential past and the present. Anyone unfamiliar with his story might have thought of him as peculiar or fazed, but to Jim it seemed understandable that Antonio should appear fractionally removed from reality.

'I can remember', Antonio said, looking up from his reading, 'discrepancies in the likeness of the portrait I had sent to Rome before my arrival there. You wouldn't have known me from a girl. Heaven knows what they made of it. The painting was probably burned after my death or eaten by time.'

'And what was the mysterious illness from which you were suffering at the time?' Jim asked, curious to draw him and remembering the allusion to sickness being the cause of the slow journey to Rome.

'Probably what you've suggested,' Antonio said, putting down the papers. 'Some sort of sexual bug picked up on the way. Diagnosis was hit and miss, but I recall instinctually knowing at the time that the cause was sexual.'

'What about the famous eclipse of the sun that coincided with your being proclaimed emperor? Was that a fiction or did it really happen?' Jim asked, wondering if his own sanity wasn't in question for taking Antonio so seriously.

'It was something very significant. It helped trigger the revolt against Macrinus. The troops were superstitious and saw in it a sign. These sort of things happen, and it played into my cause.'

Jim looked away for a moment, knowing he couldn't fault Antonio in his historical recollection. He was confused, but even in his sceptical moments, when the thought crossed his mind that Antonio might be no more than a weirdo who obsessively identified with the most bizarre of Roman emperors, he still continued to believe in the authenticity of his friend's claim.

While Masako sat riffling through a fashion supplement Jim continued to observe Antonio in profile as he started reading again. The horizontally pencilled eyebrow, the eye coloured like a foggy day in Venice, the feminine profile fused into masculine characteristics, the almost puckered set of the lips, all combined to create the irregular features of someone used to fielding looks. Jim had noticed how people stared at Antonio in the street, not in a threatening manner but more out of a sense of being thrown by his appearance. It wasn't that he had inherited the legacy of Quentin Crisp's draggish affront – on the contrary his clothes were elegantly quiet – it had more to do with the air he carried of being a stranger on earth. The word alien seemed to have been invented to describe him as he walked with apparent tunnel-vision through the Piccadilly crowds. It was his alienness that attracted attention, and people turned away from it, uncertain how to react.

He read quickly, like someone already acquainted with the text, his eyes registering agreement, surprise and amusement at what he encountered. For Jim, sitting there at a tangent, the process was like watching film, only the situation was all too disquietingly real. Of late his whole life had come to assume the pattern of being nudged in and out of a questionable take on reality. There had been times recently when making love to Masako that he'd felt on the verge of disappearing through a window into an altered state. Orgasm had seemed to have the lift of a jet nosing through free-associated cloud. He had almost succeeded in simultaneously climaxing with her but had pulled back, frightened he might be drawn into the weird electrics of her interior. That she had access to the paranormal didn't so much scare him as have him feel uneasy in ways he couldn't rationalize.

Antonio was immersed in his reading and clearly some place else. Jim was left to wonder what his supervisor would think if he told him that he had an inside knowledge of his subject, having met the reincarnated Heliogabalus. Any such claim would put an end to his academic credibility and call into question his state of mind. Not that he any longer entertained illusions about joining the dead world of academe. On the contrary, he now saw institutions as the enemies of imagination, devoted to reason rather than the thrust of live energies that came from risking the edge. The changes that had come about in his life had taught him that reality was multi-track and that each conscious state is selected from a repertory of billions of alternative possibilities. He could no longer believe in a world of commonly shared experience. He had been thrown out of his pre-conceived notions of reality and bounced like a car shaken off the road's hard shoulder into the boundary ditch. All the ideals of security he had shared with Danny, and of carving out a niche somewhere in the system he now viewed as valueless. He had even played with the idea of deconstructing his thesis and converting it into a novel. He didn't want to be part of a scheme of stored knowl-edge, pedantic footnotes and quotations shoplifted from the correct sources. He wanted to break loose and discover the real meaning of life within himself. That Masako and Antonio were both part of his new, revised existence he didn't doubt, nor that some sort of inter-active psychic link had brought them together.

Masako caught his eye and smiled at him as easy as sunlight streaming through a high window. He could feel the little telepathic flutter that travelled through the airwaves at their shared contact. He wondered if this was what it meant to be in love and to share a sympathetic thought-field with another. Masako seemed to him to be so genuinely at ease with herself, so comfortable with her bound-aries, that her interchange with life was simple, like a foot fitting a shoe.

'You've got a novel here,' Antonio said, reading the idea that had been circulating in Jim's mind. 'My advice would be to colour it up.'

He put the dissertation down, and Jim could almost hear the little click in consciousness that had him reconnect with real time and place as he stared up at the late afternoon light rinsing the sky-light. Masako suggested they took a walk over to Fresh and Wild in Brewer Street to pick up ingredients for the dinner she proposed to cook that evening. She had it in mind to make a poppy seed and sour cream pasta, and needed a lemon, miso and chives. 'I'd like to show Antonio the shop. It's quite something.'

'It's the place for the health-conscious,' Jim put in, at the same time getting to his feet as a sign that he was ready to go.

Antonio, who missed no opportunity to increase his store of places visited in London, needed little encouragement to go out. He slipped the copy of Jim's thesis into his valise with the promise that he would return to it later and put on a black Armani jacket over his purple shirt.

The three of them went out into the unseasonably chilly evening. They made their way towards Berwick Street Market just as the stalls were closing. Masako's eye was drawn to the flower stall, and they stopped to admire coral-coloured hubs of sweet williams, shocking-pink gingers, blue-mooded cornflowers and feathery ash-blue nigella. Jim followed behind, reminded of how he had walked these streets with Danny and of the good and bad times they had shared together. The route they were taking had once formed part of their Soho walks, and Jim felt scorched by the betrayal of his trust. It hit him hard to know that probably for the entire duration of their relationship Danny had been unfaithful. He knew he should go and have himself tested, and the resentment he felt at having been exposed to the risk of infection only increased the sense of paranoia that came over him at times.

Masako must have read his discomfort, for she took his arm almost, he imagined, as a defence against the searing intensity of the flashbacks that continued to trouble him. They made their way through the pimp-monitored artery of Tyler's Court, pointing out the landmark Raymond's Revue Bar to Antonio, bypassed an acned teenage prostitute clearly working to finance her crack habit and joined the busy crowds along Brewer Street. Antonio spoke of the little adjoining streets that he had explored in his morning walks – such as Bridle Lane, Silver Place and Lexington Street – their names pointing to an older, historic London. Jim scored points by telling them that the avant-garde 1960s publisher John Calder had kept an office there for three decades above a strip-joint. 'There's the famous story of how William Burroughs went around there one day with a shooter, locked him in his office and at gunpoint had him sign a cheque for the royalties outstanding on *The Naked Lunch*.'

They walked up the street at the leisurely pace of tourists, Jim still deep in thought, and observed copies of 1960s' *Playboy*s in the shop Vintage Magazine before picking up on the audible hum of Piccadilly Circus to their left. Its noise hung on the air like surf breaking somewhere across a white beach. Jim recognized the sound as the one to which he had gravitated on first coming to London. He remembered the rent boys he had encountered at the meat-rack and how they had come from all over the country to congregate there outside Boots. He could see them now, standing out of the rain, sitting in café windows or trying to pull a trick on the street. He had known boys who had struck lucky or rich by meeting an opportune stranger, someone only too happy to take them permanently under his wing.

He distracted himself with these thoughts as they walked along, Masako's arm secure in his, the city resonating with its rush-hour crisis. When they got to Fresh and Wild on the corner of Sherwood

Street they found the store buzzing with the health-conscious, most of whom had long ago wised up to the detriments of eating non-organic. Antonio was curious about everything, and it was becoming clear to Jim that his new friend clearly didn't get out and about much in Rome, given the element of surprise he showed at even the most commonplace items for sale. For all his cultural sophistication he lacked the big-city predatoriness of shopaholics and of those out to substitute things for the emptiness within. He had, Jim observed, an almost child-like naïvity when brought face up to the world, as though he had never really lost that element of wonder which is so much part of childhood. His eye took in everything from the diverse range of multi-grain breads to the palette of vegetable colours, right down to the exhaustive variety of supplements, aromatherapy products and biofriendly household cleaners suitable to those who lived green. Masako picked up her simple purchases, while Antonio's eye went on a rapid klepto-maniacal round of virtual shopping.

It was Jim who led the way out to the evening street and suggested they stop off at Oddbins to pick up a couple of bottles of red. As was his way, he couldn't resist glancing up at the sky, and his eye was rewarded by thin rafts of alto-cirrus streaking a thin blue sky. There were evening clouds starting to traffic the airways, and he turned away from his survey, having made a necessary contact with the big spaces windowed above the city.

He walked slightly ahead, aware of people directing glances at Antonio, little darts of curiosity prompted by a passing fascination more than anything else. He still felt down in himself over Danny. The walk had been responsible for putting him too closely in touch with a past he was trying to forget. He stood with his hands in his pockets waiting for the other two to catch up and for some reason looked across the street. He instantly froze in his tracks. There, standing slouched on the corner of Bridle Lane and looking directly at him, was Slut. His denim jacket was slashed open on his tattoo-splashed torso, his ripped hipster jeans were slung above his crotch and, as always, he was barefoot. He looked even more wasted than how Jim last remembered seeing him, hoisted on a tree in the

Hampstead woods with smoke billowing from the fire. Jim continued to stare, unable to break the hold the man had on him. He watched Slut raise a finger to his lips, evidently warning him not to tell. The implicit gesture had Jim recoil, and for the moment he thought he was seeing things and hallucinating Slut into existence. Time seemed to have stopped in its frozen impact.

He was recalled to himself by Masako tugging at his arm and saying, 'What's wrong, Jim? Are you all right?'

He managed to break free of Slut's fixed stare and whispered to Masako, 'Don't look, but see that man over there. That's Slut.'

'Why don't we go back and call the police,' Masako said anxiously, trying not to look.

Before Jim knew what had happened Antonio had crossed the road and made a beeline for Slut. He couldn't believe it as he saw Antonio go up to Slut and talk to him on what appeared to be an intimate level and after a brief exchange of words return. The whole gesture was so ambiguous that he couldn't be sure whether Antonio had issued a threat or made an assignation with the self-styled gay saint. It had all happened too fast for Jim to get any clear take on the incident.

'What did you say to him?' Jim shot out in panic. 'Do you know who that is?'

'Slut,' Antonio replied, in a way too knowing for comfort. 'The one who's been bothering you. I recognized him immediately. It's all part of my being able to tune into your thoughts.'

Jim found it hard to conceal that he knew Antonio was lying. He didn't believe him for a moment and thought his answer was a convenient way of concealing the truth. At the same time he remained baffled by his friend's motives in approaching Slut. Nothing made sense. When he looked over again Slut was gone. He could just make out his impossibly thin denimed figure disappearing down the Soho sidestreet, leaving him to wonder if he hadn't imagined the whole thing.

'Do you want us to go back?' Masako asked, increasing her hold on his arm.

'No, let's get the wine first,' he replied, purposely turning away from Antonio. He felt like hurting him for the complicit way in which he had gone over to Slut. Something in him had turned and he knew he would never quite feel the same about Antonio again, no matter his motives for acting in the way he had.

Ignoring Antonio, who hung back outside, he followed Masako into the wine store where they picked up a couple of bottles of a black Chilean wine called Casillero del Diablo, one they had drunk before, admiring its down-there depth-notes. Jim purposely lingered in the shop, hoping his anger would cool. When they went back outside he ignored Antonio who was browsing in the window and who showed no sign of having taken offence at being excluded. On the contrary, he appeared his usual correct, if slightly inhuman self. Making no gesture of atonement Jim took Masako's hand and without saying a word headed off down the street. Jim made his resentment towards Antonio his focus and correspondingly tightened his grip on Masako's hand. Still undecided as to whether to head back home, he steered them into Great Windmill Street, glancing around as he did to see Antonio tucked in behind a Chinese couple but still following. Like Jim's mood, the sky had clouded over, lending a blue tint to the narrow street, with girls standing outside the entrance to strip-clubs.

'It'll be all right,' Masako said by way of encouragement, as they cut aimlessly into Rupert Street with its largely faceless buildings creating a disused, anonymous feel to the place.

'Why on earth did he do that?' Jim questioned, still chewing on what he took to be a violation of trust.

'I don't know. Does he know this man, I wonder?'

'It's a mystery to me. I'll have to speak to him about it or I'll never be able to trust him again.'

'Do you want us to go back or just walk? Masako asked, as Jim showed signs of unbottling his anger.

'Let's carry on for a bit,' he said, glancing back to discover that Antonio was no longer there. 'Where's Antonio?' he asked, the surprise in his voice making Masako turn around.

'He's probably realized he's not wanted. I'm sure he'll be there when we get back.'

'I suppose I've gone and offended him. But not without good cause.'

'Mmm. We've got to do something about Slut,' Masako mused. 'Go to the police, Jim. I'll come with you.'

'I'd still rather not,' Jim replied, giving off signals that he'd rather keep his life private.

'Mmm, but this man's turning into a stalker. We can't get rid of him.'

Jim warmed to the intimations of solidarity in her voice and to the fact that she considered them together. It made him feel less alone and in a weird way less afraid of being attacked. He put his arm around her narrow shoulders, taking in her entire being as he did so, and brought her up close. He could feel the energies in her spiral towards him like the force bringing clay alive in a potter's hands.

'I'd like to stay out for a little while,' he said. 'That's if you don't mind.'

'I'm happy just being with you. My only worry is Antonio.'

'But he can go back to his hotel. He'll be all right. It's not like he's dependent on us.'

'I don't want to worry you, but did you ever give Antonio a key to the flat?'

'Why would I do that? We don't know him that well.'

'Well, he let himself in the other day. I didn't think anything of it at the time.'

'Let himself in?' That means he must have had keys cut.'

'But why?' Masako queried, trying her best not to alarm Jim by sounding over-anxious.

'Your guess is as good as mine,' Jim replied, sensing that things weren't quite as they should be and immediately reinforcing a connection between Antonio and Slut. He hadn't liked the expression on Antonio's face after he had come back from speaking to the man. There had been a self-satisfied air about him, one of having delivered the goods.

'What should we do?' Jim asked. 'Should we go back just in case?'

'I can't think what he'd want in the flat,' Masako said. 'He has a copy of your dissertation. There's nothing else to interest him.'

'But he must have had the key cut for a purpose,' Jim said, stopping as they came to the end of the street. 'Whatever his motives, I don't trust him. I think he's got some explaining to do.'

'Let's go back then,' Masako said, her fingers making soft brushstrokes in Jim's palm.

'I suppose we'd better. But I'm not sure what we can do.'

'Mmm. I still think we should go to the police,' Masako urged. 'They may have a record on him.'

'On Antonio?'

'On Slut. He's evil.'

'I'm glad in a way you've seen him,' Jim said. 'Now you can share my feelings about this psycho.'

Together they made their way into Old Compton Street. The street was busy with predominantly gay bustle, a file of clones slipping in and out of bars or shopping at partisan Prowler or Clone Zone, a snappy tang of citrus cologne wafting back at them as slipstream. Jim was once again overcome by feelings of unreality. He had the impression he had shifted into parallel and lost track of time and place. Everything seemed filmic. The crowd resembled footage framed in a slowly evolving narrative. He had the idea that he existed only because of his part in the film being projected. For a second he feared losing contact with Masako. He was a point in recession, while she remained fixed. He felt himself being sucked backwards into a vortex and was powerless to resist the pull. It was scary, and when he did fight free it was not without rebound panic.

Sensing his alarm, Masako said, 'We'll sort it out. We need to get this man Slut out of your life.'

Jim felt his balance return, as though the street had righted itself after a tilt. Nothing appeared outwardly to have changed, but that didn't take away his terror of Slut. The thought that the man could be somewhere, anywhere, in the Soho grid made him feel acutely uneasy. Nor could he rule out the possibility that Danny was in some way linked to Slut's reappearance. He was distracted from his immediate anxieties by Masako pulling him with her into a newsagent, ostensibly to pick up the new issue of Japanese *Vogue*.

Once inside, she riffled through a slew of glossies, pointing out images that appealed. 'Look at that dress. It's got to be a Galliano,' she said, holding the illustration of the ruffled pink flourish up for his attention.

'It's as good as a sorbet,' Jim said, as an excited Masako made a quick raid on the contents.

'All my money goes on magazines,' she laughed. 'I'm addicted.'

'But they're essential. You know what they say. Artists need luxuries and not necessities.'

True to form, Masako settled for copies of Japanese and Paris *Vogue*, as well as urbane *ID* and the equally state-of-the-art *The Face*. The instant hit that came from making spontaneous purchases showed in the rush of excitement to her eyes. Unable to resist adding a copy of British *Vogue* to her slab of image-conscious must-haves, she reproached herself for her impulsiveness and took her stack to the counter.

Jim took hold of Masako's carrier of goodies as they returned to the heady jostling crowds streaming both ways up and down Old Compton Street. The collective buzz tapped into Jim's consciousness as they crossed over Dean Street and made for home. Soho had this charge about it, one that got into the nerves and stayed. Often, sitting at home, he could feel it inside him, so strong that the force-field seemed to have been absorbed by his tissues. It had never been more intense than now, as they stood outside Masako's front door, while he apprehensively fitted the key to the lock before leading the way upstairs to her flat.

No sooner were they inside than he sensed a disturbance in the airwaves. He knew somebody had been in by the roughed-up vibrations and the displacement of the familiar patterns he recognized as home. Even before his eyes met with the evidence he guessed that person was Antonio. Scrawled in red felt-tip on a piece of paper torn from Masako's sketchbook and Blu-tacked to the wall, Antonio had left his message: *I, Heliogabalus, will be sacrificed tonight on Hampstead Heath.*

Jim stared at the writing in disbelief. As far as he could see nothing else in the flat had been touched. It was like finding a suicide note, only there was still time in which to act. The fact that Antonio had warned him of his intentions struck him as a cry for help.

'What on earth is this?' Masako exclaimed, as she came up behind Jim and stared at the hurriedly executed message. She placed one hand on his shoulder and stood back from the red slash signalling from its improvised spot on the wall.

'We've got to act fast,' Jim said. 'We need to find him before Slut pins him up on the orgy-tree.'

'I'm not with you,' Masako said, her voice dropping a tone.

'I'm sorry. I'm talking out of my past. Heath-goers select a particular tree as a site for group sex and christen it the orgy-tree. The place may change from night to night or remain constant for weeks or even months.'

'Then how will we find it?' Masako asked, clearly puzzled by the notion of this shifting location.

'Instinct. I'll know from the lie of the land what's in use.'

'It's too dangerous. Let's notify the police and stay out of it. It may be a hoax.'

'I need to do this. It'll be light for at least another two or three hours. My feelings are that Antonio is already on his way to the Heath. Now is the time to find him.'

'I'll come with you. You can't go alone, Jim. I won't let you.'

Jim accepted the offer without hesitation and before he had time to reflect on the risk involved they were already headed towards Tottenham Court Road tube station.

They went down into the fetid, heat-inflected Underground and took a packed train north. Progress was slow on the crippled Northern Line, and there were inexplicably long delays at each station, the packed carriage smouldering with resigned frustration. Someone had thrown themselves on the line at Camden earlier in the day, and services continued to be interrupted.

When they got out at Hampstead and took the lift up to the street Jim felt ovened by the suffocating Tube. To his mind, its high-risk circuit could fry at any time. The place smelled like a mortuary, and he was glad to be out in the air.

The streets were still busy, and they took a right turn out of the station and climbed the hill towards Jack Straw's Castle, the familiar landmark that signposted the way towards gay activity on the Heath. It was still daylight, and Jim clung to the notion that they might flush Antonio out of the woods before Slut and his circle arrived. It was a risk but one he knew they had to take.

He led the way through the car-park behind the pub and down a footpath that prefaced the entrance to a deep oak wood. Glades of balletic silver birch rippled in the wind as he tried to push the idea of danger from his mind. What he dreaded even more than a confrontation with Slut was the possibility of encountering Danny. He regretted allowing Masako to accompany him to a place territorialized with the imprint of nocturnal sex, a precinct given over at night to outlaws, queer-bashers and a retinue of the desperate.

The sky had clouded over and, although it didn't look like rain, Jim was sensitive to the change in light. A woman with a greyhound on a lead nodded to them in passing, and he wondered if she had any idea of the use to which the woods were put at night.

They went through a tunnel into the trees, his foot turning up a KY Jelly tube as a sign of the previous night's activity. He kept his eyes on the ground, eager for clues that would point in the direction of the proverbial orgy-tree. A littering of used condoms, stranded like dead jellyfish in shallow undergrowth, were additional reminders of the orgiasts who came here under cover of darkness.

Although it was early and still light Jim felt apprehensive as they entered the wood. He called out Antonio's name once, twice, convinced he would suddenly come out of hiding. Jim kept close to Masako as they stepped in under the shadow of a group of giant oaks, trunks sculpted by the centuries into elephantine markings. He could hear the wind trapped in the dense foliage overhead, like the sea exploring the interior of a cave. The place seemed both a refuge and a potential arena for conflict. He looked down at the impacted layers of acorns, crushed under-foot, which must have been accumulating there autumn after autumn. They formed a dense, hard pattern, a decaying substratum that felt wooden underfoot.

They went deeper into the trees, and he called out Antonio's name again, this time more assertively. He heard the sound chase off down wind before fading in a series of dramatic die-offs.

He continued to read the territory for give-away signs to recent activity. He knew that since the advent of the plague things were more organized in the community and that a night-watchman usually sat in on proceedings, his tree-post lit up by green fairy-lights. He had caught sight of this strategic point, from which condoms could be obtained, right at the entrance to the wood, the lights slung up in the tree like the snaking length of a vine.

Jim and Masako came out from the first dense grouping of oaks, crossed a clearing and went deeper into a recess of trees. Even though they were only half a mile from the main road the stillness of the place had Jim imagine they were in deep countryside. They had literally entered another world, a zone unofficially occupied by a gay community who had succeeded in making it their own. He had heard from a reliable source that even the Heath Police in their white van had been told to relax their vigil on this area of the woods at night.

'It's spooky here,' Masako said, hacking into Jim's thoughts. 'But pictures are coming to me. I know he's here. I'm getting flashes.'

'What do you mean?' Jim said, as he continued to study the ground for footprints.

'That Antonio's not far away. I'm getting a signal. It's coming to me.'

'You mean you've tuned in?' Jim said excitedly.

A skinhead clone, dressed in paramilitary gear, came out of the trees and disappeared again into another part of the wood. Jim was reminded that the area was probably full of such figures, either concealed in the bushes or cruising the territory for a chance encounter. He simply wanted to find Antonio and be out of there before dark.

'I can see him in my mind,' Masako said. 'He's dressed in something long and purple. He's gone back to being an emperor.'

'I don't understand. When we left him he was wearing his black Armani jacket.'

'I'm only telling you what I see. We need to cross the stream and go further over to the right.'

Jim followed Masako as she began to pick a tentative course over a narrow stream that led into a still deeper grouping of trees. The oaks appeared even older here, ancient custodians of a place that had remained unchanged by time. There was something about their durability that struck him as oddly menacing, as though they saw off humans while remaining indifferent to anything but their own permanence.

Jim followed through a raffish tangle of brambles and bracken and succeeded in getting snared as they forced a way into the opposite wood. For the first time tonight he felt genuinely afraid. He was on the point of suggesting they turned back but kept on, unwilling to show his fear.

'We're not far away,' Masako said, stopping in her tracks and staring across at a cluster of trees. Jim came up and stood at her shoulder and looked towards the oval-shaped arch into the wood. The setting sun was concentrated on the entrance, its red-gold strobe directed in a single powerful beam.

'Maybe we should turn back,' he said. 'It's not safe for us to be here with the light going.'

'This won't take long,' Masako assured him. 'Trust me. I know he's in there.'

'You mean he's waiting to be sacrificed,' Jim said, the reality of the situation starting to hit home.

They crossed the remaining distance in silence. He could hear his heart beating so loudly that it hurt.

When they went in through the arch his eyes had to adjust to the change of light. They found themselves in a circular space scored with footprints and instinctively he knew they were closing in on the orgy-tree. The ground was rutted from activity, and the remains of a fire had left its scorch-mark under a massive beech forcing its antlers upwards into the light.

'He's in here,' Masako whispered, her voice dropping to accommodate the stillness of the place. She led the way forward towards a giant oak which seemed to have split itself into two distinct trees in its industry of growth. A squirrel bolted across the foreground pursued by another in a rapid, screeching foray. As they drew nearer Jim could see Antonio's clothes neatly folded in a parcel on the ground, the black jacket on top of the purple shirt and grey trousers, all arranged with obsessive tidiness as though placed on a chair overnight at home. As they closed in he saw that a knife had been punched through a heart cut into the oak's warped bark. The blade had been forced in deep and had clearly remained undetected by the Heath Police, as there were traces of rust along the cutting edge. It was, he realized, a symbol that stood for a minority which lived outside convention and the law.

Quite suddenly he felt Masako place her hand on his thigh to arrest his progress.

'Jim, quick. Look over there,' she said, pointing to someone sitting with his back to a tree and partially concealed from view. The figure was wearing what looked like a long purple gown, the hem picked out with gold.

Jim knew immediately it was Antonio and in astonishment called out his name.

Antonio didn't move. He sat there staring in front of him, like someone in trance. Jim wondered if he'd been drugged or had taken something to prepare himself for the violence he was anticipating. He looked every bit the sacrificial victim awaiting Slut and his coterie.

When he didn't answer they went up to him, thrown by the force of his catatonic stare.

'Antonio, you've got to come with us,' Masako said, extending a hand. 'Trust us. You're with friends.'

'All we've got to do is go back to the road and find a taxi,' Jim added. 'You can't go through with this. These men are evil.'

Antonio still wouldn't respond, and Jim could see that he was naked under the silk gown and shivering from the chilly night breeze that had sprung up.

'This place puts a spell on people,' Masako said. 'You'll break it by coming with us.'

Jim held out his hand, and to his surprise Antonio tentatively gripped it. He was clearly unable to stand by himself, but with Masako's assistance Jim succeeded in getting him to his feet.

'What have you taken?' Jim asked. 'We'll get you checked out by a doctor, when we get back.'

Antonio said nothing. He continued to stare at some imperceptible point in consciousness as Masako quickly retrieved his clothes, stuffed them into their accompanying carrier-bag and returned to help Jim walk Antonio out of the wood. Each took an arm as they moved slowly forwards, a cerise slash of sky up there in a ruckus of grey cloud being all that remained of the sunset.

With each painfully manipulated step forward Jim felt safer. He jostled with alarm as they almost tripped over two clones having sex in the grass. He took the precaution of keeping clear of the main footpath leading to the car-park, certain that Slut and his gang would use this route. The dark was coming on, and there were men in the shadows like predatory wolves. He could see and smell their presence in and amongst the trees. He wondered when the night-watchman would arrive and switch on the green fairy-lights and the whole scene would come alive.

Their progress was slow, but Jim knew they were going to make it. He was struck by the dark humour attached to the situation in their supporting someone who looked like a drag queen out of a place notorious for its subversive sexual rites. He widened their arc, even though it meant making a longer journey. He wanted to keep away from the ruins that extended into the woods, for he knew men would be waiting there, sniffing out their strategies for the night. He stopped abruptly in his tracks, startled by a noise, but it was only an owl coming on with a soft oboe in the twilight. All around them a nocturnal underworld was alerting itself to the steady arrival of night. Foxes were out and so, too, were men in their pursuit of undercover sex.

Antonio said nothing, and when they stopped and rested by a cluster of bushes Jim heard the piercing notes of a whistle issue from the direction of the orgy-tree. Its shrill alarming imperative sounded to his ears like an urgent summons. In his paranoid state he imagined they had been spotted. But it was dark now, and he took comfort in the knowledge that it was unlikely they could be seen from the woods. Way over to their right, his eyes picked out the tunnelling headlights of the Heath Police on their night patrol. It looked like they were purposely keeping clear of the centre of gay activity, the van nosing down a footpath like a white shark cruising the depths.

They weren't that far from the boundary road and, despite the hard work involved in supporting Antonio, he was certain they would get there. If anything, Antonio seemed more responsive now and their progress a little more fluent. Jim could hear traffic on the other side of the trees and knew that a whole different world existed once they came off the Heath. Masako was right, he told himself; the place felt as though an electromagnetic field was drawing those who came here to its centre, like aircraft disappearing in the Bermuda Triangle.

'We need to get you dressed,' Jim said to Antonio as they paused again beneath the trees. They sat him down, stripped him of his toga and managed somehow to get his clothes on.

'No taxi will stop for us with you looking like that,' Jim said, as Antonio allowed himself to be dressed. As an afterthought he took the toga and spiked it on a bush, hoping the garment would surprise someone out walking their dog in the early morning. If the place had a bad name, then he would add to it by leaving behind this mischievous pointer to the night's sexual activities.

He froze, hearing someone coming towards them on the path, but the figure kept a wide berth and headed off in the direction of the woods. He could see headlights now and hear a steady stream of cars burning along the road's hard shoulder. His ankle hurt from having twisted it in a ditch, but that was something he would attend to later when there was time.

As they came out through the trees, the moon had risen, and its light hit them full on. Antonio was able to walk by himself now, and the three of them stood back, all focused on a particular moment in time, through a shared vision. The light was momentarily dazzling, before heavy clouds obscured the view.

They came off the Heath and, taking advantage of a pause in

traffic, crossed over the road to the other side. Jim looked at Masako for a sign that the spell had been broken. Already he felt lighter and freer, as though Slut no longer had the power to draw him into his circle. For the moment he stood there, waiting for a taxi with its orange light to materialize out of the dark, grind to an abrupt halt and, headed their way, take them the one route home.

Also published by Peter Owen

Not Before Sundown

Johanna Sinisalo

0 7206 1171 7 • paperback • 224pp • £12.50

'Unsettlingly seductive . . . elegance, authenticity and chilling conviction' – *Independent on Sunday*

'A thoughtful, inspiring and rewarding work' – *Gay Times*

'An eerie blend of traditional troll lore and cool urban thriller' – *Independent*

'A wily thriller-fantasy . . . each discovery sounds like the voice of a storyteller reminding us of how the gods play with our fates' – *NY Times*

WINNER OF THE FINLANDIA PRIZE

Angel, a young gay photographer, finds in the courtyard of his apartment block a small, man-like creature – a young troll, known from Scandinavian mythology as a wild beast like the werewolf. Angel gives the troll a name, Pessi, takes him home and hides him.

The first thing Angel does is to research everything he can about trolls from the internet, nature journals and newspapers – but he doesn't discover that trolls exude pheromones that smell like a Calvin Klein aftershave and that this has a profound effect on all those around him.

Shooting an assignment for the ultra-hip 'Stalker' jeans, Angel finds himself fast-tracked into a dangerous liaison with Martes, the art director of the advertising agency, while a couple of his friends in turn fall in love with him because of the troll's scent.

What Angel fails above all to learn, with tragic consequences, is that Pessi the troll is the interpreter of man's darkest, most forbidden feelings.

Cassandra's Disk

Angela Green

0 7206 1144 X • paperback • 240pp • £10.95

'An exceptionally clever, vivacious account of sibling rivalry'
– *Spectator*

'A vivid voice combined with real confidence and control'
– *Times Literary Supplement*

'Engaging and ingenious . . . the comic writing is highly accomplished, as are the more lyrical passages' – *London Magazine*

'Angela Green is a wonderful storyteller . . . Stunning!'
– *newBOOKSmag*

In a white, cell-like room on the Greek island of Ithaca, photographer Cassandra Byrd – giantess, eccentric, sexual siren and twin – races to fill her computer's blank disk with a raucous account of her highly unprincipled past.

Realizing that her twin sister Helen has been born with a double share of beauty, calcium, talent and maternal love, the young Cassandra reinvents herself on her own terms as the vulgar, uninhibited Big Bad Baby. When Helen survives their catastrophic childhood to become a successful actress, Cassandra sets out on a rampaging odyssey through New York, London and Paris, secretly following her sister's sexual trail in order to prove her own attractiveness and worth.

Outrageous, wise and infinitely touching, Angela Green's first novel is a darkly funny and humane story of memory, myth and meaning.

Angela Green's second novel, *The Colour of Water*, is also published by Peter Owen (£11.95, ISBN 0 7206 1204 7)

Also published by Peter Owen

The Miscreant

Jean Cocteau

0 7206 1173 3 • paperback • 163pp • £9.95

'Ultra-contemporary' – *Time Out*

'Butterfly-like, brilliant, febrile . . .
Cocteau's famous novel was all but a
bible to avant-garde intellectuals of
the 1920s' – Elizabeth Bowen, *Tatler*

'It is the book's universality that
engages us: its persuasive account of
Jacques's first love affair with the
revue artiste Germaine and his discovery that sexual behaviour is far
too complex not to contradict the
dreams of an adolescent'
– *Times Literary Supplement*

PETER OWEN MODERN CLASSICS

**Jacques Forrestier, the central character of Cocteau's
famous first novel of 1921, is a bisexual parasite and
dilettante.**

Leaving his provincial family he comes to Paris to study for his
degree. Indulging in a life of dissipation with a group of
students and their mistresses, he falls in love with Germaine, a
chorus girl kept by a rich banker. The affair, doomed from the
start, forces Jacques to come to terms not so much with society
as he finds it but with himself.

A sparkling evocation of the Parisian scene of the 1920s, The
Miscreant is also a study of loneliness and youthful
disenchantment. It is a perfect showcase for the savage irony
and epigrammatic wit that consistently distinguishes Cocteau's
brilliant and highly individualistic prose style.

Translated from the French by Dorothy Williams

With illustrations by the author